— THE —
AMBASSADOR

BRIAN C. BAKER
A NOVEL

ACKNOWLEDGMENTS

Some give of themselves in ways that are both selfless and beautiful. Across the years and miles, these souls have given the gifts of joy, and wisdom, and support. Thank you Angela, Callie, Carla, Carolé, Chris, Connor, Destin, Diane, Katelyn, Kathy, Meg & Khris, Lauren, Sheila & Lee, Michael, Sue & Pat, and Richard. But not Shelby. Shelby you're a bad cat.

The author wishes to extend gratitude to the team at Enchanted Ink for lending their expertise and their artistry to this work.

ENCHANTEDINKPUBLISHING.COM

THE
AMBASSADOR

Copyright © 2022 by Brian C. Baker

All rights reserved.

Cover Design | Editing | Formatting
Enchanted Ink Publishing

ISBN: 978-1-957759-00-5 (Hardcover)
ISBN: 978-1-957759-01-2 (Paperback)
ISBN: 978-1-957759-02-9 (Ebook)

Printed in the United States of America

DEDICATION:

There are parts of our lives that leave bruised and bleeding memories beneath the veneer of everything that comes after. For my sisters and for me, our time in the crucible was never alone.

This is for my mother. A woman who showed us how to find joy despite the aching hunger of our austere years. A woman who paints and writes and sings and dances and in no way is immobilized by the scar tissue earned from fighting for her children. Where this story gets it right, it is because she role-modeled the love and the courage required to vanquish monsters.

THE ——

AMBASSADOR

Chapter 1

BESIEGED

THEY WERE CAMPED ON THE front steps. News vans from the locals and at least one independent station lined the street, broadcast dishes elevated from their steel and fiberglass spines like Hollywood animatronic giraffes, gaping toward satellite views in a moonlit sky. My office within the West Virginia Governor's Mansion overlooked the clutter of camera-mounted artificial light and the puffery of reporters who touched up the creases sweat had eroded in their makeup. I touched the windowpane as I watched them. The heat of my palm rose in a fog that haloed the glass.

My name is Jackson Ford. I'm a politician. I could once enunciate that word with the inflection of a priest invoking the word *shepherd* before their metaphorical flock. *Politician.* Guardian of the common weal.

As I stepped back from the glass, a hawkeyed cameraman relieving himself in the bushes saw me in the curtained window of the executive office. He yelled, and his exposed member sprayed urine across one leg of his cargo pants. Cameras swung their brilliant beams upward. As shoulder-mounted optics dilated and zoomed, I felt akin to Pericles, uncomfortably exposed atop Athenian ramparts, besieged from without, rotting from within.

By the time they focused, the governor of the state of West Virginia was gone.

The rotunda of the governor's mansion is flanked by twin staircases leading to offices and private quarters. Descending either stairway gives a view of the rotunda. Beneath a domed skylight, the center of the marble reception floor is dedicated to a humidity-controlled, argon-filled display case that once was home to the Declaration of Independence before the National Archives upgraded their steel case to one made of titanium. My predecessor authorized $23,000 from a discretionary executive fund to purchase the old steel case. He used it to enshrine his law degree from the University of Virginia.

My election to office, first term, was a rout. My predecessor took the UVA law degree, but state troopers prevented him from taking the case.

My home is a perceptive land where people judge you, quietly, by what you do. The first day of my term, mansion staff were waiting beside the empty case when I entered, waiting to see what I would enshrine.

Very gently, I laid cloth.

The regimental colors of the Seventh West Virginia Infantry. First raised in the cauldron of succession from Virginia, their banner rallied 1,010 brave men at Antietam, Gettysburg, and Cold Harbor. Two years and a dozen intervening contests reduced their strength to eight hundred ghosts and one steely regiment of survivors that would be renamed the Bloody Seventh. Confederate volleys had shorn the standard to a blue cobweb darkened at one corner where a fourteen-year-old standard bearer had wrapped himself in familiar cloth and died.

Now, Micah looked at the glass as though he could still see the halo of a fallen soldier. The elderly veteran was six feet and two inches tall. Head bowed, he angled his body with the awkward gait of someone for whom mangled legs had never healed.

The glass reflected his image and mine. His face shared a commonality with images that depicted the visages of Arapaho tribesmen, Dust Bowl farmers, and Laotian refugees. He carried the lined countenance of someone who had suffered through a crucible of desiccation and pain, and had emerged lean enough and pure enough that petty torments could find no purchase.

Torments like reporters. Litigators. Lobbyists.

When he spoke, his eyes never flickered, as mine did, to our reflections in that viewing pane. Two men, one white, one dark, looking at the legacy of war.

"Some nights, I look at it, and it seems them stars are real." He shifted, looking up at the dome above us.

"Like they come down from outside that window and landed here. Like fire and heaven are in that cloth."

I looked at the battle standard of my Republic. Hand-sewn. Stains like wine where a child died. I could not draw from it the same significance Micah did. Then again, Micah was a veteran of one of America's lost wars and a graduate of camps where the North Vietnamese guards schooled their captives in degradation, torture, and privation. And he was a survivor of multiple horrific surgeries that had attempted to lace titanium with reluctant bone. He understood pain.

Micah had been a particularly comforting presence for my wife.

Both during her treatment and in the aftermath of my wife's consumption from the cancer that had spawned in her left breast, I was shamed by the self-aggrandizing way men defined nobility and by the doe-eyed way those without the perspective offered by radiation and tamoxifen used the word "sacrifice."

The best part of my existence lay in somber earth beneath her headstone. In the intervening distance of years, I had filled the void of her absence with grief and a variety of self-destructive associations intended to perpetuate the brightest and best of the things she'd helped create. Along the way, I became—in my own estimate—something worthy of loathing. I lived with the acknowledgment that I had become something half-human and half-farce. Micah had watched my descent as an unwilling and sober witness. He knew the skill with which I could deflect questions from reporters and independent grand juries. Perhaps in my current silence, he perceived a moment that could support the burdens of honesty.

Micah shifted his weight, trying to find equilibrium between scarred muscles and ill-knit bone. "Other nights," he said, "all I see is the blood. I think on that. I think on how somebody carried it till they couldn't carry no more."

Leeland descended the shadowed stairway like a wraith. Black suit. Glittering gold tie. Plucked eyebrows. A shaved and glistening scalp. His Cambridge class ring rose like a bronze tumor from the pinkie of his left hand. Its citrine center allowed a glimpse of what I assumed was a molten core. He had been my aide for two years— the "troubled years." His position was meant to serve as an ostentatious gift from a political supplicant to my administration in the hour of our greatest need. In truth, he was a conduit of sensitive information to entrenched business interests and the blunt tool these men used to direct my wandering attention.

Since Elise had died, there was little that interested me.

Micah was an exception. He had known my father. Had fought beside him until North Vietnamese T-34s had ramped over barbed wire and sandbags and overrun their position at the Lang Vei Special Forces Camp. Micah had tended my father during their trek to Hanoi and during their privation there. Other veterans, in cracked and wavering voices, had spoken to me of the way Micah had cradled my father after infection spread from his wounds. Micah had soothed his brow with a rag dipped in water hoarded from his own ration. He'd bathed my father's gangrenous body until the fever peaked and my father grew cold.

The vets said their gentle efforts to get Micah to release him had failed. Then the guards had come, fearful of disease, gagging against the stink of putrescence. They beat Micah with a three-foot length of rebar in order to prize my father's corpse from his arms. They immolated my father with diesel fuel. The choking smoke belched soot across the hard clay of the prison yard. When other prisoners were finally allowed to drag Micah away from the black stain that stretched twenty feet from my father's ashes, he left behind a splayed mirror of his image. Micah's shadow was a patch of brown soil amid the soot stain on the earth. The shadow was prostrate, one hand stretched toward my father's ashes and bones.

Leeland snapped his fingers—the same gesture other men used to summon their dogs.

"You know what I'd do?" Micah was looking at me now, wide-eyed and sincere in the transparency of his emotion as Leeland pointed to his watch.

I blew out my breath. Blinked away the tension coiled in me. I had no doubt Micah's gaze was the same one he'd directed at my father as he whispered about how they were both going to go home. About his personal faith that all things noble were rewarded in God's own time.

"No, Micah," I said. "What would you do?"

"Tell 'em all go straight to hell. Then I'd chase them bloodsucking lawyers out the building wit' my carbine."

My hand fell upon his shoulder. I'm a physically big man. And I am governor. Under my grip, I have felt men quail and sway. Micah didn't move. Like a pillar, he bore the weight.

"If we chased all the lawyers away, that'd leave just you and me."

"And Mr. Ricker." Micah said it without indictment, as though my campaign manager, my friend, was in the room.

I let my hand slide away. "And Steve."

Micah called out as I reached Leeland and the door to the mansion. "Mr. Jack." Micah worked his cleaning cloth in his hands. He laid the cloth on the wheeled waste container with a broom, mop, and dustpan hooked to its sides. "I don't believe none'a them liars." Micah bit it out like he was snapping off shots at a distant tree line. Staccato. With finality. "None'a them."

Then Leeland had my arm, and we were through the door and onto the mansion steps.

"Too bad he's not on the grand jury," Leeland said. His breath was heavy with nicotine and bile.

Any response I may have made was overwhelmed by shouts from the press of reporters clamoring against the forest-green uniforms of the state police. Scarlet strobes swept the night sky from the cruiser detailed to escort my limousine. I smiled. Waved. Wondered how many leering faces behind the lenses and extended microphones had actually voted for me. Inside the limo,

I looked up at the open skylight. Cameras strobed the stars to invisibility. With a touch, Leeland pushed a button, and the sky was cloaked by glass as opaque as the bloodstains that had limned the Bloody Seventh's regimental flag.

CHAPTER II

SILENCE

STEVE RICKER HAD BEEN A managerial accountant. CMA. The absolutism required of public and financial accounting had not fulfilled his love of numbers. In the more speculative world of management accounting, he had found release in the future-oriented perspective required of those who use balance sheets and income statements as a crystal ball. What do the numbers tell us, Steve? Where are we to go? CEOs had asked him that. Men who wielded power as surely and remorselessly as tyrants wield whips and chains.

He'd told them. And he had been right.

Numbers never lie. They may be manipulated, misread, or ignored. But for Steve, there was always something in the hind part of his brain that whispered correctly the statistics that would whirlwind future probabilities into events of right-damn-now.

When he married Claire, he had known. Of four sisters, it would be one of the girls that felt a nodal lump within her breast with the same revelatory horror that their mother had experienced. Nowhere on the pink ribbons does it mention the cruel genetic legacy that imperils some family lines, the shell game that condemns daughters to generational self-destruction.

One frosty January Saturday morning, he'd put down his drill with a four-inch deck screw on the magnetized bit. He laid down the cedar post that marked the midway point of what would become a six-foot fence to keep deer and the neighbor's snot-nosed bulldog out of their garden. From the French doors off their patio, Claire had beckoned with a smile, her hair pulled up from the soft white of her exposed neck. She wore an unadorned white cotton robe and exuded the barefoot luxuriance of someone who had slept until dreams could keep her no more.

She'd taken his face in her hands and led him into their little Charleston ranch home. He remembered with implacable certainty the way in which the fence posts behind him had reflected in the glass of the French doors as he passed through. Skeletal spikes. A gap-toothed frame that cut against hilltop and sky.

He'd felt the warmth in Claire's left breast. It had been imperceptible to his hands roughened by cedar, but as he kissed the soft dark areola and her hand stroked him to erection, he felt the warmth against his cheek. It was subtle. A hot spot that heralded the division and exponential growth of cancer cells. He felt it and slackened within her grip. Withered away with dread and fear at the certainty of what lay before them.

That was before he met Jack Ford. Both of them husbands with wives battling the same foe. It was before the years had twined to the circumstances of today. Circumstances that had put him inside West Virginia's Mount Olive state penitentiary.

Steve placed his glasses upon the bandage covering the bridge of his nose. Beneath that gauze, fourteen black threads stitched together the lacerated flesh that a shank had made as it lashed toward his eyes. He had gotten between three Crips and their target as they rushed his cell. Their target had been his cellmate, an Aryan Brotherhood gang member. They'd beaten Steve into unconsciousness, then eviscerated the Aryan with razor blades embedded in the thick plastic handles of toothbrushes and a steel screwdriver that had been sharpened by whetting the tip and edge against the concrete of a cell floor.

A guard stepped away from the phone bank and nodded for Steve to use the line. Steel bars reflected in the glass privacy screen between his phone and the one bolted next to it on the cinder block wall. For a breathless moment, Steve was transported back in time to that moment before Claire had opened the doors of their Charleston home. The instant when, looking up, he'd seen the four-by-four posts rising up across the border of their yard reflected in the glass of the French doors like a serpent's spine. He blinked the memory away and shifted so that the bars were replaced by his aged visage and slumped shoulders. In that moment, he knew the sadness coiled within him was not made restless by his captivity.

The sadness flailed in his chest and rose to squeeze his heart, because in that moment, when his wife had opened the doors of their Charleston home, his life had known only hope. It was the time before cancer. Before suffering and loss led him to this place. He touched the prison phone, some part of him struggling to put a name to this place as a location in time, as a waypoint in the narrative of his life.

Sacrifice, he thought, and then . . .

Hope.

Where it pressed against his cheek, the dark brown receiver felt warm. Steve listened to something subtler than the curses of three Hispanic cons rounding on the elderly black trustee mopping the cement floor at the far quadrant of the pod. Then the sadness that gripped his gut and heart spoke to him in its own insidious voice, whispering about the inevitability of pain and loss.

He looked through the star pattern of his shattered eyeglass lenses and dialed.

Chapter III

BOY SCOUT

THE STATE PATROL CRUISER BLIPPED its siren at the intersection ahead. We braked hard enough to launch Leeland from his seat opposite me in the limo. He cursed under his breath and pounded on the divider that segregated us from the driver. A right at this intersection would take us to the dual-laned fury of I-64. Twenty minutes of sirens would bring us to Route 60, thence east into Smithers and the joyless two-lane strip of road that conveyed the incarcerated to Mount Olive state penitentiary. Despite its Mayberry-esque name, Mount Olive was anything but banal. Layered away from polite citizenry by barbed wire and tall walls, Mount Olive contained the worst of West Virginia's murderers, rapists, and thieves.

It would be inadequate to say that Mount Olive was a troubled supermax prison. It housed a violent population that compounded as the opioid crisis unfolded across the state. West Virginia's prison population was the most diverse of any state. Diversity created a fractured system of gang affiliations, all vying for dominance, none in ascendancy. The population, conflicts, and understaffed corrections staff made Mount Olive a crucible.

That is why Steve was confined there for contempt of court. I was in negotiations; he was my opposition's leverage. They wanted me to see him suffer. So they whispered in Judge Perdue's ear, but not in a way that would make the old justice a co-conspirator. Their words were like the heated and sterile tip of a lance. They punctured an abscess. Out erupted a surprising vanity that had lain festering for years.

"*Ricker mocks you*," they whispered.

Perdue was not one to be mocked. Perjury, the old man would have understood. There were ways to deal with claims of ignorance and obfuscation. But for a man to just up and say he wasn't going to talk about something the special prosecutor wanted to talk about, to sit there, silent as stone, without even invoking Fifth Amendment privileges or raising the tentative shield of a hired lawyer . . . That was a bald challenge to Perdue's legitimacy, to his power, and to the machineries of justice. Steve Ricker would serve as an example, Perdue had argued, even over the special prosecutor's request for incarceration at a more genteel location. The number-crunching little bastard would abide with men doing hard time until he deigned to speak openly about the presumed crimes of Governor Jackson Ford.

I could be at Mount Olive inside thirty minutes, watching the warden's trembling hands turn a key. My mind played through the images of a cell door thrown wide. Conveniently, as with all fantasies, the images ended there, with freedom and self-righteous aggrandizement. Heroism is easy in our fantasies. But like a good movie, thirty minutes would just be the first act. I was on my way to an impeachment vote in the House of Delegates. If I veered from this course and released my friend, I would guarantee my impeachment and unleash a legislative maelstrom that would engulf and destroy all the things that still mattered.

Steve understood that.

He was buying time.

I saw the strength that resided in my friend. It was a quiet and abiding force that lent solidity to those around him in times of chaos, uncertainty, and crisis. If, at the end of our days, there is a final measurement of all that sums us, when Steve stepped on the scale, the surrounding shades of men that held their own at places like Verdun, Bastogne, and Khe Sanh would recognize a kindred spirit that understood what it takes to hold the line.

"They're postponing the vote until you're there." Leeland straightened his tie and smoothed the thin remnants of one brow. "Makes for better drama." He smiled. Saliva slicked a yellowed incisor.

The sirens whooped, and we picked up speed. I-64 dwindled in the darkness. The ring of Leeland's cell was plaintive against the Doppler whine from a pair of motorcycle escorts dispatched by the Charleston Police Department. One of the helmeted motorcycle cops rode close to my window. His head swiveled as though he could see through darkened glass. He spoke into his chin mic and throttled away. Somebody was getting anxious.

Ahead, the West Virginia Legislature held a late special session. The House of Delegates convened to consider my impeachment. Despite their two-year terms of office, some of these delegates had a venerable history. A half dozen had served under Governor Arch Moore, convicted in 1988 for taking bribes from coal barons. At least one recalled William Wallace Barron, convicted in 1971 for jury tampering in his own bribery case. The current House of Delegates was more proactive than their forebears had been. The special prosecutor had yet to indict me, though the suspicion of bribery, vote tampering, and illegal campaign contributions hung like stale smoke in their caucus rooms wherever conversations aired my name.

"Are you insane?" Leeland half turned as though he could conceal the identity of his caller. "Do you have any idea where we're going right now? No . . . No, you can't—"

I held out my hand. Leeland cradled the phone to his chest, gestured *No*. My hand did not move. He relented and slid the cell into my palm. It was silver and shaped much like a cigarette case. The chrome was smudged with Leeland's fingerprints. It smelled of his cologne—a scent of mulched pine and freshly turned soil, humid and fertile as cemetery earth.

"Steve," I said, "your calls are taped."

His voice was distant and frail: "I know."

"Perdue's going to blink. Trust me."

"I do. I do." He repeated it like hitting a nail already driven home. "How are you, my friend?"

I almost laughed. A man who'd stood before a wrathful judge and resolutely, calmly refused to indict me, a man who was calling from the grim abode of a state supermax prison, wanted to know how I was.

I knew exactly how he was. State Delegate Stan Habauch had used his influence with Mount Olive's warden to bunk Steve with an Aryan Brotherhood member who'd just been released from solitary after beating a Crip so badly the gang member had been blinded and paralyzed. The warden bunked Steve and the newly released Aryan on a tier populated by Crip allies like the LPT and Nuestra Familia. Discretionary use of guard man hours had created a window of opportunity for the black inmates to execute the unrepentant racist. They'd wounded Steve and beat him into unconsciousness when he tried to stop the lopsided battle.

When he regained consciousness, Steve had crawled across blood-slicked cement to try to save the dying man. Such was his humanity that he'd wept as he bundled up the unrepentant racist's disgorged intestinal tract in a towel and laid it across his gaping abdominal cavity.

This event had had the effect Stan Habauch hoped for. That was the day I made the concessions that he could sell to the cabal behind his political machine. Tonight, he would meet me at the top of the capitol steps, and we would clasp hands like old and familiar cronies.

"I'm getting you out, Steve. I made a deal." Before he could voice his protest, I said, "I didn't give up Hope."

"Jack," he said, "don't." His voice sounded distant, as though space was sliding between us as surely and inevitably as leagues unfold between two different moments in time.

"I'm going to need one more night to finalize the deal," I said. "Can you do that? Can you make it one more night?"

Steve watched the black trustee turn his back on the heckling crew from La Eme. The trio of Mexican Mafia enforcers followed the trustee, shoving the five-foot-two black man. Water sloshed the old man's pants when one of the Hispanics kicked his rolling bucket.

"Sure," Steve said. "You know me. Making friends. There's a guy on the lower tier. Screams my name at night. Like a banshee." He switched hands and watched the unfolding assault.

The guard station was vacant.

"Listen to me." Jack's voice hissed across the line.

At the opposite end of the pod, a group of black inmates took two mops and rolling buckets onto the floor. One of the buckets hit a picnic table bolted to the floor. No water sloshed out.

"We're going to beat this thing," Jack said. "It's hard right now . . ."

One of the black cons had a series of tattoos across his face. They were thick welts that ran in crosshatched vertical and diagonal lines. Raised belts of scar tissue. Like the Itsekiri tribe of Liberia, whose tattoos were made by slashing the skin and forcing scar tissue to grow. Steve and the convict locked eyes. Without a sound, the man wrenched off his T-shirt in one fluid movement. The mutilation extended down his neck, across his broad shoulders, and cascaded across his chest. Crosshatching like griddle marks. Each line was a cut that had bled, knit, and been cut again and again, until the scar knotted ripe and purple against the ash of his skin.

"You hear me?" Jack was saying. "From tonight, it gets better."

"Y'know"—Steve smiled and nodded as though coming to accept something—"that's what I used to tell Claire."

The black cons were closer now, with their mops and empty rumbling buckets. The Liberian looked at Steve like a hungry man who spots sustenance.

"Hey, Jack," Steve said, "you think the girls found peace? It's just, some days, I wonder."

Protestors chanted while waving *FORD OUT NOW* signs. A phalanx of Charleston cops nudged them back. Counterparts to the news contingent we'd abandoned at the governor's mansion were already in place doing live feed from the maelstrom of citizens that seemed to recognize me as the resident evil. Several of Stan Habauch's campaign aides waved impeachment signs and marshaled the auditory might of the crowd.

If they had been clear-eyed observers of good and evil, they would have shrunk back from the visage atop the capitol steps. Stan Habauch's 265 pounds of sloth and largesse were draped in yards of fine white linen. He likened his suits to the toga candida, the whitened robes worn by Roman citizens to mark themselves as candidates for elected office. One short-lived newspaper pundit had compared his suits to the iconic garb of Colonel Sanders. His editorials ceased when two men pulled him from his vehicle in the driveway of his home and used a ball-peen hammer to shatter, one by one, each finger and then the thumb of his dominant hand.

Habauch's jowls rolled back into the wide smile of a Mercedes salesman as I climbed the steps. Leeland remained in the shadowed cavern of the limo, no doubt reporting to the same cabal of mine that daily tallied the number of strings that tentacled from their fingers to the delegate's spine.

Habauch's grip was a meat vise, porcine and damp. He posed, holding my own knotted fist for the cameras. "Don't you worry none, Governor. We gonna unload this bad freight."

Bad freight. Programs that subsidized school lunches for children, that enforced labor laws the feds had never deigned to apply to the remote hills and shantytowns of Appalachia. Pollution controls that kept the toxic dross in mine towns from injecting downstream aquifers with lead, arsenic, and carcinogens.

A political lifetime of progressive legislation.

I would barter all these things for Steve's freedom and protections for Hope.

The Hope Scholarship legislation had been Elise's baby. At tremendous personal cost, she had led the lobbying effort to use lottery proceeds to pay for scholarships. The scholarships covered the cost of college books and tuition at any of West Virginia's twelve public four-year universities or nine public two-year community colleges. Any West Virginian with a high school cumulative grade point average of B or higher qualified for the scholarship, which would pay for their two- or four-year degree.

It was a popular scholarship.

There were no tax increases.

Enrollment spiked upward by almost 20 percent. In the first year, it made college possible for eleven thousand children that otherwise would not have gotten in the door. But those lottery revenues had previously been in demand elsewhere. In giving the lottery funds to our future generations of West Virginians, Hope had denied it to the House of Delegates and Senate, where it had once paid for what the politicians called "constituent projects."

The Hope legislation was enacted midway through my first term. Each year, we had a legislative battle to protect it. Stan Habauch was the corpulent center of the opposition that sought to claw back the funds. One year, Habauch sought to exclude tuition at community and technical colleges. Another, he sought to raise the qualifying grade point average from 3.0 to 3.7, an act that would have reduced the eligible students by three-quarters. Another, he sought to limit the Hope Scholarship to covering only the second half of a four-year degree program. His argument was that student loan debt for freshman and sophomore year tuition would create a greater appreciation for their free ride during the junior and senior years.

Now, he wanted it gone entirely. Habauch—and the men that controlled him—had other designs for the funds that were currently designated as an investment in our children.

In order to protect Hope, Elise had launched a constitutional amendment drive close to the end of my first term. It would have protected the Hope Scholarship from future erosion. By the eve of her death, we'd been on the verge of seeing the ratification of that constitutional amendment.

After her funeral, the momentum evaporated. As did my focus. As did my will.

That was the past.

Now, three years into my second term, I was at the last in a series of trades. Everything else was on the table. I would get Steve out of prison. I would protect Hope.

And there would be no further efforts to force me to admit my personal wrongs. By personal wrongs, I mean my appointment of Habauch cronies to critical posts in the executive branch of state government. If corruption was a cancer, my participation had metastasized that corruption across the state agencies that regulated Habauch's sponsors. At his request, I appointed his slate of nominees to the senior leadership of state agencies responsible for mine inspections, labor disputes, and environmental concerns. I had also turned a blind eye to the extortion that fueled Habauch's political machine. Businesses made payments to Leeland in cash at the mansion. Leeland deposited a fraction of the funds to my personal accounts to ensure I would be a named co-conspirator and funneled the rest to Habauch. Steve had uncovered the deposits in his quarterly audit. Every personal account I could access was tainted. The moment I spent a dollar for myself, I would be as dirty as the rest. It was one of the secrets I'd asked Steve to keep.

In return for our roaring silence, Habauch left Hope alone.

Bad freight.

Habauch turned and entered the capitol, leaving a stale vacuum in the air. It was the fetid void that comes when something of great and lethal mass sails past without causing the damage that is its potential.

I followed.

Inside the building, state delegates rose, silent, as I walked the aisle. Faces of men and women I had known personally for twenty years cast their eyes away from my own. Men whose corruption and ineptitude I had railed against in the days when my wife walked this aisle at my side met my gaze and smiled. I stopped beneath the Speaker's dais and faced the hundred souls who had convened to cast a roll call vote on the matter of my impeachment. This was the culmination of an investigation that leveraged charges of obstruction of justice and criminal conspiracy, all stemming from reports that I had taken illegal campaign contributions to gain reelection during the tight race that had coincided with Elise's illness and demise.

It was irony that the charges were untrue. I carry regrets, corruptions, and personal failures like a devil burdened with a sack of sins. The impeachment charges were not among them. I think Habauch found humor in that. They were articulated so plausibly, inclusive of paid witnesses, because Habauch's cronies had used that process to fund his own campaign. Both my governor's races had been against Stan Habauch.

It was no coincidence the trial's proponents had been marshaled by him.

I turned and faced the assembled delegates. There was a nervous shuffling in the front row. Someone coughed. The Speaker of the House was a member of the opposition party, but he hailed from a different era of politics. In his eighty-four years of life, he had never wavered in his dedication to the service of citizens in his small Appalachian district. He did not describe a man by his party but by his actions. He'd sat in the minority and in the majority, and now, in the fullness of his years, the elderly Turner Roy Barnes had been a well-respected leader of the whole of the House of Delegates for the past half decade. He looked down at me from the podium, white-haired as Cato's ghost. He covered the microphone with his calloused hand and spoke to me as though I were his own child.

"Caesar's problem was, he stood there countin' knives. Don't tarry, Governor. Not here."

I heard the rasp of his hand releasing its hold on the surface of the microphone as I paced through the door to the stairway that led to a private observer's gallery. It was a balcony room that overlooked the assembly. From somewhere in the auditorium, laughter came, raucous and derisive, until Barnes' gavel cracked with the finality of a gunshot.

Originally, there had been but one chair in the gallery. It had been called the Governor's Gallery, intended as a ceremonial portal for the chief executive of West Virginia to look upon the musings of the legislative branch. I hadn't used it until Elise fell ill, four years ago. During contentious and partisan wrangling over omnibus legislation that would have provided public funding for breast cancer screening, pre-K literacy programs, and the Hope Scholarship, Elise and I had walked the aisle.

Very few legislators had known we would be coming. Stan Habauch's pets gaped at us. One who owned twelve fast food franchises spit on the carpet as we walked past. His venom reflected a sincere desire to keep the youth behind his fryers ignorant to life's other opportunities.

The reporters present did not witnessed his gesture. They did, however, notice the Governor's Gallery held a solitary chair, intended for the head of state.

Elise was not a political animal. She had not been versed in the moral convolution and compromise that enacts legislation. Her standards had been framed before kindergarten under the guidance of a Marine's wife widowed during the Vietnam War. The unrelenting hope and resolute conviction that caused her mother to refer to her husband as missing in action and set for him a place at every meal as though he would be shortly home framed the inner strength that carried my wife through much of her chemotherapy.

I begged her to take the solitary seat within the gallery. Instead, she placed her frail hand in mine, and her eyes, sunken from fatigue and the ravages of battling cell division that had metastasized to a dozen different parts of her form, looked up at me. She shook her head. She would not sit while her husband stood.

Turner Roy Barnes had gaveled then as well, rolling across recalcitrant delegates who demanded time on the floor with the admonition: "Not today, sir. The lady waits." Reporters Stan Habauch had positioned to record the trouncing of my keystone legislative agenda spent their time framing close-up photographs of my wife, standing with a solitary chair at her side. It was visual fodder that spoke of sacrifice. It had the visceral import that only the courage of a dying woman could lend to political affairs.

After the vote was won, Elise's grip slid from my arm. Her cheeks were blushed with exertion, her forehead damp. I caught her before she fell. In my arms, she murmured an apology. To me. She apologized *to me* . . .

I carried her from that goddamn gallery, sickened that I had allowed political process to burn through my wife's last reservoir of strength. Down the stairs, down the aisle, I walked through a torrent of applause while the sergeant at arms and state police cleared the throng not for anything I could have possibly done, but for the woman cradled like a child in my arms. Once we were gone, Stan Habauch had personally seen to the installation of a second chair. Both were bolted in the spot where we'd stood, preempting a similar display from ever occurring again. As a final touch, attached as a rider to an appropriation's bill, he had inserted legislation that renamed the Governor's Gallery a generic Balcony Space Number 2.

In BS 2, in the chair that occupied the place where my wife had stood as men and women cast ayes and nays on the floor below, Sarah Everly sat with her foot propped against the balcony rail. She hulled peanuts from a sack and dropped the shells onto the carpet as though it were a barroom floor. Her hair was discordantly short. Her signature three-piece suit had become the hallmark of a state prosecutor who was at once venerated for her prowess, even as she was excoriated for her harsh sentencing demands.

I sat beside her. Took a peanut from her sack.

"Better wash your hands," she said.

"Stan Habauch's a respected legislator."

"Convicted murderers have told me his handshake was the single most unpleasant experience of their lives. They said it was like losing your fist in a mountain of dung. That what it felt like to you, Governor? Like you were falling in shit?"

I crushed the shell. Rattled the nut in the hollow of my fist. On the floor below, Turner Roy Barnes had begun the process of impeachment with the reading of the charges. Sarah Everly looked at me, her jaw set in a hard line. One of the rare interviews Sarah Everly had granted during the course of her independent counsel investigation of my last campaign had summed her in a word: resolute.

When she was a child, Prentiss Everly, her alcoholic and gambling-addicted father, had been caught on the doorstep of his Cora Alley home and maimed by a man he owed four hundred dollars. LeMarcus Ray was a loan shark who knew the toothless used-up old man had far more value as an object lesson to others than as a reliable source of vig—interest payments on the loan—so after methodically shattering both of Everly's kneecaps with .22 magnum rounds, he laid the smoking barrel against the gibbering man's temple. A dozen crack dealers and whores who were content to watch the murder from the alleys and stoops where they conducted their trade reported what happened next.

Little Sarah Everly stepped between them. LeMarcus was six feet two, 225 pounds, and had welted scars on his face and knuckles from the days he took alley fights for the price of a pork chop. As an enterprising loan shark, he had once used a bolt cutter to remove the thumbs of a man who'd been late delivering vig. His capacity for capricious acts of violence, massive size, and venomously long memory had made him the scourge of Logan County.

Eight-year-old Sarah Everly looked up at this massive man, who was as tall as the stars and as dark as night, and her child's hands gently drew LeMarcus' revolver from Prentiss Everly's temple and laid the still-warm barrel against her breast. One prostitute later reported that they stood that way longer than it takes her to service most of her clients against the rough brick wall of the alley from which she viewed the encounter. Then the hulking brute, who would later extinguish his own flame in a siege shootout with Charleston SWAT, knelt and spun the butt of the .22 revolver so that it came down in Sarah's palm. What electricity must have shimmered between those two as LeMarcus Ray guided the muzzle over his own black heart and held it there for a full minute before nodding in some unspoken acknowledgement, rising, and slouching into the darkness and away.

Those who know Sarah Everly well enough to be privy to such things swear she carries an unregistered .22 revolver in her purse, even in the courtroom, and that the cylinder holds four ancient cartridges and two spent shells.

I opened my hand and let the nut and crushed husk drop to the floor among her detritus. Sarah looked at me without blinking. From the legislature floor came the diminutive ayes and nays of a voice roll call vote. "You have influence with Perdue," I said.

"No."

"If you ask him . . ."

"No."

"*If you ask him,* he will raise the contempt order."

"You think the vote down there's going to end anything? Whether they impeach you or not, I have a job to do."

"Steve Ricker's in Mount Olive. You know what they'll do to him!" I was out of my seat now, glowering and in full view of the legislators below. Stan Habauch's neck hung in rolls over his pale collar. He nodded up at me, as though I'd given a sign, then turned his massive head to the right. A display flickered the changing tallies in red lights.

That moment marked the high-water mark of impeachment. The ayes faded and were replaced by a succession of nays cast by political sops, Habauch cronies, and legislators from whom the man in white had called in furtive debts—all to retain me in office as a man similarly cowed and collared. Sarah touched my hand. Her nails were blunt cut, unadorned by polish.

"Jack, he wouldn't even condescend to lie."

On the floor, the momentum picked up. Nay . . . Aye . . . Nay . . . Nay . . . Nay . . .

"Steve's protecting you. Not your office. Not political power. He's protecting the man who picked him up from a thousand goddamned barroom floors. He's protecting the man that held him together while his wife died, painful and slow."

She saw what the words did to me and rose.

"You may think you're protecting something else, but it's not noble. You may think you're saving an ideal, but it's not truth or justice or even the potential for a child to go to fucking school. I can only guess at what you think you're going to save here. But I know for certain what you're sacrificing. He's in jeopardy because you asked him to lie."

Sarah's hand slipped into a pocket for her phone. She turned her back on me as she answered a call. I watched the vote progress. My political career was saved. I hadn't even begun to tally the price of that victory when I heard her whisper an end to the call and felt the weight of her stare. When I turned, her lips were pursed, like a doctor's before they deliver sorrow prefaced with the self-serving disclaimer: *We did everything that we could.*

Chapter IV

JANET RENO

MICAH HAUNTED THE KITCHEN DOOR. He'd been there before the first hints of sunrise burned the sky and dissipated the faint crystals of frost that had etched the kitchen windows overnight. There were other staff out there with him. He'd allowed none but the cook entry and then only to ignite the gas stovetop and sizzle bacon and poach eggs over electric-blue flames. The elderly woman placed the plate before me with all the reverence of a penitent and then retreated out of range of the recorded ovations that came from the small television atop a DVR in a niche within the kitchen wall.

It was a recording made at my first election celebration nearly seven years prior. We were on stage together, smiling. Elise and I. Steve and his wife, Claire. Remission was our future. Four years in which to improve our world. Beside me, the eggs had congealed and grown cold. The bacon lay in dark strips writhed by heat. Through the kitchen window, I could see an elderly state trooper hoist the US flag against the dawn.

On the television, Claire Ricker wore a multicolored turban and a wan smile. Elise clasped hands with her. They waved. The crowds cheered as I took the microphone and spoke of dreams that were even now fragmenting in the glare of a new day.

The plate moved as Leeland's fist closed on cold bacon. He chewed as he spoke, watching the tape. "What's this?"

"My first campaign."

"You haven't seen the news." He was gloating, rocking heel to toe with an energy that spoke of more than caffeination. "Impeachment fails. Ricker's dead. Independent counsel's choking on her own vomit. This morning's press conference is gonna play better than that inauguration speech. I'm drafting your statement."

He slid a sheet of paper before me, then stabbed the volume on the set so that my recorded voice rose above the muted hiss and click of the DVR's antique gears. "... *this is our covenant, one with another. These my friends, my fellow citizens of the great state of West Virginia, these are my promises to you.*"

"They lapped it up. Such bullshit." He muted the tinny applause and the voice that had once been my own. "Who wrote that?"

I looked at the half page of text he'd manufactured in Calibri eleven-point font. "No one," I said.

The side entrance to the press conference room was a public corridor within the governor's mansion. Beside me waited the elderly trooper who had raised the flag, campaign hat pulled low upon his brow, his expression carefully neutral. His name was Toby Withersbee. As senior trooper, he served as honor guard. Each dawn, he would raise and unfurl the colors of the United States and the state of West Virginia. It was he who had laid the flat of his palm upon the sternum of my predecessor when he attempted to take the display case from the lobby, tactfully snaking out the steel of his baton in his free hand when "movers" attempted to force the issue.

In the years I occupied this mansion, I'd made it a point to rise predawn and run the grounds for exercise. I timed the two-mile circuit to coincide with the flag raising. Each morning, I would conclude the jog, winded, at a place where I could watch Withersbee raise the flags. My hand would rest over my heart, feeling the rapid trip and thud that reminded me that I was alive.

Each morning except the day Elise died . . . and today.

Withersbee averted his eyes when I looked at his face. There are some people who possess a moral compass that forever points true north. It's inevitable that they should judge those of us who lose our way. Lights from camera crews and the strobe of photography haloed the pressroom door before us as Leeland went ahead. From within came the cacophony of questions punctuated by Leeland's evasions. He called it foreplay. I read his statement on the single-typed page again.

The words blurred.

"Does it speak of loss?"

Trooper Withersbee blocked Sarah Everly's path. She stood in the corridor, hands on hips, eyes narrowed with the shadows and lines that could've only come from a sleepless night. "Most of all, a eulogy should do justice to the dead."

"Trooper, she doesn't need to be back here."

I turned away from her as Withersbee took her by the arm.

"It's not too late, Jack . . ."

The pressroom door opened at my touch. It was a transition. From cloistered serenity to a swirl of faces and light. From introspection to voices shouting noise. But none of them shouted loud enough to overwhelm the words Sarah snapped over her retreating shoulder as Trooper Withersbee walked her toward the stairs.

"Clear his name, Jack!"

Leeland looked up from the limelight like he'd been slapped. His surprise was momentary. "Ladies and gentlemen, the governor of West Virginia!"

I stood behind the podium. The prompters were off. Leeland slid a new sheet of paper into my hands. "Revised draft," he whispered.

I read, mechanically: "Last night, as you're aware, my former campaign manager was fatally injured. This individual was being held at the Mount—" I looked at Leeland. "You didn't even use his name."

The room was quiet except for the hum of cameras. Leeland looked away.

Slowly, my gaze swung toward the cameras. Toward the men and women who waited.

I barely recognized the sound of my own voice. It was low. Funereal. Laced with regret and the ache of loss. I felt the paper Leeland had given me crumpling in my hand.

"Waco," I said. "Remember the federal raid on Waco? Blood and fire and death. When the smoke cleared, when the ATF's dead were draped with flags, everybody was pointing a finger. But not the attorney general of the United States. No. She stood in front of God and everybody and said, 'I am responsible.'"

I paused. Cameras whirred.

"That didn't bring back the dead. Nobility won't bring back the dead."

Leeland inched toward the podium. The lights were bright. The room felt hot and crowded. Inside, I felt the slow unburdening of something that had weighed upon me for a thousand days.

"Consider how povertied your stories would be if we all raped and murdered and stole, then said, 'I am responsible.' It's not the way our society functions."

Leeland stepped up beside me. His hand hit the mic with an audible pop and feedback. "Folks, the governor's been up all night. We're going to postpone—"

"No."

He found my ear, then came a furious whisper. "You're coming apart!"

I leaned close to him. Into his aura of dead trees and fetid earth. "Then you shouldn't stand so close."

I looked at the reporters. Opened my clenched hand. The crumpled statement floated to the ground as Leeland backed away.

"I knew Steve Ricker eleven years. We met in this crummy little schoolroom in Opeha, West Virginia. That's where the support group would meet. It was for . . . It was for women who had breast cancer. Steve and I were the only husbands who went. Always found that odd. Most of those women were married, but we were the only men in the room, listening to wives and mothers and daughters talk about what it takes to face death."

I thought of Micah and the way he must have held my father. I thought of cradling my wife in my arms, her head lolling against my chest, as I held her in the Governor's Gallery. I thought of the look on Steve's face as rose petals sifted from his hand and onto the burnished walnut curve of Claire's lowering coffin. From dim memory, my own Election Day voice came to me: *"This is my covenant with you . . ."*

"When I was elected," I said, "I made promises to each of you. I promised there'd be no lies between us. No excuses. No dishonor." I gripped the podium harder, as though it could bring stability to a disintegrating mind. "I could not keep those promises. Effective immediately, I am resigning as governor."

A barrage of questions. Two of the evening anchors were out of their chairs, elbowing their way toward the dais. I felt Trooper Withersbee's hand on my arm, guiding me off the dais and toward the exit as his other hand warned back reporters that surged toward us. A freelancer caught me at the door, one hand on my shoulder as Withersbee turned to shove open the exit. The reporter wore the camouflage and tan boots of a Middle East embed. "Put it on the record, Ford! Did you take bribes?"

I looked at him. He revealed the digital recorder in his clenched fist.

"Can you bring back the dead?" I asked.

His hand fell away. I moved past and out of the hallways of power.

Chapter V

CLOSING DOORS

THE WEST VIRGINIA GOVERNOR'S MANSION grounds are bounded by a wrought iron fence six feet high. Sharpened black steel spikes top each post—a compromise between the desire to present an open and visually appealing aesthetic to the public and security consultants that advocated coils of razor wire atop the barrier.

I stuck to the shadows along the fence line. It was two years after my disgrace and resignation. I had first been replaced by the Speaker of the Senate, a wizened and respected member of my own party. Then, in a general election, by newly elected Governor Stan Habauch.

I would definitely be regarded as an intruder.

At a side gate, I ducked into the alcove beneath a wrought iron ivy-covered archway. The delivery gate could be unlocked electronically by the security office or by pressing a code into the old mechanical combination keypad beside the gate.

I had the code.

I bundled my frayed suit against the winter air and stepped into the alcove.

A dim blue light illuminated the new badge reader. I felt the surfaces around the badge reader for any indication of the old mechanical keypad. There was nothing. The red LED on a new security camera blinked steadily.

A sudden and unreasoning rage boiled across my innards. My fists rose, ready to pummel steel and stone.

Click.

The gate swung open and revealed a familiar form.

"Micah."

"Mr. Jack." He glanced at the surveillance camera. Moved to ensure he wasn't in range. He had his full cleaning cart out by the gate. The walkway was uneven. The cart hadn't been made to travel the grounds. I understood in a heartbeat that it'd hurt like hell for Micah to bring it a hundred yards from the mansion to the gate, and as he bent to remove a tin foil-wrapped plate of food concealed on the cart, I also understood why.

He offered it to me.

Heat rose from the foil. The scent of bacon and eggs reminded me how long it had been since my last meal. The tremble in my hands as I took the plate reminded me how long it had been since my last drink.

"Micah. Thank you."

"Been a week since . . ." He looked away. I hadn't realized it'd been a week since my last visit. Alcohol does that. It gnashes away chunks of your life and swallows them into a vast maw of darkness. Never to be sated. I wondered how many weeks I'd surrendered in the interval since Elise died.

"The new governor, he says I can't let you in no more." Micah shifted, uncomfortable, his eyes down on the flagstones. "Not even when it's cold."

He was saying goodbye.

Micah pulled a bundle from the cart. Over my protests, he placed a heavy coat into my hands. "This one always kept the cold off me."

"Micah," I said, "you're a higher class of person than the ones around you. That includes me."

His face moved with an expression that looked like physical pain as I walked back through the gate. As it swung closed, he raised one hand. The gate locked with a click. I sat in the alcove under the ivy sky and watchful gaze of the security camera and tore into the plate, ravenous.

I shrugged into the coat Micah had given me. In one pocket, there were fives and ones, folded neatly under a rubber band. In the other, a flask emblazoned with *De Oppresso Liber* of the Fifth Special Forces Group. It was heavy with liquid. On the walk back from the gate toward my flophouse, I saw state troopers raising the flags against dawn. I came to attention, hand over my heart as they crested the pole. As the troopers departed, my hand slipped to the flask. I unscrewed the lid and raised it to my lips in a gesture that was in no way a salute.

I sneezed. Sarah Everly slid a tissue from the sleeve of her judge's robe and extended it to me like a dealer offering the one card I really need. She held it there, outstretched, as I raised a finger for her to wait. I held her in that frozen pose of offering. It appealed to me in some manner. I wish I could say it was because she had taken so much from me, but that wasn't the case.

I sneezed again.

"Jesus fucking . . ." The tissue fluttered down before me. "Just take 'em all." Quicker than thought, her hand flashed into the sleeve, and a travel pack of tissues skidded across the desk to me. She walked back around to her chair. The tissues slipped past my hands and fell beside my shoe. By the time I rose from picking them from the floor, she was in her chair, glaring.

"So, I did good?" I asked. "You heard from 'em, right?"

I saw from her expression that I had not. So I tried a different approach. Gratitude is usually a good play. "First off, thank you for getting me on the stage, but, I mean, they liked—"

"No, Jack, they didn't like the speech."

"What? Who? Tell me who the hell wouldn't—"

"None of 'em. But mainly senior citizens. That's who. A lot of them voted for you. Both terms."

"Yeah, so, that's just . . ." I fumbled for a word and could only find the one my own plaintive voice of self-recrimination and doubt vocalized like a mantra.

"Disappointing." I huffed into a tissue. "What didn't they—"

"You, Jack," Sarah said. "They didn't like you."

I looked away. She must have taken it for a flinch. Maybe it was.

"It's not your fault." She was up again. Out of the chair and pacing the judge's chambers. "It's mine. I'm the one that sent you in there. I really thought it'd be different. For Christ's sakes, it was years ago. Twenty-four months is a political eternity."

"Because I resigned?"

"It was how you resigned, Jack!" She paced in a way she couldn't when she was behind the bench. "You turned your back on everybody. And swear to God, like that wasn't enough, you opened the sewer on your way out!"

She wheeled on me, and for a moment, the assistant district attorney was back. "To this day, I don't understand the deals you made. How you could sell out to so many fucking unrepentant and horrible criminals. You kicked the governor's mansion doors wide, and as they walked in, you resigned the highest office in this state without saying a word. Even Dick Nixon walked out protesting his innocence and waving to the crowds. Remember that? He said he wasn't a crook! Your abject goddamn silence said you were."

"That's all?" I asked. "They want me to wave?"

"They want closure! These people know how it ended. They want to know if you're dirty too. Like it or not, this is what your life has been reduced to," Sarah said. "You're a suspect who's only interesting because of the inference of guilt."

Some people feel bad about spilled milk or kicked puppies or lost and crying children. Sarah Everly is one of those people. I didn't move. Didn't change my expression. In all my years of working closely with the narcissists and manipulators and self-dealing personalities that infest the corridors of public office, I had learned to take the impact of a truck without showing the pain. I held a stoic expression in place, ready for the rant to rise again in a new storm wall of fury. But that was it. Sarah paused, as though in her own estimation, the dose of honesty she'd delivered may have been more than my fragile system could take.

"I'm sorry. Look, I'm not independent counsel anymore. My investigation's over. For that matter, I don't know why you came to me looking for—"

"I went to everybody, Sarah," I said. "Everybody. I'm disbarred. I got no savings. No pension. No home."

She watched me intently. I could see the prosecutor's mind at work. Never crowd the witness. Wait until they're done.

"And you're the only one who'd see me," I said.

There was a tap at the door. We both knew what that meant. The bailiff was there to escort her back to the courtroom. But she didn't move. She crossed her arms.

"That's not why you came to me," Sarah said.

"Oh? Then why am I here?"

"It's something a priest once told me. Confession's good for the soul."

"What'd you tell the good father?"

"Not a thing. I listened. Then I prosecuted him. He got twenty years. Even a pedophile understands. Confession's an act of responsibility. It's a testament of remorse. That's something you never did. You never once said, on the record, what you knew."

"Are you trying to be my priest?"

"No. I'm not even trying to be your friend. I saw how you treated them."

I flinched.

"If Elise could see the state you're—"

My reaction was visceral and swift, my words clipped: "Leave her out of it."

"Why? Don't you think she'd have something to say?"

I rose, turning my back on her. Unwilling to answer that.

"Jack."

Her voice stopped me as my hand touched the door. For a moment, I'd have sworn the oak trembled, as though it sensed the environment it inhabited. As though somehow, the suffering of thousands of broken lives that had shambled into this courthouse seeking some measure of repair had flowed into the building itself. As though the suffering trembled new life into the parts of the building that had once been green and living, and now, sometimes, those parts reverberated with the pulse of human tragedy and pain.

Then the solid red oak was still again beneath my fingertips. Behind me, Sarah spoke. It was an apology.

"I've run out of fundraisers and church groups that'll pay to hear a disgraced governor talk about the state we coulda been."

"I understand," I said. "Y'know, for what it's worth, I always thought you woulda done all right in politics."

I turned. She was at her desk. Knuckles to her eyes. Lips pursed in a fine frustrated line.

"No chance in hell," she said. "I saw what those bastards did to you."

Then her eyes came up, and I saw that she was offering me something. "Maybe . . . There's this thing tonight. I can't make it. You'd be doing me a favor."

The two bailiffs watched a small color television perched on a cabinet that held state forms so outdated they had carbon sheets between the triplicate layers. CNN threw world headlines against the screen in a display too small to be seen. The bailiffs ignored us while the clerk frowned her way through hand writing an address. She paused her scribbling twice to take calls. I stiffened each time, but it wasn't because of the interruption. It was the senseless pileup of actions unfulfilled. The two calls had been met with indifference, then immediately shunted into hold on her multiline phone.

"Superior Court," she said as a third caller rang. She didn't even give this penitent an opportunity to voice their request. "Please hold."

With the flick of a finger, there were three blinking lines. She looked at me over pince-nez glasses as she handed me a slip of paper with an address. "This is the venue." Then she gave me a check. "And here's your stipend."

I looked at the date. It wasn't made out for today. "Excuse me. This check—"

"Postdated." She nodded as the phone rang again. She held it up, covering the mouthpiece. "Judge Everly said you'd want to cash it tomorrow."

"I see. Could you—"

"Superior Court, Clerk's Office. Hold please." She flicked the fourth call into the electronic bullpen. One light went out, marking the demise of the first caller's patience.

"Could you tell me who . . ." Then I let the question trail away as the clerk smiled, as though that was what she had been waiting for.

"Oh, about a hundred," she said cheerfully. "Defense attorneys." Without another glance at me, she went to the most recent caller, intoning again as they came off hold, "Superior Court, Clerk's Office. How may I help you?"

"Great," I said as the bailiffs ignored me and the clerk cleared calls using the hellish inequality of a last-in-first-out method. "Lawyers."

The open sofa bed behind me was an unkempt sprawl of blanket and sheets. The frame was bent, casting the bed on a slight cant downward toward one side. The apartment's wall was a neutral beige. There was no art on the wall. No degrees or decorative sconces. The paint was adorned only by the play of shadow and light from a curtain-framed open window at the fire escape. It was a scene of solid black and white lines and gray flurries of motion on an eggshell canvas. I watched the movement behind me in the mirror atop the dresser that faced the lopsided bed.

My hand trembled toward the bottle on the dresser, even though the glass beside it still held a finger of scotch.

I paused, closed my eyes, and considered the reasons alcohol was a part of my life.

It wasn't for enjoyment, though it once may have been.

It certainly wasn't for companionship. Though I had a physical need for it, that addiction wasn't the "why."

Above me, voices increased in volume, cursing in Spanish.

There it was . . .

I understood what they said—the benefits of classical training in college and a year of immersion studies abroad in Madrid. That intimate knowledge of Spanish language unveiled the depravity of the people above me. In a world where every argument has two sides, I knew too much to empathize with either of theirs.

As their anger grew to become a chorus, I drained the finger of scotch. There. It. Was.

Her shrieking demeaning taunts, his vile threats—they were flushed to a septic and distant place by the warm amber wave.

I inhaled. A deep and cleansing breath. My hand came back to the edge of the dresser.

Begin anew.

"My name is Jackson Ford," I said. My voice was low, a murmur moving in my throat with a familiarity that comes from having self-introduced to strangers and masses for thirty years. "I was a two-term governor of the great state of—"

The voices overhead grew louder. It's easier for those not fluent to escape the tenor of voices in a language not their own. I took a second to disconnect from their new argument.

Begin anew.

"Hi, everyone! Jack Ford, two-term governor of the great state of—"

Sirens blipped outside my open window. As though in response, the wind picked up, and the curtains curled, their shadows overwhelming the shadows of the fire escape ironwork against my wall.

A vase shattered overhead.

"Course, they know who you are. Goddamnit." My hand was halfway across the dresser. Something ached in the back of my throat. I shook my head, like erasing a board.

Anew.

"Good afternoon, ladies and gentlemen of the bar. I've been asked by my dear friend, Judge Sarah Everly, to speak on her behalf at this auspicious gathering . . ."

Outside, another set of sirens blipped to a halt in front of the apartments.

"Auspicious gathering . . ." I repeated, my thoughts trailing, "of . . . distinguished . . ."

I could hear them thumping up the stairs beyond my front door. From the landing outside, there was a murmur and static of radios. Then the shriek of unoiled hinges on the stairway door. I imagined the cops muttering as they bypassed the elevator I had never known to be in service. The next time I blinked, my hand held the glass. The scotch was gone except for a rivulet retreating to the bottom of the tumbler. My throat was warm and thick with words.

". . . liars," I continued to the imagined audience of over a hundred solicitors. "Cutthroats. Thieves. How many of you bastards screwed your best friend's wife this week? How many of you corporate pricks are fucking over customers and citizens like they were your best friend's wife?" I gestured, raising the empty glass high, a thin sheen of gold at its bottom not escaping my notice as my right hand grasped the bottle, urging my audience to action.

"Come on, now," I coaxed. "Show of hands."

I nodded, surveying the venue in my mind's eye. The forest of raised hands.

"Jesus. All'a ya."

I poured cheap scotch and drank. It was gone in the twinkle of an eye.

"All. Of. You," I said.

Outside, more cops thundered up the stairs past the door with the screaming hinges. Shouts came from outside the apartment above mine, then an exchange in English and Spanish from both sides of what I knew to be a locked door.

I gestured to my audience with one crooked finger. "Judge Everly asked me to beat some sense of responsibility into your reptilian hides. Some cognizance of right and wrong so you might recognize the point at which your own manipulative interests must bow to the greater good. For society—"

The woman upstairs screamed. Short. Sharp. And then there was a silence that lasted until the crash of a police battering ram hit the reinforced metal door they'd installed in the unit after being robbed by rival dealers.

It was a tremendous blow. The kind some big linebacker cop had torqued just right and leveraged all his strength and weight into what should have been a catastrophic point of impact, where the blunt end of a forty-pound sledge should've torn inadequate bolts from the strike and deadbolt plates. It should have been followed by the sound of splintering wood, the crash of a ruined door slamming into drywall, and the tramp of feet moving into the apartment. And then by voices calling out in a cadence of inevitability as they cleared each room, one by one.

Instead, the sledge clanged against steel—a reverberation that went into the reinforcing plates they had screwed into studs and the frame.

The cops yelled. The sledge hit again and again in an increasing rhythm of desperation. Somewhere in the apartment above, a window shattered. There was a clatter on the fire escape. Then a confusion of light and motion along the wall behind me.

He was half my age but heavier, hunched over, half on the fire escape, half in the open window. He held a bloody knife in one hand. His other hand clutched the sheer fabric of a curtain. But not for balance. He was perfectly balanced there, on the cusp of entry, and the only thing that held him frozen was my presence.

As we locked eyes, the bottle rose in my hand. Effortless.

"For society," I repeated, to a live audience this time.

The bottle came down hard on the edge of the dresser. Shards exploded across the dresser top and into the mirror, along with the precious little scotch left. I felt a pain across my palm. But sharp things should slice both ways, lest we forget what it's like to be cut.

"For the victims," I said in Castilian Spanish.

Upstairs, metal pounded metal. A tinny rhythm creaked toward the only conclusion possible as the door screeched and slowly yielded to the combined efforts of men.

His eyes traced the jagged edges of the bottle I held—a mental calculus that no doubt took into account the thin red scrawl of my own blood down the length of the cracked neck, off the lowest tip of the ugly shard halo, and onto the dirty carpet.

Then he was gone. The curtain waved a new stain. Boots tramped across the floor above my head, and shouts came from the fire escape.

"For the victims," I repeated, laying the broken bottle on the dresser, savoring the sensation of alcohol in my wound as the slice opened across my palm. With my other hand, I held the tumbler below a rivulet of scotch that dripped from the dresser's edge.

From lower on the fire escape came the shouts of men. Cops thundered down the fire escape and past my window.

I lifted the glass and drank.

"For the dead," I said.

There were more shouts, then gunshots echoed from the front of the building. Sharp staccato bursts that implied the choice to put down a knife is not as simple as it seems.

I looked in the mirror. Silence pervaded after the last flat crack of a firearm. The interplay of light on the wall behind me had taken on a red tint as sunset began to color the sky.

Begin anew.

"Good evening, ladies and gentlemen of the bar. Tonight, I'd like to speak to you . . ."

". . . about responsibility," Jackson Ford said before the microphone shorted and feedback squealed from the speakers. A handler walked onto the stage beside Ford, beckoning the sound engineer, who brought another microphone pack.

Al Nivens watched them swap the microphones on the former governor from a table fifteen yards from the speaker's raised dais. The podium pressed against Ford's gut with the same firm restraint as a roller coaster's stabilizing bar. It indented the wearied black suit Nivens guessed was the same one Ford had worn to Steve Ricker's funeral. The former West Virginia governor was underdressed for the event. The banner across the stage behind him proclaimed the event as black tie for the Urban League of Defense Attorneys. It showed a happy collection of thirty-something models with legal pads and smiles but without dark rings under their eyes or the latent reservoir of despair that accumulates from years of eighty-hour weeks.

At Nivens' right hand, a gray-maned partner at a venerable Charleston firm stole a glance at the woman sitting at Nivens' left. She smiled slyly at the old power broker. His eyes drifted along the curve of her neck, lingering on the diamond stud earrings that had likely been one of his first gifts in an affair she would remember. They had entered together but had pointedly settled without comment on either side of Nivens at the table where seats had been subscribed far in advance.

He knew what that meant.

Al Nivens was a buffer. His presence would provide the two the barest veneer of propriety at an event where the gray mane's partners were in attendance with their wives, even if his own had been "unable to attend." Nivens kept his focus on Jackson Ford while he privately bet the old man would leave ahead of the young woman—just to sell it—before they met in a loft he kept nearby.

"As defense attorneys, you have an obligation," Ford was saying. The new microphone wasn't working yet, but Ford could project. The first two rows of tables had no problem hearing him, even without the speakers. "A sacred trust to uphold your client's rights against the onerous machinery of the state. That's what I used to be. The state."

Laughter echoed from a guy two tables over. Up on stage, the handler and sound engineer detached and reconnected wires. Ford forced an apologetic grin at the audience while they worked.

"Should have indicted that bastard," said the gray mane. Nivens looked at the old man, but eye contact wasn't there. He was gazing upward, pontificating, as though seeing a tableau presented against the venue's ceiling. "His campaign manager and chief of staff are both crooked," the partner continued, "and Ford doesn't know?"

The young associate at Nivens' left uncrossed her legs and leaned in toward the table. There was laughter as, on stage, the sound engineer made Ford raise both his arms, as though the cops had him cold and he was surrendering.

"Yeah, it's all fun and games," Ford said, "until someone gives you a Miranda."

"They say contractors used to walk into the mansion with bags of cash," the associate said, rubbing her thumb across her fingertips in a universal symbol, speaking past Nivens as though he were invisible. "Can't claim ignorance about something like that."

"Don't be so sure," Nivens said.

They both turned to him, as though noticing him for the first time. He looked at the associate. "You're too young to know, but you"—he looked at the gray mane—"you might've met Elise Ford. Such a fucking brilliant mind. And beautiful. Even without her hair. Even with chemo burning up her veins. Beautiful. At the end, you coulda waved a million dollars in that man's face, and he wouldn't have seen a thing. He was transfixed, see? Because when you love someone—I mean, truly love someone—you don't fucking blink while they slip away."

Nivens reached into his suit coat, as though fumbling for a good cigar. The associate sat back, glared, and recrossed her legs.

"What firm are you with?" The gray mane searched Nivens' face, looking for a memory that seemed on the verge of recollection.

Nivens placed a digital recorder on the table. The associate's eyes went wide. The gray mane pursed his lips and made the connection.

"Associated Press."

The speakers popped and hummed. The sound engineer and handler vanished.

"That's better," Ford said. He nodded to the engineer and handler in the wings. "Thank you."

"You all know why I'm here," Ford said, turning back to the audience. "It all comes back to responsibility." His gaze roamed a world Nivens knew must be darkened by the lowered house lights beyond the stage. "I remember back during the Clinton years, there were scandals. It's true. Every presidency has them. Jackson, Grant, Harding, Nixon. Jesus, we won't talk about Bush two or any of the others. That's when it got to a whole other scale. But the Clintons. Those were classic scandals. Whitewater. Jennifer Flowers. Stains on a cheap blue dress. Clear-cut scandals about the failures of a man. And see, that doesn't interest me. I mean, to each their own. I know people who could analyze Clinton and cuss all day. Not me though. Because his was a personal failing. Me . . . I care more about political scandals. See, that's when you get the failure of a system. The failure of everything we've planned and built and hope to God will last, and the neat thing about those is that you get new leaders. That's the sort of crucible where great people are born. So I'm not really talking about Clinton right now or even the fucked-up ATF middle managers trying to mount a raid to impress people at budget time. No. I'm talking about Waco."

On either side of Nivens, the associate and gray mane shared a look. She picked up her purse, preparing to leave. Nivens realized he was about to lose a bet with himself.

"Waco," Ford said. "That was the place. Fucked-up standoff between a bunch of lunatics led by a guy who thought he could have a harem and a bunch of federal agents trying to do their jobs in a situation with zero tactical surprise, a hostile local population, and inadequate firepower. You know the thing that impressed me? It was this obscure prosecutor from Miami they'd appointed to the post of attorney general. Waco exploded. Federal agents died. And then, when the fires were out and the dead were draped with flags, everybody was pointing a finger. Everybody, except this one lady. Janet Reno. Not her. She was a believer, see? She believed in the absolute dignity and power that comes from saying 'I am responsible.' Sweet Jesus. I can still hear her say it. Solemn-like. Like she was in church instead of in front of a phalanx of reporters. When was the last time you heard that out loud? Any of you hear that from your clients?"

There was more laughter. On either side of Nivens, the associate and partner rose and exited into the wings, apparently not caring that their indiscretion would be witnessed and later, remarked.

"But Janet Reno was mistaken in her beliefs," Ford said.

On the table, Al Nivens' digital recorder shone a dim red light, capturing the words.

Ford squinted into the darkness. Then he closed his eyes, as though shutting down. He said the last part quietly, almost low enough to escape capture by the microphone: "No amount of nobility brings back the dead."

Outside the hall, I sagged against an iron fence and watched the valets running cars as more lawyers climbed the hotel stairs toward a celebration at which I'd been just the warm-up act. I could feel the cold through my suit and see my breath congealing thin white vapor in the air, as ethereal as a wraith.

Then I saw him coming down the hotel steps. A white puff of air marked my curse as I turned and slouched toward the bus stop from which I would be carried away.

"Governor! Governor Ford!"

I hurried. Not looking back.

"Governor!"

And then he was beside me, jogging along with a grin, confident in his quarry.

"I'm not governor anymore," I said.

"That your idea of a return to the stump, Governor? Abandon morality? Deny accountability? Nothing brings back the dead? What about the living? Do you owe anything to the living?"

"No. I paid the living," I said, and I meant it.

"You didn't pay them with the truth, Governor," Nivens said. "This is your chance to set the record straight. You know, hold the corrupt officials accountable."

"I got nothing to say."

"Hey, the administration's looking at Judge Everly for the federal bench. You wanna endorse—"

"No." I stopped in my tracks. It caught him off guard. He continued for two more strides before swinging around to face my outstretched finger, pointed at his heart like a dagger. "Don't you ruin her chances by using my goddamn name."

"Aren't you here at her request?" He raised a digital recorder. "I mean, when we get a new federal judge, isn't it fair to ask with whom she associates?"

The digital recorder blinked at me, waiting for a reaction.

I swung hard.

My open palm hit his hand, and the recorder spun from his grip and out into the street. It shattered when it hit.

Nivens didn't even glance at it. He pulled a reporter's notepad and pen from his suit pocket. He glanced up at me as he scrawled on a page. "You spell *goddamn* with two Ds, right?"

Chapter VI

THE INVITATION

"NEW ZEALAND?" MATTHEW POPE WAS up, pacing now, eclipsing views of fire and flood and famine being broadcast on a wall of television screens behind him in the White House conference room. "You even whisper the word 'Wellington' to this guy, and he's going to drop his fucking money behind somebody else. Any-fucking-body else! What?"

The president's chief of staff stopped pacing and glared at Tony Ball, deputy director for the committee to reelect the president. Ball had his hand up, more like a penitent than a student. Wildfires lit several of the screens, throwing a hellish red glow across the thick sheen of sweat on the political operative's bald pate.

"Wellington's not the offer," he said. "We couldn't get the embassy."

"Fucking Auckland, New Zealand?" Pope glared at Ball, then at Christine Harper, who sat on the far side of the conference table, a selection of dossiers fanned out before her like oversized tarot cards, each with an abiding revelation. Harper shot a condescending glance at Ball, who ran his fingers alongside his smooth head as though he could still feel the memory of hair.

"It was the—" Ball started.

"Do you think this guy doesn't know the fucking difference between a consulate and an embassy?" Pope demanded. "What'd you ask State?"

"He didn't ask," said Harper, tapping the table with her fingernail. It clicked like glass against more fragile glass. "Tony was specific. Ambassadorial postings."

"First world embassies," Ball said. "I swear. I spelled it out for them."

"You know, the Maxwells have a place in Saint-Germain." Harper smiled, sitting back in her chair like the problem had been solved. "Sixth arrondissement."

"Paris? No," Ball said. "State would never go for that. Besides, the president has already nominated—"

"What's it worth?" Pope asked.

Ball blinked. "What?"

"Not you. Shut up. What's it worth?"

"Forty-six million." Harper smiled. "It's big for the sixth, but not Saudi or Russian oligarch-big. It has a 3,000-square-foot private garden and a separate structure for his dinosaur bone collection."

"The Senate's going to vote the French ambassador

next week," Ball said. "If we ask State to pull back their nominee—"

The wall of televisions flickered. A figure rose from a chair at the edge of the room and moved across the screens behind Pope, looking from his phone to each screen. Pope snapped his fingers to refocus Ball's attention from the man.

"Hey, fuck State for throwing Auckland at a donor with a net worth greater than the whole fucking island. We're changing strategy for the ambassador to France. That's Maxwell now. I'll communicate that to State."

Pope looked at Harper. He gestured to the dossiers. Behind him, the images continued to revolve. Fire. Famine. Flood. The man stood behind Pope, watching the screens. "What about Malagar?"

"Couple options there," Harper said. She slid a dossier to the edge of the table and stood up, leaning over to flick the folder open to reveal photos of a man waving to crowds. "The favorite is option one. Alex Williams. Former US Representative from Florida until he lost re-election."

"No." Ball glanced at the photo. "He'll be in jail."

"What?" Harper sat back in her chair. "We didn't—"

"He took bribes when he was on the House Armed Services Committee," Pope said. "The Bureau sat on it for us, but a DoD audit caught up to the contractors. They're rolling on him, and it's not gonna go away. We can't use him for anything for at least a year."

Harper opened the next folder.

Pope shook his head as soon as the photo became visible. "No. This asshole was against us on the Everglades thing."

"But that was two years—"

"I don't forget." Pope glared. "Next."

Harper spun the first two dossiers toward Ball as discards. He moved both away from him, one at a time, with a finger and a look of distaste. Harper flicked the last dossier open, showing a ruddy man in a suit turning a spadeful of soil at a ribbon-cutting for a highway toll booth construction project.

"Former New Jersey Senator Marlin Fisk," Harper said. "IRS is looking at him for tax evasion and—"

Pope cut her off: "Mob ties. We can't have that kind of exposure. Next."

Harper frowned. "Those were the only ones that would consider going down there."

Ball cleared his throat. He raised a finger. "I have someone."

From a coat pocket, Ball fumbled open a printed copy of a newspaper article. The headline proclaimed: *JACKSON FORD WINS TIGHT RACE.* The image of his victory was a balloon drop, with hundreds of balloons cascading down around Ford and his wife.

"Jackson Ford," Ball said. "West Virginia University. Two terms in the House of Delegates. Then he went national and served two terms in the US House. After that, he went back to West Virginia and won the gubernatorial race on a reform platform. His first term, he instituted some environmental and labor protections and a statewide scholarship program."

Ball unfolded and slid another sheet of paper onto the table. The second headline announced the funeral for Jackson Ford's wife.

"He barely campaigned during the second-term race. His wife was in chemo. Plus, they ran on a bootstrap, and the opposition outspent them in media like twelve to one. Ford won with a two percent margin. If his wife hadn't been dying, he wouldn't have had that. He buried her about a year into the term. Couple months after that, independent counsel began looking at him."

"What were the charges?" Pope held the article up, looking at Jackson Ford with his head bowed at his wife's gravesite.

"Bribery. Extortion. Illegal campaign contributions."

"That's what? A fine and house arrest? Did they get him?"

"They didn't get anyone," Ball said. "His chief of staff died in some kind of prison riot while he was being held in contempt for not talking to the grand jury. After that, Ford resigned."

"Didn't have the nerve to ride it out?" Pope frowned.

"Or he knew when to quit," Ball said. "He's a pariah now. Living hand to mouth."

"Is he hungry enough for the job?" Harper asked.

"Only one way to find out," Ball said.

Pope looked over his shoulder at the man who stood transfixed before the television screens. "Mr. President?"

The president of the United States did not turn his gaze from the screens. "Maxwell goes to Paris," he said. "As for Malagar . . . we cannot fuck that up. Vet him some more."

"Yes, sir," Pope said. "Now, who do we have for New Zealand?"

I followed a clutch of elderly women past the tall white columns fronting the portico of the venerable Kanawha Garden Club. The columns bore a patina of white paint that had yellowed and cracked with age. The women moved through a glass set of double doors that gaped wide, propped open with a rubber doorstop on one side and a folding chair wedged against the metal handle on the other.

I paused at the entrance. The women continued onward down a corridor, then turned to the left. Their voices diminished and were gone as they vanished around the bend. There was silence then. I turned away from the entrance of the place where I would provide my next speech. The garden club had once been in a residential neighborhood, but Charleston's urban sprawl had overtaken it. A granite and fieldstone purveyor operated on the left of the little half-acre enclave now. Piles of river rock summited above the six-foot fence. Somewhere over there, machinery growled to life, and a thin gray plume of smoke rose, marking the sky as a tractor moved between the piles.

Heat shimmered up from the blacktop parking lot, where two dozen cars were angled neatly between diagonal lines. The lawn was patchy. At the front of the building on either side were skeletal hedges. Tufts of unmown grass rose from the mulched barrier where only the hedges should have grown. A fly moaned past my ear.

To the right, a sign rose above the fence: *Ted's Tavern*. I blinked at it, then closed my eyes. My fingertips trembled slightly as I snugged my tie tight against my frayed collar. I didn't drink at the venues. I didn't drink prior to going to the venues. But after . . . after was fair game.

"Hey," someone said. "You the speaker?"

I opened my eyes and turned from thoughts of escape. A twenty-something woman with the nondescript business casual attire of a county employee and the patience of a German train conductor looked me up and down. Without waiting for a response, she crooked a finger at me. "In here."

"Be right in," I said. "Just marshaling my thoughts."

"Yeah," she said. "Well, we're all here, and we're waiting." She turned on her heel. Her shoes clacked as the carpeted entryway ended and she moved down the hallway's hardwood floors and out of sight.

I followed her into the darkened recesses of the Kanawha Garden Club. Down the corridor and to the right were offices and a bathroom. To the left was a large meeting space. The building doubled as home for the

local VFW and county extension. Hardwood floors in
the meeting space were taped off for what looked like
a fraction of a basketball court's dimensions. A portable basketball hoop sat at the corner of the room, where
a Hispanic woman coiled the long electrical cord for
an upright vacuum cleaner. A group of elderly women
milled around the twenty-something. She chatted as
she moved through them, laughing in a style I recognized as the best of extrovert craft in action. She was
working the room.

I moved to a table where coffee and tea decanters and
bottles of water sat along with the remnants of a box of
donuts. The Hispanic woman cleaned up detritus from
the top of the table: stirrers and torn sugar and creamer
packets. She dropped them into a fifty-five-gallon garbage can that sat three feet from the table. I knelt and
picked up a stirrer and empty sugar packets from the
ground beside the table and nodded to her as I tossed
them into the garbage. She tilted her head sideways, her
lips parting, as though about to share a thought but uncertain of her words.

My thoughts were elsewhere. The twenty-something
strode toward us.

"Governor," the Hispanic woman said. It wasn't tentative. It was the voice of someone who had found her
voice. "You are Governor Ford."

I looked at her and nodded. Recognition like this seldom went well. "Hi. It's just Ford now." I smiled at her.
"Jack Ford."

She held out her phone. On the screen was a photo dappled in sunlight. Greenery surrounded the mother and daughter in a way that seemed a mockery given the untended and arid landscape that sat outside.

"Is this your daughter?"

"Yes," she said.

There are some parents you would never know have children. They comport themselves in their workplace behind a mask that's more than professionalism. It's an armor that allows them to work so hard in difficult, sad, and sometimes degrading environments because they want to provide their children with sustenance and a stability that otherwise would not exist.

Elise surrendered the ability to have children. It was the price of her first remission. I would pay that toll a thousand times again. Perhaps though, it predisposed me to notice when the stoic veneer faded, as it did now in the Hispanic woman's face as she pointed to the girl in the high school graduation cap and gown.

"This is my daughter, Emilie," she said. "She has such good grades."

Her eyes lit up, her smile bright. I understood and smiled in return.

"Which university?" I asked.

"Marshall," she said. Her lips moved without a sound, but I knew the words: *Muchísimas gracias.*

"No thanks needed," I said. "Your family and your daughter did all the hard work."

Her hand fluttered to her lips, and she looked at the image of her daughter again.

"Hey," someone said behind me. I turned. It was the twenty-something.

"Be right there. Just getting something to—"

She didn't even blink. "The Ladies Auxiliary is a dry function."

"Of course," I said. "Of course it is."

"I'll have someone bring you a water." Then she took a wireless microphone from her purse and put it in my hand. She held an arm out, as though clearing a path through the elderly for me to vault onto the stage.

Thirty elderly women clustered into their seats in a space with twice that many chairs. On the stage, the twenty-something flicked a switch, and a single spotlight glared down on the podium. She checked her watch like there was a limit to the patience of the world.

"We're running behind schedule. Can you adjust the length of your . . . talk?"

"Sure," I said. "You have the . . . Uh . . ."

She swung her purse from her shoulder and palmed an envelope from the interior. I took it and counted. Four twenties. This had come out of petty cash.

The mic squealed in my hand as I approached the stage. Someone in the audience coughed. Light reflected across the white cinder block walls as someone else came in through the double doors. I turned on a smile and waved with the microphone in my hand as the twenty-something walked to the edge of the stage. The microphone hummed with the movement, generating feedback from speakers perched on unpainted plywood boxes.

"Good day to you, ladies!" I boomed. Campaign mode. Friendly. Reaching deep to tap reservoirs of enthusiasm that grief and disuse had filled with silt. My smile faded as I looked at the room. The elderly women watched me without interest. A bald man slouched down into a chair at the very back of the group, focused on his phone. I winced for him. Someone's son or son-in-law roped into driving the family matriarch to her outing.

"Thank you for having me!" One more rally. Waiting for some level of reaction. Or any interest from the group. "I'm here to talk to you about—"

The twenty-something was back at my side, one hand a vise on my wrist. The other covered the microphone. "Introduce yourself," she said. Then she waved again. The elderly women waved back, and then she was gone.

I stood there, in a halo of light, in a hall of strangers.

Ted's Tavern was the sort of hole in the wall that excluded the light of day. The place had cinder block walls, like the Kanawha Garden Club down the street. But the owner had painted his interior a matte black and drilled holes in the blocks from which he anchored old black-and-white movie posters in cheap plastic frames. I sat at the bar on the Bogart side, with *Sahara*, *Casablanca*, and *The Maltese Falcon* at my back. There was another customer in the last of a row of unoccupied booths along the wall behind me. Each booth had a light that mimicked a candle flickering at the end of its wick. It was a dim ambiance. At least at the bar, the lights weren't flickering. In the dim but constant glow, I could see the dark walnut grain of the bar through the bottom of the empty glass before me.

I fished a twenty from the envelope in my coat pocket and laid it on the bar.

"You know who I am?" I asked.

In that moment, sunlight dazzled the glass bottles perched high behind the bartender, then winked out again as someone came in and the door swung shut.

The bartender snagged the bill. "You're Black Label, very little ice."

"Yeah. That's who I am."

"Same here." The bald son-in-law to some elder matriarch sat on the stool to my left. I glanced at him. Surprised at the need for intimacy in a room where there was one other customer, fourteen booths, and at least nine other stools. Then the flint-eyed woman sat on my right, and as she took a long hard look at my imperfections, I knew I'd missed something essential.

"He's buying," the bald guy said and nodded his head toward me.

The bartender looked at me. I narrowed my eyes and frowned. "Buy your own damn liquor," I said.

The woman on my right tapped a single manicured nail on the bar. She nodded sideways to the bartender with the lilt of a smile on her lips, and he took the cue to busy himself elsewhere.

"That's no way to treat your friends, Jack." She fixed me with her gaze. She was in her thirties and had a beach volleyball physique packaged in a suit that would be at home in court or Congress.

"Gotta give a little to get a little," chimed in the bald guy.

"Or a lot, Governor," she said.

"I'm not governor, and you're no friends of mine."

"You sure?" she asked.

"I resigned the office. Buried all my friends. I'm sure." I looked at the bartender as he slid three glasses before us. "I ain't paying for theirs."

The bald guy slid a hundred-dollar bill on the bar. "Keep 'em coming."

"You're too rich for reporters." I leaned back, examining them both. "Suits are above pay grade for state cops. That makes you feds. Is the Bureau taking an interest in all failed politicians or just me?"

"Governor Ford, we're not—"

I raised my hand to the bald guy. "Just Ford. I don't want to say it again."

When I turned back to look straight ahead, I caught her expression out of the corner of my eye. The woman was smiling, as though she'd caught on to something I hadn't intended to reveal.

"That irritates you," she said. "Doesn't it? A surrendered title."

"Loss of privilege," the bald guy helped.

"The absence of power." Her nail clicked against her untouched glass. Mine was at my lips. I could feel the smoke in my mouth. The warmth. The hint of vanilla in my throat. Then it was gone. There was no pleasure.

No numbness. No solace. In my mind, I blamed my company.

"Who are you?" I asked.

The bald guy tossed back the contents of his glass in one easy swallow, as though something that had aged a mere twelve years wasn't worthy of being savored. He shrugged and looked past me to the woman.

I turned my gaze to her. Her eyes met mine, and I got the feeling she had the visual acuity of a raptor, able to spot prey emerging from a dirty little hole while soaring miles away.

"Jack," she said, "we're an invitation."

Chapter VII

THE SHORT TERM SWEET DEAL

THE GREAT SEAL OF THE United States was inlaid in the floor like a harbinger. A warning I should heed. The eagle wore a breastplate of the Republic. It clutched an olive branch in its right talon and thirteen barbed arrows in its left. Its gaze was directed to the right, sweeping across the olive branch in a manner that symbolized the nation's desire for peace. The Latin banner cried out *E Pluribus Unum* beneath a rising constellation of thirteen stars.

Out of many, one.

Our nation's seal could have been very different. On July 4, 1776, the Continental Congress passed a resolution that specifically tasked the revolutionary trio of Benjamin Franklin, John Adams, and Thomas Jefferson to generate the emblem that would be used on official government documents. Franklin advocated for a scene of Moses parting the Red Sea, inundating Pharaoh and his pursuing armies above the motto "Rebellion to tyrants is obedience to God." Not to be outdone for biblical flair, Thomas Jefferson lobbied for a scene of young Americans being led by a pillar of fire in the night, like the lost children of Israel in the wilderness. To complete the trifecta of proof that not all ideas of the Founding Fathers were the best ideas, John Adams suggested a more classical Greek motif. He wanted the seal of the United States of America to feature Hercules resting on his club.

Fortunately, it was six years and several committees later when Charles Thomson, Secretary of the Continental Congress, designed the 1782 seal with the American eagle casting its gaze toward the optimism of an olive branch.

The eagle looked away from our direction of travel. Ahead, past the arrows of war, a security checkpoint was manned by Diplomatic Security Service guards. One with a slung M4 watched me pointedly.

The federal analyst that had escorted me through the maze of the Harry S. Truman building to this subterranean space stood on the eagle's beak, her square-toe black pumps scuffed the *Pluribus*. "We're running late," she said and beckoned me toward the dual glass security doors ahead. From an egress, two old men in suits and an Air Force military attaché exited the secure area and walked across the pronged arrows of war.

"Sure," I said. "The die is cast."

Then I walked around the Great Seal, mindful of the role of symbols in our lives.

The analyst signed a log for me, and the DSS guards did what guards do. I made it out of the sniffer and metal detector and visual pat-down process without a belt for my pants but with a red visitor badge on a lanyard around my neck. The guards gave me odd looks of disbelief when I said I didn't have a cell phone. Apparently, they see more people without kidneys than without electronics to enter in the bank of temporary lockboxes just behind their security station.

We stepped through another set of twin glass security doors. The corridor beyond hooked left. It was carpeted in a deep blue plush that absorbed the tap-tap-tapping of the analyst's pumps as she led me past a sign that said *Operations Center* and into a bullpen of workstations reminiscent of the Apollo launch command at Houston. Department of State personnel worked at stations labeled for the six geographic Department of Defense commands: Northern, Southern, Africa, Central, Indo-Pacific, and European. People clustered the central command node, where a series of computer screens showed smoke billowing above the wavering outline of flames. As we approached, someone duplicated the view of incineration on the bank of screens consuming the far wall visible to everyone in the ops center. Analysts at other nodes paused what they were doing and looked up at the black smoke spewing from the carcass of a cargo truck that sat astride fractured cement barricades. The analyst leading me halted at the edge of the clamor of phones and voices and pointed me toward the man at the center of it.

"Pope," she whispered, then stood back, her hands touching and then coming apart, like she had somehow taken me off an invisible leash. I was now free to go to my new master.

"Do we have a handle on the Lebanese response?" Pope yelled from a position before the massive screens. "Was anyone important on the grounds?" Without missing a beat, he locked eyes with me as I approached. "You're late. You know who I am?"

"Matthew Pope," I said. "President's chief of staff. I was told I'd be meeting Lillian Schaeffer."

Someone shouted: "Orion in range! We're getting satellite images!"

A subset of the screens at the front of the room flickered and changed to a top-down perspective, zooming incredibly fast through a peninsular view down to a city, then to a street, where the guts of the truck vomited smoke. One screen identified it as a Renault truck chassis. From the sat view, it was easier to make out the strew of charred bodies and see the pixilated images of running figures. At the lower left corner of the screen, I could make out the slower, more forlorn movement of a man crawling away from the wreck, trailing stains as he made swimming motions against the cracked and pitted pavement.

"Madam Secretary's in Beijing for three weeks of talks to appease Microsoft," Pope said like we were shooting the breeze in a boarding area while waiting for the pregnant people, wheelchair travelers, and un-accompanied minors to get on. "Met the lady? Fluent in nine languages. Every word meticulously planned. She hates this place. Too much chaos. Me? I come down here for kicks. Fucking rejuvenating. This is the pulse of the globe."

"Where's this?" I asked, nodding to the scene of carnage. The wounded man at the corner of the Orion spy sat image flailed one last time and then was still except for the almost imperceptible adjustments the screen made as the satellite tracked overhead.

"This time? Lebanon," Pope said. He smiled, watching the fires rage. "You're looking at the outer perimeter of our embassy in Beirut."

"Can't locate the ambassador!" an analyst called. "He was hosting a reception for the Lebanese prime minister."

"Avrahim drags half his cabinet with him," Pope yelled. "I want to know if anyone relevant died today!"

More screens flashed up as pictures within pictures on the main wall. Grainy feed from the embassy's security cams collected images at the street-level as analysts prioritized the information. Other screens targeted bodies in the street, and identification software began to pair the slumped forms with a flickering cascade of database ID photos.

"They're all relevant," I said as three, then four, then nine bodies were identified.

"Huh? Somebody convinced a Lebanese boy the best thing he could do with his crappy life was turn a Renault into the surface of the sun," Pope said. "How relevant was he?"

Embassy staff and Marines and Lebanese security forces showed up on the screens, triaging wounded and tolling the dead.

"Tell me what you know about Malagar," Pope said without looking at me.

"That'll be a short conversation. It's a country in South America. Borders Ghana, Brazil, and, ah . . ."

"Suriname. And it's not so much a country as a shitty little dictatorship. Get's more interesting when you realize they've got a wealth of natural resources comparable to Venezuela. Morally, they're way more conservative than Brazil. But who isn't? I hear there are great beaches. But it's the ports we care about. We need them open for American exporters. We have an opening." He looked at me, arms folded across his suit. "Frederick Hinkley was our ambassador. He's coming home for early retirement."

"That's a poor euphemism for scandal."

"You should know," Pope replied.

There was a moment of silence as more cameras came online from the embassy security boundary. Then what looked like body cam footage from one of the Marines coordinating the response became the primary source across the wall. At the periphery, screens continued to depict the actions of the computer recognition program as it flicked through the Renault's carnage. Body parts. Twisted and smoking metal. Then it froze on a dead-eyed face grimacing up at the Marine's body cam.

"The embassy Marines caught Hinkley with an eight-year-old girl," Pope said. He was looking at me like there wasn't anything at all on the wall. "She was the daughter of a Malagayan Army noncom that provided external embassy security. If not for diplomatic immunity, Hinkley's head would be on a pike. We're looking at a couple names. People who could go down there and keep a lid on things."

"Couple names," I said.

"You're one."

"What qualifies me?"

Pope looked at me. I mean, *really* looked at me. I was painfully aware of my frayed suit. My bloodshot eyes.

"Need," he finally said. "Yours. Not mine. See, this is the part of the interview where you—"

"You want stability, right? I can give you that." My pulse quickened. The post of ambassador carried with it enough to light fires in my breast. Pay. Authority. An eventual redemption. "You want quiet. I'm a mouse. You want . . . Whatever you want, I can do it."

Pope nodded. "I'll bet you were something back in the day. Am I right? Begging for an ear and a vote. Door to door across WVa," Pope said, sounding out each letter: *double-you-vee-ay.*

The Marine feeding us images must have been on point to reinforce the perimeter. We could see him gesturing other Marines and Lebanese security guards into position facing the hole the Renault had blown in the embassy's barriers. There was no traffic on the broad roadway. The wind had changed. The smoke had flattened across the roadway like a fog. He and his body cam stared intently at the fog. His hands came into view, raising a 9 mm pistol.

"I used to do that. Every house would smell different," Pope said. "Different sort of stink. Remember that? Old people'd walk you into their dusty parlor. You'd sit there with pictures of the dead all around you and a cup of bitter coffee. What'd you tell 'em, Jack?"

Out of the plumes of smoke, something writhed. The movement was like ghosts trying to part the billowing veils obscuring our mortal view. Frail souls warning us with soundless voices and misty hands that leviathans were rising from prisons black with bile and hatred.

"I told them I'd pave the roads," I said.

The body cam Marine took a shooter's stance, his finger along the tan frame of the pistol. It pointed without wavering as a cement mixer erupted from the smoke, drum rotating. The front of the truck carried the grimace of rough-welded metal plates across the engine compartment and cab.

Muzzle flame blossomed on the screen. Shell casings flicked up and away in streaks of brass light. The Orion top-down view showed the truck racing in a headlong sprint toward a collection of figures from whence sparkles of gun muzzle flame illuminated.

"I promised decent pay for honest work," I said. "That their kids wouldn't get sick from drinking the water or going outside, and when they did go outside, they could play in the park without finding crack pipes or needles."

Beside the body cam image, a monitor flashed up the Marine's ID. He couldn't have been more than twenty-five.

"I promised if they worked hard and graduated high school with good grades . . ." There was a rasp in my voice, but I knew no one else heard me. "If they did that, they'd be able to go to college."

As the cement mixer hurtled toward the camera view, rounds found the slits the driver was using to see. Bullet impacts threw gouts of glass from behind the plates covering the windshield.

"Mostly," I said, almost a whisper, "I promised not to let them down."

"My God, you're Miss America," Pope said.

"I made a difference," I said. "For a while."

The cement mixer veered past what remained of the Renault's burning carcass. Bullet impacts flared across the plates, then some found tires. Both front tires exploded. Black rubber flew from the spinning rims, followed by sparks as steel rims hit the pavement and momentum kept it coming. For a moment, it seemed that what remained of the outer barriers would be enough as the cement mixer hobbled to a stop short of the embassy's line of security.

On the screens that occupied a wall, the Marine thumbed a release, and the 9 mm's empty magazine fell, twisting, as though time had slowed. The Marine's free hand rose to insert a new one.

Light flared from the truck, blinding all screens carrying the body cam feed. The Oasis quadrant of screens also turned white with the brilliance of detonation. The screens on the wall automatically calibrated brightness to diminish the effect as it became static and white.

Pope was looking at me. The screens that had once shown the world of a Marine in Beirut were static-washed now and unambiguous in their absence of any sign of life. Then the Oasis feeds returned to show a crater more massive than the Renault's in the roadway. Where there had been a line of men at the perimeter of the embassy, figures and pieces of men now curled against the ground, unmoving. At this distance, they were unrecognizable as things once alive.

I tore my eyes from the monitors. Pope nodded. It was an appraisal.

"How relevant are you now?" Pope asked.

I looked at my profile in the window glass of the Air Force Gulfstream. I was clean-shaven. I mean barber shop, soak under a steaming hot towel clean. The suit was off the rack but new. The shirt still possessed the fold lines made during manufacture before being inserted into a clear plastic package in Mexico.

A crewmember leaned forward and took my empty glass and napkin with the Great Seal within a circlet made up of the words *Department of State, United States of America*. He put my empty glass on his tray.

"Another club soda?" he asked.

I shook my head.

"The weather let up just a bit," he said. "We're on the ground in twenty minutes, Mr. Ambassador."

Then he was gone, and I looked past myself at the black veils of clouds pluming across the landscape. Farther out toward the horizon was the thin rim of the Atlantic. For a moment, I contemplated calling him back. I imagined the cool of the glass in my hand and envisioned the way the liquor would tremble slightly as we hurtled through the high and still sky.

I inhaled. Closed my eyes. Then opened them again to a view of the world from seven miles up. Exhaled.

Begin anew.

Even as the words framed in my mind, something dragged my eyes away from the vista outside the window. My hands clenched into fists, then relaxed. They trembled slightly, even though there was no turbulence.

Chapter VIII

DULCE ET DECORUM

Beryl Allister walked along the fence at the perimeter of Malagar's military airport. He wore his duty uniform with the sergeant's stripes, even though he was off duty. He wore his sidearm in a leather holster that put the 9 mm low on his hip, even though the lieutenant had ordered him to turn it in at the armory and report to his new post at the border checkpoint with Brazil.

The transport left without him. Within a day, they would know he was absent without leave. He had one day to make things right.

Beryl walked the fence line as though it was the inspection a NCO would make once each month, checking the wire and supporting posts, even though the inspection was not due for two more weeks. The guard shack controlling the entrance the Americans would use was only three hundred meters away.

He paused, clipboard in hand, and pretended to worry the fence away from the metal bolts that kept the bottom links anchored in the soil. He had time before they arrived.

A breeze slid past. The papers on his clipboard rustled. The top sheet flipped upward, revealing the photograph Beryl had placed there.

For a moment, Aurelie smiled up at him.

She and her mother were in sunshine, the sand at their feet copper and coarse. Aurelie held up two gray rounded stones she'd found in an inlet where cold highland waters ran into the ocean. She had the lighter skin of her mother, but his daughter had his black hair and broad smile.

Beryl stood, one hand on the fence, one hand holding the visage of his daughter, and he felt more than heard the sound that caught in his throat—half sob, half her name. It surprised him. Then the breeze passed. The page uncurled and covered the photo, as though nature itself knew the photo of Beryl's dead child had the unique power to shred his coherence into equal parts grief and rage, and that if those dark aspects of sorrow were released, he would not be able to do the things that must come next.

Beryl blinked the images away, his voice quiet in the admonition: "Not yet."

When he looked up, he saw it darting across the sky, as though the clouds had parted just to give him a glimpse. Then it was gone again, in the midst of a descent pattern over the airport that would lower the jet with the blue and white livery of the United States toward the runway.

In the tattered thought process grief allowed, Beryl had planned something simple. Get inside the airfield and on the landing pad. Be there when the Americans arrived. Though he knew some of the Marines may recognize him, he couldn't put the overriding desire from his thoughts. He wanted to get close before pulling the trigger. Close enough for recognition. Close enough for Beryl to see the fear.

The first American Humvee roared past behind him. He turned from the rain-slicked runway as an armored Suburban trailed the Humvee down the access road, followed by a second Humvee carrying armed American Marines.

Guards at the shack raised the gate to allow the Humvees and Suburban access to the airfield. Beryl controlled himself as the vehicles drove to the edge of the tarmac designated for smaller jets to park after they cleared the runway. Overhead, the ragged remnants of storm clouds scudded low and into the mountainous peaks at the far end of the valley. A storm had washed the area hours before. Lightning had danced across the sky, but in an ominous portent, the rain had not come down in anything more than frustrated fits. Steam rose from the isolated puddles. Sunlight lanced through a break in the moving clouds and reflected brightly from the Suburban's tinted glass.

Beryl took the photo of his daughter and folded it into the breast pocket of his uniform. He fought the impulse to run toward the shack protecting the access road. There was still time. There was still a chance.

Daniel Nokes stepped from the darkened confines of the Suburban and into sunlight that momentarily dazzled. A break in the clouds swept the light over and past him, throwing gems across standing water rippling in a depression on the tarmac. Another break rolled across the far end of the runway, illuminating the military flight line and throwing a rainbow high above a squat row of Bell UH-1Y Super Huey helicopters. The air smelled faintly of the ocean, even though the military airfield was twenty miles inland from Malagar's coast and the deep-water harbors that funneled a nearly constant flow of American-engineered and Malagayan-made products to ports in Charleston, Wilmington, and Baltimore.

He shut the door on the Suburban without a backward glance and ambled over to the lead Humvee, where Gunnery Sergeant Joseph Gaines stood watching sky at the far end of the runway. At four points around them, Marines with slung Mossbergs and M4s scanned the landscape.

Daniel stood beside Gaines, aware of the incongruity in their appearances. Gaines was a figure cut from a six-foot-two block of onyx. He was somewhere between his late thirties and immortal. He had a linebacker's build in the blue coat and sky-blue trousers, with a gunnery sergeant's sense of decorum. The other Marines were in camouflage or duty uniforms as they posted security. Gaines and the Marine driving the ambassador's armored Suburban were dressed for a formal occasion, even if the occasion was a passing of the torch between emissaries to the shittiest little part of the world.

Daniel was the same height as Gaines, but he carried it stoop-shouldered in a lanky Alabama sharecropper frame. He had the lean corded muscles and splay-footed gait of his forefathers. The cargo pants he wore were the cleanest he had available, and he'd donned his third-best Hawaiian print shirt. He slipped a pack of gum from a pocket and extended it to Gaines—a silent gesture of goodwill and camaraderie Gaines ignored.

Daniel held the gum out just long enough to be annoying, then shrugged and pulled a stick for himself. He folded the gum into his mouth and chewed before inclining his head toward Gaines, as though to share a confidence.

"Gunny," Daniel said, "wishing it won't put a man in hell."

Gaines inclined his gaze upward just a fraction. The broad white wings of the Gulfstream left the cloud layer as the pilot jockeyed the craft toward the landing strip. The wings wimpled under the movements, swaying up and down, white vapor spiraling away from the winglets in plumes of mist that trailed their descent from the sky.

Daniel put the gum away as the jet touched the runway. A pall of mist and smoke rose behind the swaying tail as air brakes rose from the engine cowling on either side of the fuselage. The reversers howled a dark turbulence into the humid air. The jet slowed with a ponderous reluctance.

Gaines turned and looked at the Suburban.

"Ready!" he called.

Private Riley stepped from the driver's side of the idling vehicle. Like Gaines, he wore dress blues. Riley walked around to the rear door of the Suburban as the Gulfstream slowed its roll and navigated a turn from the active runway to the taxiway that would lead to the apron beside the embassy vehicles. The air reverbed as the jet eased up. The nose dipped slightly as the pilot braked to a halt. Gaines murmured into his radio earpiece. After a moment, he raised his hand to the cockpit and signaled that they could open the jet's door.

The aircraft door indented and then swung downward, extruding stairs as it lowered. A crewmember stood in the slant of light beyond the open doorway.

Gaines looked at Riley. Riley stepped to the Suburban and swung the rear door wide.

Former Ambassador Frederick Hinkley stepped out of the darkened interior as though he hadn't a care in the world. He wore a double-breasted navy suit with an Ian Fleming bow tie and suspenders. His was a jowled countenance akin to the look of a televangelist disheveled by sin. One eye was half-lidded, swollen with a blue-black shiner. Thin black threads of a suture protruded from a gash on his lower lip. He made it a point to step around the puddle that lay just beyond the vehicle door.

Riley held the door open, frozen in place, eyes staring at a point on the horizon that was not to be confused with a line of sight to Hinkley's squint. Hinkley blinked upward at the gray sky. Then his hand swept back the stray shocks of his cotton-white hair.

The Marine watching the access road and security checkpoint along their egress raised binoculars to his eyes. He tracked the movement of a lone Malagayan noncom walking the exterior of the security fence line to the guard shack controlling the access road.

Hinkley walked to Gaines. Unlike Riley, Gaines kept his eyes on the former ambassador. Daniel saw the big man's right hand twitch slightly. Hinkley licked the suture in his lower lip as he approached, wincing as though he savored it. He looked up at the Marine.

"What's the matter, Gaines? No fare thee well?"

Gaines didn't move.

Hinkley frowned, then stepped past Gaines to Daniel. Daniel inclined his head to the Gulfstream as the engines diminished to a whine, then fell into step beside Hinkley as they walked toward the jet.

"Danny boy," Hinkley said, "this misunderstanding will pass. Don't know when we'll have a chance to work together again, but I want you to know I regard you as a friend. I'm gonna miss your sense of social order."

"Thank you, Ambassador," Daniel said. "Maybe you'll take some friendly advice?"

"Of course," said Hinkley, his tone and demeanor making it clear no words would ever move him.

Daniel put his hand across Hinkley's shoulder, stopping the old man. Anger flashed across Hinkley's bruised face, but Daniel tightened his grip as he leaned close to the old man's ear. "From now on," Daniel whispered, "answer the door with a gun in your hand."

He placed the heel of his palm against the former ambassador's bony spine and shoved him toward the jet. Hinkley lurched forward, his mouth a grim line, nostrils flaring. He recovered and walked toward the descending airstairs without a backward glance.

Behind them, the Marine sentry watching the access road peered through binoculars as the Malagayan noncom dropped his clipboard on the roadway and went into the guard shack, where two soldiers were on duty. He swung the binoculars to take in the airfield's perimeter road. An olive drab defense force Humvee rolled between each guard position on a regular patrol. When the Marine swung his view back to the shack on the access road, it was in time to see a figure exit and walk down the access road toward them.

"Gunny, Ramriez," the Marine murmured into his radio. "Got one armed individual walking toward us from the roadway guard shack." He refocused his binoculars on the figure, who was still two hundred yards away. "Got a holstered sidearm. Appears to be local security."

We walked toward each other as though it were a prisoner exchange. The wind blew his hair, lifting and tossing white strands with an undulation befitting a specter come to speak of mistakes, loss, and regret. His face was mottled with swelling that made one eye larger than the other. Both squinted at me with a hostility I did not ignore. He kept his gaze locked on my own as we neared.

As we came abreast of each other, Frederick Hinkley raised his fist, two fingers extended, and prodded my chest. "Welcome to Malagar, Ambassador." Then his fingers moved across my suit coat, as though brushing away something unseen but nevertheless deleterious to my health. "Do remember to lock your boudoir."

He staggered past me, and the man with the mane of hair like a Dickensian ghost vanished into the jet's cabin.

Ahead, a tall lanky man wearing a Hawaiian print shirt and straw Panama hat signed for a diplomatic pouch one of the crew had run over to him. He retreated to the back of the Suburban while the crewmember jogged back past me and up the stairs. The whine of the jet's engines increased as I reached the only figure on the tarmac that seemed posed to receive me, a Marine in dress blues. He watched me with stony neutrality. I oddly preferred Hinkley's resentment. At least with him, I knew where I stood.

Usurper. Pretender to his petty little throne.

"I'm Jackson Ford," I said as I reached the Marine. I extended my hand.

The Marine's eyes focused past me. I glanced. The airstairs were gone, and the door had recessed back into the fuselage. The nose wheel turned toward the runway as the jet's engines roared with something like urgency.

I looked back at the Marine and saw something I hadn't expected. He stood a little taller, as though unburdened. Then his eyes flicked to me, and I caught a fractional movement in the muscles at his jawline and in the focus of his gaze. He didn't look at my extended hand and did not appear to notice when I dropped it by my side.

"Mr. Ambassador, Gunnery Sergeant Joseph Gaines," he said. "We should go, sir."

Gaines gestured to the back of the Suburban as the four Marines at sentry positions jogged back to their Humvees. At the back of the Suburban, a Marine private held the door open for me. I paused as I reached him. He was also wearing dress blues, had sandy hair, and couldn't have been more than twenty.

I extended my hand. "Jack Ford."

He looked down, uncertain. Then he reached forward and took my grip. "Private Richard Riley Jr., sir. They call me Little Dick, but, ah, you don't have to, sir."

I grinned at his honesty. "Mind if I call you Richard?"

"No, sir. I mean, I'd like that. Sir."

The corporal at the gate was suspicious. He met Beryl outside the gatehouse. The private inside the shack watched them both.

"Gate inspection," Beryl said. "Logs and equipment lockers. Let's see it."

"We passed inspection two days ago," the corporal said.

Beryl didn't like the way the corporal's eyes raked across him, as though trying to remember something. "Let's go," Beryl said, gesturing with his clipboard. "I got three more gates. Either you're prepared, or you're not."

The corporal turned, heading back for the shack. "Hey!" he shouted to the private inside. "Radio the duty officer. I want to—"

Beryl let the clipboard fall. The sap was in his hand before it was halfway to the ground. By the time the clipboard clattered against pavement, Beryl's swing arced a half pound of lead shot sewn into a leather pouch. The pouch narrowed to become a handle. At the end of the leather handle, a loop allowed him to insert his pinkie or ring finger. It kept the pouch from slipping from his grasp when it became wet with sweat. Or blood.

The sap caught the corporal against the flat of his skull, just above the ear. He dropped half-in and half-out of the guardhouse. The private's eyes went wide, his hand frozen in mid-reach for a radio on the desk. His mouth fumbled to form words.

Beryl was inside in a heartbeat. His boot slammed into the small man's chest. The private flew into an equipment locker, dislodging something inside that clattered down. He struggled back up as Beryl swung with the sap and hit the private's forearm. The man cried out in pain and then was silenced as Beryl hooked a fist into his chin. Beryl spun him and caught him from behind in a choke hold. The private struggled, clawing at Beryl's grip, until he entered a world of darkness and his hands fell away by his sides.

Beryl stood and straightened his uniform. He took the battery from the portable radio before he stepped out of the gatehouse and closed the door. He retrieved the clipboard, tossed the battery into the grass, and walked toward the Humvees and jet. He had taken too much time. Hinkley was already out of the American vehicle and walking toward the aircraft that would carry him to a place beyond Beryl's reach.

Beryl loosened the Beretta in the holster on his hip, but the range was too far. There were fifteen rounds in the magazine. Even with careful aim, he couldn't hope to put an ounce of metal into the hindbrain of Frederick Hinkley at this distance. The Marine watching him with binoculars would alert the others, and they would form around Hinkley like a shield wall to protect the bastard responsible for corrupting his daughter and casting Beryl into a realm of loss and pain.

But he had no choice but to try.

At a range of sixty-five meters, Beryl sank to one knee and raised the Beretta in his grip, the iron sights rising to obscure the moving gray halo of hair so far away. The air grew still. He half exhaled.

And that's when he heard it—the swift and nearly silent thudding of boots running across the grass.

Beryl looked up in time to see the corporal. A crown of blood that had flowed from where the blow had split his skin down to the skull. It matted the hair on one side of his head and neck. The blood had run in rivulets to frame his lips and jaw. He ran, intent, and the thin black graduated line of a baton uplifted in one hand began its descent.

Then the corporal was on him. The world exploded in a pure white light as the tip of the baton smashed into Beryl's temple, and he was conscious only of the slow and melancholy spin of the world as the earth rose up to receive him.

We rode out in single file. Riley drove; Gaines rode shotgun beside him. We didn't slow at the open exit gate. As we flashed past the checkpoint, I caught a surreal image of a guard beating another guard with a baton. Blood rose from the metal tip in a castoff arc that sprayed high in the air as the baton rose and then flashed down, again and again before, being lost behind us.

On the roadway beyond the airstrip, two olive drab Ford F-150 trucks hurtled past, blue dome lights flashing, each with soldiers hunched against each other in the back beds. Through the rear window, I could see the trucks angle to a stop at either side of the security gate and the shapes of men as they leapt to the ground and ran to the gate, rifles up. Beyond them, in the sky past the gate, the Gulfstream streaked upward from the end of the runway before becoming lost in the overcast.

The man sitting beside me in the Suburban had opened the diplomatic pouch and was rummaging among the papers. He withdrew a box sealed in bubble wrap and tape, and flicked open a knife from somewhere under the loose-fitting Hawaiian shirt depicting golden sunsets and black palm fronds. The blade was a razored extension of his finger as it separated the tape and wrap from a red oak box with the words *Johnnie Walker* charred into the side in an ornate calligraphy that was not something I had ever seen affiliated with the brand.

He folded the blade away, and the knife vanished again. He pushed his Panama straw hat up. Brown hair curled against his forehead. He spoke without introduction. Without explanation for his actions. He hadn't made eye contact yet, but when he did finally address me with his gaze on the golden hand-tooled clasp at the side of the oaken box, it was with a familiarity that could've convinced an observer we were old and trusted friends.

"This is good. I mean look at this, Jack." He delicately opened the box. It was a presentation case, with twin blue glass tumblers perched in foam next to a pristine bottle of Blue Label scotch. "See, there's a right way and a wrong way to do things. You don't take the devil something they know, right? You don't just throw a bottle of something at Los Generales without putting a little spin on it."

He hefted the box, smiling at me like a professor delivering his capstone lecture. All the wit and wisdom from a lifetime of training was mine to hold now, if only I paid attention.

"Like this." He gestured to the case. "Expensive bottle. Johnnie Walker Blue. Right? But anybody with a couple hundred bucks can get this. The presentation here? This is an Etsy creation. Blown glass. New York artist. Only maybe a dozen ever made. He signed the glass when he blew it in his kiln. Didn't even know that was a possibility. That's cool. I'm not going to even touch it. If they see a fingerprint, I want to be able to say it's from the artist. They'll eat that up. I guarantee you, no one else is going to show up with this at a party."

He blinked as I stared at him. In the absence of a re-action, he nodded as though satisfied I understood the lesson thus far. He continued speaking as the Suburban swayed on the rutted roadway. He swung the box lid closed and latched the side.

"They don't care about the liquor. They got plenty of beverages. They don't even care about the glass or whether it's beautiful, even though it is quite nice." He placed the box back in the diplomatic pouch at his feet. "What our partners care about is being wooed. You're going to find them very receptive to overt gestures of courtship from the senior-most American on station. That's your takeaway. You're gonna have to devote a lot of time and effort into holding their hands."

"You're Nokes," I said. "The spy."

"Please—Daniel," he said. Then he sucked air between his teeth. "Somebody actually said the word 'spy' out loud after using my name? No. No. No." Daniel leaned forward, wagging a finger. "Though, yes, I did once have a mistaken dalliance with the good folks at Central Intelligence. And before that, I guess I had the equivalent of a long marriage and soul-crushing divorce from the part of Uncle Sam's Army that likes jumping out of planes. But that's the past about which we do not speak. Your RSO is in Brasília. That's 'Regional Security Officer.' He thinks he actually is a spy, even though he's nowhere near anything or anyone with actionable intelligence. I'm your economic section. Bilateral and multilateral trade. Civil aviation's a good example of what I do. All those next-gen Hueys on the airport flight line are my good work. Oh, I'm your foreign agricultural section. That's USDA's outreach to the primitives that're still using sticks to plant seeds. We're gonna take away their little fertility idols and sell 'em tractors."

"Sounds like you don't think too much of the people down here."

"I offend?" Daniel leaned close. "Stop kissin' babies, Jack. You're an ambassador now. You got a constituency of one. Long as you don't fuck little girls, the president won't give a damn how you spend your time."

The landscape changed from forest to a series of cinder block slums that rose three stories from the brown earth of clear-cut jungle floor. The narrow areas between shanties were wrinkled with rain ruts and evidence of travel. Some had rough-hewn board walkways between the hovels. Others had eroded to the point that the nearest structures on either side had collapsed. Children played amid the detritus of broken cinder blocks, splintered wood, and rusting and warped corrugated metal roofing sheets.

We rumbled over a Bailey bridge that spanned a drop of fifteen yards to a creek swollen with muddy runoff and tainted by effluents from the slum. A brown froth covered the lethargic water that curled in eddies. As we crossed, an old woman looked up at us as though she could see me through the tinted glass. She stood knee-deep in the creek, a rusted gasoline can held to capture water.

Thick black power lines passed over the slum without stopping. They rose over a series of fence lines at the edge of a fresh clear-cut in the jungle. Razor wire protected the transformers, which were the end point for the power lines. Beyond the transformers, I glimpsed a series of hangars and industrial buildings. Massive orange chimneys rose above one building. Children wearing dirty blue uniform shirts walked up to one of the massive open doors. Beyond the buildings, fitful black smoke rose from mounds of trees that had been bulldozed to one side of the clear-cuts and set alight. Near the fires, metal shipping containers dotted the muddy brown earth. Power lines ran in haphazardly from the main buildings and into the containers. They faded into the distance and then vanished as our travel took them out of view behind a screen of foliage.

Daniel followed my gaze. "What say we show you around the cesspool?" He pointed a finger toward the corrugated factories we'd passed. "The Japanese are here. Germans. Dutch. And a hell of a lotta American corps. The Spanish aren't. They're trying, but the whole place used to be a Spanish colony. Los Generales won't let 'em set up sweatshops. Feelings run high."

The Suburban slowed as we drove past another slum that was a confusion of structures extending from the roadway and up into what was once forest. There were tents, wooden structures swathed in tarps, and more shipping containers. Old tires lay flat against sheets of corrugated metal the inhabitants used for roofing on some of the structures. The faces in the encampment were old. They looked out at us past rags hanging over windows and doorways, then turned away as the Humvees and my Suburban rolled past. Their gazes had a commonality. Anyone who's been visited often enough by privation or fear or suffering can tell you that it's not those visits that leave a gaze like the ones I saw. Hunger and fear and pain are just heralds. They run ahead, warning us all of something else that's coming. Something that, once it arrives, it abides. It seldom leaves.

Sorrow.

Like a companion, it limps in the doorway as sickness squeezes water from their bowels and shivers bands of agony across their hearts. It sits down beside them with a weight and substance that burdens all in vigil at a deathbed. In the silence of the night, when even the sobs of those who've been torn from those they love most have stilled in fitful places of sleep, it whispers with a voice that penetrates all dreams. It whispers that it will never leave.

The faces I saw held sorrow. Inconsolable and enduring sorrow.

"See the pattern?" Daniel asked. "Labor. Industrial site. More labor. Another industrial site. One thing this place has is a lot of villages. It was mostly agrarian before the corporations arrived. US multinationals are the real flagship here. No unions. No health and safety. No wage minimums. It's management heaven. Fourteen billion in merchandise floats out that harbor each year. Everything. Shoes to satellite dishes. Los Generales get a cut of it all."

"The Generals," I repeated. It wasn't an unfamiliar reference to me. The Department of State briefing warned me the country was ruled by a military junta—an old-school Roman triumvirate where latter day strongmen vied like Caesar, Crassus, and Pompey in their dominion of Malagar.

"Three of them," Daniel said. "Wicked as furies. Imaginative as stone. If not for our backing, they'd have consumed themselves in petty bickering. The current administration saw promise. We cultivate that."

Up ahead, smoke rose from someplace concealed by the ribbons of forest that remained. Gaines keyed his microphone and said a word. The Humvee leading our path lurched left at a fork in the road, away from the rising plume.

"Cultivate," I said. "Like a farmer."

"I like that." Daniel said. "Sure. Like a farmer."

"Your sheet says you were at the School of the Americas. What crops do you sow?"

"Maybe not a farmer, then, Ambassador," Daniel said, "but I work with them. Closely. So the combined industrial interests of the United States can count on uninterrupted harvests from this field."

A Huey passed low and fast alongside the Suburban. The soldier in the far doorway leaned into his GAU, the barrel trained on a copse of trees at the source of the broadening pall of smoke. Riley pointed to the distance, and Gaines keyed his mic again. The Humvee ahead accelerated, and we kept pace, jouncing on the rutted roadway as we cleared the shanties, angling to the left of the fork as a soldier wearing twin cylinders on his back walked out from the trees to the edge of the road. He turned as we approached, facing the forest and pointing a black smoldering nozzle.

"I teach them how to control the pests, Jack. How to—"

A tremendous gout of incandescence shot upward from the soldier's flamethrower. It burst in fractionated light as it hit tree branches and seared huts hidden behind foliage. Each hut instantly whooshed upward in a conflagration that rose to ignite the canopy above. The inferno threw red light on the faces of soldiers moving amid the huts and dragging forms out. It shone crimson against the pall of black smoke that mushroomed into the sky and illuminated dead men swinging amid the trees, suspended by ropes tied around their ankles.

Each man twisted, arms akimbo, as though they were each in their own orbit. The dancing orange seemed to add a layer of depth and fury as it reflected from the blood, wet and red, in the places where someone had cut away their ears.

Daniel had fallen silent as we passed.

"I teach them how to remove the weeds," he continued after a moment. I heard something in his voice that had the hardness of flint. He exhaled. Blinked. Then we were past the fires and the soldiers and murder, and there were only trees and the diminishing sound of helicopter rotors fading behind us.

"Sometimes"—Daniel's eyes shifted from my face to a defocused point out the front windshield—"I pull them myself."

The flag undulated in the last winds of the storm. Whipping red and white bars at the top of a flagpole we could see in the distance as we rode through an urban sprawl of low one-story cinder block buildings. The embassy's five-acre compound was ringed by a twelve-foot wall crowned by concertina wire. Marines rolled heavy wrought iron gates apart and into recessed steel cupolas along the wall as the Humvees turned onto the grounds. The Suburban drove up to the embassy, while both Humvees gunned past the flag and veered around the building. They vanished into what must have been a motor pool area. Riley parked before the glass-fronted building on which was affixed the Great Seal and the black embossed words: *The Embassy of the United States of America.*

In front of the embassy, Gaines opened my door without a word and stood stiffly as I stepped out. Daniel came around to my side of the Suburban, carrying the diplomatic bag.

"My part of the tour's over," Daniel said. His eyes flicked to the double glass doors of the embassy. "I'm sure your deputy will. . . have some things to say. I'll see you later, Jack."

"Hey." I inclined my head toward the courier bag that held the scotch, crystal, and documents that had not been viewed by me. "Anything in there for my attention?"

"Lord, I hope not," Daniel said.

Then he was gone, walking with the diplomatic pouch past the flagpole and down toward the embassy's front gates to the city streets beyond. A Ford F-150 truck waited there for him. It was the same olive drab color as those we'd seen racing toward the airport. Marines at the gate opened a security door for pedestrians inset in the main gate. It was hinged to allow the thick iron lattice to swing wide. Daniel stepped through, and the gate snapped shut behind him.

Riley and Gaines climbed back into the Suburban without a word. It eased around the circle surrounding the flagpole, then away toward the back of the building.

From the front of the embassy, a young man frowned his way toward me. He wore a blue pinstripe suit and a gold tie between a pair of jet-black suspenders. "They were supposed to call," he said. He shook my hand, then dropped it, perfunctory. "Ambassador Ford. I'm Michael Scoggins, Deputy Chief of Mission. You can follow me."

Without waiting for a response, he turned and walked into the embassy.

Inside, he moved across an open floor. The ground floor was a large open area for an empty queue that led to unmanned and silent windows marked *VISAS*. From behind those windows, I could hear the angry clatter of a keyboard. The ground floor otherwise seemed vacant. Scoggins was halfway up the stairs to the second floor before he realized I wasn't following. He stood there for a moment, his expression akin to one I'd seen once on a man walking his dog as he jerked the leash with insistence, quickly followed by irritation and unreasoning anger when the dog refused to come.

Scoggins slowly descended the stairs. Muscles worked on both sides of his jawline.

"I'd like to meet the people working with me," I said.

"Weren't you briefed?" He tilted his head. Then he sighed, like there was a personal cost to saying what came next. "Ambassador, we're a rump embassy. This whole place is here so we can plant a flag in the ground and give the United States something kinda like what Gitmo has going for it. A place of exile."

"Is that your briefing?"

"Fine." He crooked a finger for me to follow. In three strides, he walked to a view beyond the visa windows. At a reception cubicle, a big man sat hunched over a small monitor. "Over there—Consular Officer and your ISO, Harold Dink. This is his twelfth embassy. He's had every post you could shoehorn his ass into. His jacket's nothing but poor reviews."

"ISO?" I asked.

"Information Systems Officer," Scoggins said. "He maintains the Post Communications Center on the third floor. Did you not read your briefing?"

Without waiting for an answer, Scoggins pointed to a black woman walking into the ground floor from a side door. She wore a white lab coat and spoke to Harold as she approached his window. Harold raised his hands as though to say *No*, but she leaned in and gestured, her hands making points. Scoggin's hand was aimed like a weapon. He dropped his thumb as he spoke.

"That one," he said, "is Dr. Maureen Cassidy. Used to be in Cameroon, Embassy Douala, until she started mouthing off about locals poaching from UN medical stores. Transferred for her own safety. You met Nokes?"

"I met him," I said.

"You getting a sense for it yet?"

"For what?"

"For how fucked-up you have to be to get sent here?"

"I'm here."

"Yes," Scoggins agreed. "You are."

"So are you," I reminded him.

Then Scoggins did something unexpected—he smiled. It was genuine mirth before it became something else. "Ambassador," he said, turning toward the stairs and walking up as though he were done, "every prison needs a guard."

Armando de Rosas gunned the truck down narrow streets teeming with pedestrians and competing traffic. Daniel looked at Armando's tailored Armani suit and saw himself in the young officer's mirrored aviator sunglasses.

"Colonel, you're out of uniform."

"Shhh." Armando laughed and held a finger to his lips. "This is Armani. Danielo, I am incognito."

The truck revved across an intersection. Horns sounded from opposing traffic.

"Armani. You're a regular chameleon. You look like your father."

This hit a nerve.

"You look like shit," Armando growled. "The new ambassador, he touch you? Eh? Maybe he love spies this time?"

"With you screwing me, I don't think he'd have a chance," Daniel said. "You were to infiltrate."

"That village. Why send a man inside? That says nothing. A column of smoke. Some butchered radicals. That speaks of *la guerre*. What's wrong? It is the fire in your belly. The milk, she no longer conceals the flame."

"You just added to his ranks," Daniel said.

Armando spit out the window. "Reto Poirier is a dead man!"

"Not yet," said Daniel, "and not because of anything you did today."

Harold Dink watched the new ambassador walk up the stairs to the embassy offices on the second floor. Beside him, Doc Cassidy also watched.

"He'll look great at parties," Harold said.

"You're a bitter man, Harold," said Cassidy.

"I'm a happy child trapped inside a mean fat man. Damn it!" Harold's big fingers hit errant keys on the board. His too-small chair squealed. He banged the monitor.

"Hey," Doc Cassidy said, "what's the odds I'll get a response to my—"

"You got one," Harold said.

"What?" She blinked at him, not expecting that. "My requisition?"

"Yeah," Harold said. "State says no. Make do with what ya got."

"There are no more vaccines!"

"Doc, you know what? Nobody cares."

CHAPTER IX

THE IDEAL

MAYA WAS TWELVE. SHE SCOOPED rice, chicken, and onions onto a banana leaf and folded it, carefully. The dexterity would come back in time. Three fingers on her left hand and one on her right were gone at the second knuckle. The injuries were still angry red scars.

Around her, children played. Women moved around fires, tending food. But the men of all ages were elsewhere. She took the folded leaf and walked toward the long central hut where men had gathered.

As she approached and the group of village men parted for her, she could hear him.

"Blessed are the children," her father said.

Laurent Veldago stood guard at the hut. He was as big as a bear and carried a machete others whispered he'd killed hundreds of soldiers with. But he smiled kindly at Maya and moved the cloth covering the entrance of the hut to allow her inside.

She entered, moving through the men. At their center was her father, Reto Poirier. He was not very tall. He was not very handsome. But there was something there that held the eye. It could have been the play of late afternoon light through the openings in the hut's walls. Or the way he spoke, as a teacher. Not a priest. An equal, even though he was their commander in a war that had driven them from their homes and into hiding.

"Blessed are the children," he repeated. "Our faith, our hearts, tell us this." He beckoned her, smiling. She walked across the room to him, and he took the banana leaf from her and held her maimed hands.

"They closed the schools." In the tenor of his voice was something like an apology to all the world for the cruelty perpetuated on the defenseless but had especially been her burden. "They burned our fields, our churches, our homes, and they herd us into these places to work."

Maya came into his arms and laid her head on his shoulder.

"Their factories take our children and return them like this," Reto said. "We must remind them what is right."

Chapter X

VIEW FROM THE TOP

THE UNITED STATES FLAG HUNG from a staff behind my desk. Through my third-floor office window, I could see the gray sprawl of one-story buildings that vanished into the distance beyond the five-acre embassy compound. Within the compound, the Marines had a barracks residence in a squat one-story building beside the shack that provided emergency power for the installation. Between the barracks and the embassy, there was a flat black tarmac that served as an open-air motor pool.

A Malagayan Huey rotored low over the industrial slum just past the embassy's security wall, the door gunner scanning the embassy grounds, the blunt muzzle of his GAU-21 pointing forward, in their direction of flight. Then the helicopter vanished from my field of view.

To the right of the office window, a wet bar mirror reflected sunlight hued by the glitter of a dozen bottles of liquor and wine. Tumblers and wine glasses caught the light in a way that more than dazzled. I exhaled, forcing my eyes away from the bottles, then regretting it.

Hinkley or his predecessor had oval office envy. The room mirrored that presidential enclave with a table and two sofas arrayed before the ambassador's desk. But that wasn't what made my jaw clench. The third floor housed the secure communications room and additional quarters for embassy staff, though only Harold Dink was actively sleeping on this level. The ambassador's quarters were adjacent to my office, accessible both by the corridor and through a set of double doors leading from the office.

Those double doors were splintered, broken wood visible beneath the pristine white paint and gold filigree.

Behind me, at the open door leading to the main third floor corridor, Gaines knocked. He spoke without bidding. And without entering. "Mr. Ambassador, night report. Gates are closed, the grounds secure."

"Sergeant, why are you at this post?"

"I'm a Marine, sir. I go where ordered."

"Someone said this is a place of exile. They said we're here just to raise a flag."

"I find that guilty men make their own prisons," Gaines said. "As for the flag, seeing it aloft is both my duty and my honor. I have a question for you, sir."

He was in the residence now, standing before me. Somehow, my eyes had drifted away from splintered wood and the place where a child had been violated. I had to look from a row of bottles to meet his gaze.

"Are you going to dishonor my flag?"

I nodded my head to the broken bedroom door. "See that this is fixed."

I set a photo of Elise on my desk, angling it so I could see the familiar tilt of her smile from the office sofa. I walked to the window—a six-foot glass pane that consumed most of the wall from my waist to a point just below the ceiling. Outside, the right side of the moon was a luminous silver arc, waxing crescent. High clouds obscured it, becoming luminous as they wreathed and curled in their transit.

The flagpole was barren. At the main gate, a Marine stood in a pool of golden light from the security lamps positioned on both sides of the wall. Bugs darted around the incandescent source high above the Marine.

Farther out, a break in the clouds allowed moonlight to fall on gray block walls. It reflected silver in the standing puddles of water on flat rooftops and the asphalt roadway. Where the sprawl of construction had ignored the remnants of vegetation, the moonlight reflected a dim electric green that seemed to shimmer as heat evaporated the rainfall. In that moment, with a new position and something like optimism before me, the world seemed at peace.

Laurent worked the bolt cutters quickly, snipping apart the chain links in the perimeter fence with little noise. A gap appeared in the fence as though Laurent's tool had unzipped the barrier and thrown wide the far side. Behind him, Reto, Maya, and four others crouched in single file. When Laurent finished, he slid the bolt cutters into a pack on his back and pulled the gap wide enough for passage.

Reto Poirier passed through the gap, leading his small group beyond the fence topped with inward-leaning razor wire. The angle of the wire was much like the outermost defensive perimeter around prisons the world over. The wire is angled not to keep intruders out, but to keep workers in.

When Reto Poirier's group reached the corrugated steel structures, they overpowered, bound, and gagged the sole guard. Reto forced open the door to the power transformer using a crowbar. The dull thud and creak of metal splintering wood was lost in the night. He swung wide the door to the shed containing the breakers for the complex of sweatshops that sprawled across the grounds beyond them and tossed in a sack.

Reto and his group ran, dragging the bound guard with them. They took cover behind a sweatshop building thrumming with the sound of machines. The shed erupted in white light. The sound of the explosion and resultant reports of transformers detonating echoed across the hills and startled sleeping birds upward into the night. In the same instant, it brought a consuming darkness as lights inside factories winked out and machines moaned to a halt with their work incomplete.

There were factory foremen in most of the buildings. Doors slammed open as some fled, afraid their charges would turn on them in the darkness. There were, after all, vats of acid and ten thousand sharp objects. There were machine parts that still steamed red in the darkness. Others stumbled out into the night amongst the workers. None of the foremen fought what came next.

Building by building, Reto Poirier flung the doors open, his voice booming in the noxious and sweat-stinking places as he beckoned to women and children. They stumbled out into the sudden and ringing stillness where his young daughter, Maya, beckoned them toward the gap in the fence, a child illuminated by moonlight, leading people out of servitude and into the quiet of the jungle.

"This is a new site." Daniel touched the high-definition image with his finger.

The Malagayan Army officer shook his head. Another tilted his head, also not able to see the target American intelligence analysists had painstakingly located and captured for this report.

Daniel took a chisel-tip marker and touched it to the photograph. He sketched along the hut's edges. After a moment, one officer exhaled, as though momentous things had been revealed. Daniel did the same for another hut, then a third. The other officer nodded, seeing the structures. There were dozens of them in that one high-resolution image taken of a previously uninhabited spot in the jungle in the foothills to the south.

"But when?" asked the officer, looking furtive. The satellite photo was in the middle of this man's designated patrol area. "Last week, I swear—"

"They are rats," Armando said. "Last week, they were not there. Now they are. Like an infestation. They eat what is not theirs. They take what is not theirs. They fuck and breed and spew waste across everything that is not theirs."

The officers nodded, attentive to their commander. He was deep into the Johnnie Walker Blue Label. But Daniel knew the real hit of the party was where the satellite photos revealed the locations of three new rebel villages in the foothills to the south. Armando pointed the half-full blue glass at Daniel.

"Danielo," he said, "generous gifts. Come! We make plans to kill rats!" Armando gestured, and the officers rose to leave. One of the officers clicked open a briefcase. He shuffled the sat images into the case before removing a leather bag and handing it to Armando. The officer clicked the case closed and departed. Armando bounced the leather bag in the palm of his hand as though it had the weight of a coin purse.

"You will help us," Armando said, gesturing with the bag. It wasn't a question or even an expectation. It was a command made by someone for whom ownership was a state of mind for both people and things.

He tossed the bag onto the table. Daniel made no effort to touch it. Then Armando walked out after his officers. The junior ones would already be out of the building and climbing into their vehicles, planning the incursion of helicopters, trucks, and men for tomorrow night's raid to collect the human detritus that had managed to slip away into the hills. But Armando and a few of his senior officers would linger downstairs for a while in the company of the lithe and dark-skinned girls. The brothel was one of the foundations of his relationship with this general's son.

Music murmured upward from the bar below. Daniel closed the open Johnnie Walker box, leaving untouched the second tumbler that had been inscribed by a man who blew glass into multicolored shapes half a world away. He went into the kitchen and poured whiskey into a coffee mug, followed by milk. Then he took the mug and the leather bag out onto the balcony that overlooked the street.

Daniel watched the sunset from the balcony and tried not to take inventory of his life. Beside him, the leather bag gaped just wide enough to reveal the darkening black oval of an ear that had been roughly gashed from someone once living.

Chapter XI

TIP OF A LASH

"OF COURSE, THE PRESIDENT'S VERY anxious to hear your concerns," Matthew Pope said to the collection of lobbyists, lawyers, and business leaders. He nodded to Tony Ball as the Texan opened the door to allow in a thin-lipped ancient woman. She slipped into a leather chair and laid her valise on the table.

"Ah, the gang's all here," Pope said. "How was your sleep Ms. Sawyer? There's something about staying in the Lincoln Bedroom. The very air scents of magnanimous power. It makes one feel like giving."

"Don't jerk us around, Pope," Sawyer said. "There was another attack last night. A quarter million in damages. Not to mention lost productivity."

Pope nodded. At the right of the fireplace mantel, Christine Harper rose from a seat and quietly opened the door. Across a corridor, they could see directly into the Oval Office.

"Well then," Pope said. "I see no reason to delay."

The men and women at the table looked at each other. First from one, then the others, envelopes appeared. Ball collected them all.

In my dreams, I slept on a hospital room sofa at the foot of Elise's bed. Though there was silence in the embassy during the dead of night and the surrounding lands were blanketed with the reverie that comes to industrial places when machines are still and forges grow cold, my dream clearly recalled the beep and chime of monitors and the murmur of voices from the corridor beyond her closed hospital room door.

It was a dream of futility. A recollection of the hours in which I waited for the actions of physicians and pharma to wrest control of our lives from the cancer that had metastasized across Elise's body. Perhaps it was the inevitable upheaval of uncertainty, frustration, and pain I'd compressed in the strata beneath my conscious mind after she died, and it was only now clawing upward from the abscess where it dwelled. Or perhaps our subconscious mind is an adversary that waits, biding its time, and in this moment of reverie, unfettered by alcohol, it was free to humble me on the eve of my service as ambassador to a foreign land.

More likely, it was recognition that I had been chosen by others. It was equal parts observation and warning—a cry articulated by the part of us that carries Cassandra's curse of foreknowledge: to be perfectly aware of what the future holds and yet unable to articulate a warning in any way that will be believed by those who hear it. I understood my posting was not based on my intellect. And I understood it was not offered because others had the sense I could change any particular landscape.

It was because I was least likely to disrupt their schemes. In the dream and in my waking hours to follow, I would be an impotent witness to a course of events that would proceed according to some sublime plan as subtle as the gravitational pull on the contents of Elise's IV drip and as unobservable from my perspective as the curve of the Earth.

A well-meaning priest told me once that our suffering is preordained. That only a moral life will ensure our passage to God's embrace in the kingdom of heaven. He shared that after a difficult night spent in vigil at my wife's bedside. It was a time when both I and Elise knew she was reaching the end of her fight.

I never touched the priest. Not physically.

But my words hit him like fists. I pummeled him with the certainty that if there is a devil who will punish us in hell, the fat leering bastard doesn't wait. He inseminates torments into our lives dream by dream, every night, raping the third of our lives when we slumber. That dreaming hell mocks the concept of rest and willfully frustrates any capacity sleep has to prepare us physically, emotionally, and mentally for the waking trials that provide the grist for nightmares.

Hell awaits us each night. Hell is a reality. It's a con-
dition of being alive. How inadequate must God be to
postpone his embrace until death or to create a heaven
that is so far removed from our dreams.

I awoke on my office sofa with those words on my lips.
To my shame, I didn't look first to my wife's photo. I
opened my eyes, and my gaze was directed to the bar.
I licked dry lips like a man stumbling out of the desert
toward freshwater and oasis shade.

Scoggins watched me from behind my desk, his
hands on the shoulders of the chair as though ready to
slide it back and take a seat.

"Mr. Ambassador," he said.

Then he snapped his fingers and gestured to the
desk. I frowned, sitting up on the sofa, thinking that
he'd made this gesture to me. But then there was a clank
at the doorway, and a foreign national brought in a tray
perched atop his shoulder. He lowered it to my desk,
and I could smell bacon, eggs, and coffee. The man began to lift the lid and looked at me as though to inquire
about something when Scoggins snapped his fingers
again. The man flinched slightly, as though anticipating
the crack of a whip. He stepped back out of the office
and closed the door.

Scoggins moved from the desk to the office's mirrored wet bar, his eyes touching bottles and glasses like
he was conducting an inventory. It was untouched. I
know because I had wanted to touch it. To drink without

remorse or restraint. Instead, I'd read and reread the situation reports a foreign service officer had provided when we wended our way up from Matthew Pope and the Department of State Operations Center.

Those reports were splayed on the coffee table and my desk.

Scoggins looked at me in the bar's mirror. "This is your morning briefing. Gaines reports the post is secure. There are no meetings or ceremonies for you to consider today. Take the day. Amuse yourself. I've got everything handled."

"What does that mean?"

"It means you can stay on the sofa. Shower or don't. Change clothes or don't." He extended a finger toward one label among those in the bar. "There's good stuff in here. Don't be bashful about, ah . . ."—he seemed to grasp for the right words—"enjoying the perks."

He turned and faced me, smiling with some secret mirth. "Jack, where you are now, what you do here—it doesn't have to be very different from where you were and what you used to do." He turned a tumbler on the bar right side up and slid it beside a bottle.

"Oh," Scoggins said in the tone of an afterthought, "and you're confirmed. Voice vote in the Senate yesterday. Congrats."

Then he was gone.

I ate and drank coffee. Then I showered and put on one of the three suits I'd brought. Downstairs, on the first floor, I found Harold at the visa window wrestling with a keyboard that was too small for his fists. When I asked him to show me the Post Communications Center, his first reaction was disbelief. It was the sort of hesitancy a child would show when asked if they would like some ice cream—by a dentist. As soon as I convinced him it wasn't a trick question, he relented and led me back up the flights of stairs to the third floor.

Harold was easily 250 pounds. Sweat glistened at the upper rim of his shirt collar from his exertion climbing the stairs. On the third floor, we passed a Marine guard and walked down the hallway to the metal door that opened to the communications room. It was unadorned. Harold entered a code on the keypad and swung the gray steel door wide.

"Iranians have technology on display in a museum from our old embassy in Tehran." Harold huffed as I followed him into the room housing the embassy's communication and surveillance technology. "It's probably more advanced in some ways than what we're using here."

Harold walked me past equipment that was hardwired into tables and walls. "We got high-speed internet and cell service as our baseline for ops." Two workstations sat at a table in the center of the room, with monitors and printers. Along the wall, equipment conduits vanished upward into the ceiling. A server rack blinked in an air-conditioned closet in the far corner of the room. "Connectivity goes to our stations on the first floor, the Marine barracks, and your office-residence.

At their first-floor station, the Marines have video feeds from cams along the walls and exterior."

Harold gestured to the banks of servers and routers. "Diplomatic Telecommunications Service provides the integrated networks between us and DC. That's voice, switches, and routers. Trouble is, all the infrastructure around here—except for the radio—is controlled by Los Generales. Copper phone lines, what little high-speed fiber there is. Definitely all the cell towers. It's all subject to these mysterious"—he waved his fingers in air quotes—"*outages* that seem to clear right up as soon as they've made their point." He tapped the cabinet. "We keep the embassy workstations on our own network on racks here. It's encrypted and reasonably fast, but every bit of it screams to a halt if somebody gets mad at us."

"What happens then?" I asked.

"The DTS Onyx satellite network has been helpful," he said. "Not a hundred percent sure access, but we can generally stay in touch with Mom and Dad when things get rough. Say, you're not planning to—"

"Oh, no," I said. "I'm a likeable guy. I get along with everybody."

Harold snorted. "Yeah, me too, Ambassador." His eyes examined the ceiling. "Why we're all here, right?"

"They've cut us off before?" I asked. "Los Generales."

"State didn't tell you?" Harold looked at me.

"My briefing didn't have a lot of local flavor. That's why I thought we'd talk."

"Scoggins would be the most proper—"

"Scoggins isn't here," I said. "Please, educate me."

"Last time we had a misunderstanding, we lost power and water for two days. Indie film crew wanted to do an exposé on our friends. That was the culprit—no, that was the catalyst. Yeah, that's a better word for it. Los Generales didn't want to be in the movies. Hinkley talked the film crew into departing before it got ugly. Well, most of them."

"Some stayed behind?" I asked.

"Yeah," Harold said. "Producer and his girlfriend. They, ah, went off grid."

"What does that mean?"

"Never heard from them again. Poof. No calls. No comms. No listings for their names on the passenger manifests of civilian air transport or ocean-going vessels. Hinkley said don't sweat it."

"That's the way Ambassador Hinkley used to speak?"

"No. He said, and I quote, 'We are not responsible for people who refuse to heed warnings.'" Harold turned to some antiquated computers. "Anyway, did I mention we got a new DoD multiplexer? That and a satellite receiver for the satellite dish. That's solid gold right there. We're under a big sky. I mean, there are lots of commercial and foreign satellites up there too. The receiver helps to track and lock a signal on the ones we can use. They're with the dish on the roof over your office. But the computers in here are ancient. I mean, dot matrix printers. Am I right? We got DTS authorization to pick up laptops locally and image them, but that wasn't an important part of the budget. Till we do, hooking to this makes as much sense as putting my bathtub under Niagara Falls."

"I saw there's some money for modernization in the budget," I said.

"Scoggins controls all that. Hinkley preferred it that way. They repurposed the funds."

"Yeah. Social functions at the embassy," I said. "The former ambassador was quite an entertainer. I'm more of a homebody. Tell me, Harold, you like working up front as the consular officer, processing visas?"

Harold flinched. "I know there've been complaints, but you ought to give me a chance."

"Your personnel file showed you started in IT," I said. "I am. Giving you a chance."

Harold was grinning when he came back down the stairs with me. Maureen Cassidy was speaking to a foreign national nurse at the visas window where Harold had his usual station. As we approached, Cassidy nodded, and the nurse went back outside, exiting through a side door beyond the visa lines.

"Harold," Cassidy said, "can you . . ." Then she trailed away, noticing his smile. "What's up?"

"Would love to help you, Doc, and I will, but not right now. Right now, I'm going shopping." Grinning, Harold grabbed his coat from the booth and left.

"He's on a mission for me." I leaned forward and extended my hand to her. "Dr. Cassidy, we didn't have an opportunity to meet when I first arrived."

"Ambassador Ford," she said, perfunctory.

"Please, Jackson. Or Jack."

"Maureen," she said. "You got a minute?" Then she was in motion, heading for the side exit the nurse had used as though I had agreed. "How was your first night?" she asked, not even glancing over her shoulder to see if I was following.

I matched her stride. "Sleepless."

"Sleepless, huh? That's jet lag or guilt."

"You've got something for that?" I asked.

"Just the one," she said and then hit the metal door latch with the palm of her hand. It swung wide, and I blinked as we stepped out into the dazzling sunlight. A worn blue canopy tent threw shade across a collection of women and small children. A child wailed in his mother's arms as one of two foreign national nurses examined him. The line extended from this repurposed paved parking area down the grassy slope of the embassy grounds and to an open side gate manned by two Marines.

UNICEF was stamped in dull white block letters on the tent. The fabric and the print had been weathered by time and the elements. A rip in the fabric flapped and puckered the length of the I as the wind moved.

Cassidy stopped in the shade of the canopy. A little girl stood nearby, her back to us. Her mother held an infant as a nurse examined the baby.

"I see a hundred children a day in danger from diseases considered exotic in the United States," Cassidy said. "We inoculate for diphtheria, tetanus, and yellow fever when I can get it. In between, we provide rudimentary medical care."

The little girl dropped a figurine. It clattered with a sound of wood against the pavement. She stared at it. As though lost.

I took a step away from Doc Cassidy and picked up the figurine. It was a man on one knee, his hands upraised. It could have had religious overtones, but for me, in that moment, it was just a plaything. A toy I was holding out to a child.

Her eyes were large and brown, her expression alive and uncertain at the sight of me. Then her arms came up. White bandages. Nubs where her hands should have been. She took the figurine, and my mouth opened, but nothing came out as she delicately positioned the figurine in the crook of one arm, as though it were an infant to be cradled and protected from harm.

"Blunt force trauma's the leading cause of injury," Cassidy said from behind me. "It's amazing what the world looks like without OSHA." She nodded to the figurine as the little girl moved to join her mother. "The figurine is Papa Poirier. Local hero."

I reacted to the name. "Poirier's a Communist insurgent," I said, reciting the words from my briefing documents almost verbatim without wondering seriously about their accuracy or provenance.

"He's a schoolteacher who refused to move. Labor's a package deal down here. When a factory site goes up, Los Generales provide the land and a working population. They forcibly relocate a village into shanties near the factory."

"Poirier refused to go?"

"Oh, no," Cassidy said. "At first, he went. His daughter worked in one of the factories until she was maimed. That night, he led the entire village into the jungles. They say personal tragedy is the catalyst of rebellion."

"The Department of State says Marxist doctrine is the catalyst of rebellion," I said. "Protecting American interests here means we're to encourage the local authorities to apprehend Reto Poirier."

"Did your little primer on in-country issues mention the cholera outbreaks? Each hot spot winds up being centered in shantytowns that support the industry our hosts are so fond of. They move the people out of agrarian settings and into places with no food and dirty water. I'm out of vaccines in two days."

"I thought the World Health Organization provides the vaccines."

"The State Department administrates," Cassidy said. "Right now, there are a forty thousand vaccines sitting on the grounds of Embassy Douala. They're supposed to be for us."

The side door to the embassy boomed open behind us. Out of the corner of my eye, I saw Scoggins step into the sunlight and shield his eyes, also dazzled.

"That was your last post," I said. "Isn't there someone you can—"

Scoggins spotted us. He pointed to me and gestured for me to come. From the back of my mind, unbidden, came a memory of the snap of his fingers.

Cassidy frowned at me. She looked at Scoggins. "Didn't Scoggins tell you why I left?"

"For your safety. Locals were poaching—"

"No." Her mouth pressed into a fine line of exasperation. "I left because the deputy chief of mission couldn't keep his hands off my ass. They hear my name, the line goes dead."

I nodded. Scoggins waved again. "Thank you, Doctor. I'll see what I can do."

She put a hand on my chest, stopping me before I could leave. "Ambassador, that was the punch line to Hinkley's favorite joke. How does a diplomat say, 'Fuck off'?" She walked away from me and to the tent, where she joined the nurses as they provided rudimentary medical care to the poorest of the people around us.

When I reached Scoggins at the door to the embassy, my gaze fell on him like the tip of a lash.

He reacted to my look. "What?"

CHAPTER XII

THEY ARE LIKE YOU

RETO LOOKED DOWN AT THE little group clustered on
the floor and against the walls of the shanty's windowless back room. They slept on the dirt and rough-hewn
wooden benches pushed against the walls, exhausted
from their trek away from the factory site and their sub-
sequent trip to take the children they'd rescued to one of
the sanctuary villages in the foothills.

He slipped past the black tarp that hung over the
doorway. The outer room was lit by daylight from a single window. At the window, Shallah tilted his head to
one side of the rags that blocked his view. He was fourteen, with a big 1911 .45 caliber pistol clutched in his
small hand.

As Reto approached, Shallah inclined his head down

the street. Through the rags, Reto could see two Ford F-150 military trucks.

"Two patrols," Shallah said. "They drink beer."

"You have sharp eyes, Shallah. Like your father."

Shallah gestured with the .45. The hammer was back. "I make them pay," he said.

"I miss him too," Reto said. "But he understood. The soldiers are children, like you. Los Generales, they are the ones who must stand for what they've done. Done to him and to you. Each time we close the factories, Los Generales pay."

Reto took the .45 from Shallah's grip. The boy did not resist. He watched as Reto eased the hammer down. "Not in blood," Reto said, "but they pay."

"One day, I will stand before them."

"On that day, they will see how very tall you have become."

CHAPTER XIII

THE REFUGE

DANIEL REMINDED HIMSELF THAT EVERY new administration enacts some level of change. Rarely transformative. Often superficial. But when he walked into the embassy and saw the line at the visa window, he paused, grinning. Michael Scoggins worked inside the booth, coat off, sky-blue suspenders visible across his bony shoulders. His countenance was red with the subdued fury of an effort Daniel knew Scoggins felt beneath him. A line of fifteen locals queued before Michael's window.

Daniel moved past the line for the stairs. He called out as he went. "Hey, Mikey!"

Scoggins' head swung up, frowning at Daniel's voice.

Daniel grinned. "Piss somebody off?"

I was on the phone in my office. It was an archaic model—corded with a block of touch-tone buttons on the face and a thick glass block of buttons at the base that could activate separate lines. Harold had assured me there were no other lines, and if I pressed anything other than the first block, I would be talking to myself.

Harold had placed the call for me, then departed to the communications room to perform tasks I'd set for him. I was just wrapping up the conversation when Daniel walked in. He wore freshly pressed cargo pants and a green-and-black Hawaiian shirt. He tossed his Panama hat onto the sofa as he walked in and placed a bottle of Glenfiddich on my desk.

"Yes, General," I said into the receiver. "I'm looking forward to making your acquaintance . . . No, I have a driver . . . This evening, then."

Daniel's eyebrow shot up. He watched me place the receiver back in the cradle. "Tibideau's the friendly one. Was that him?" He took my look for assent. "Yeah, he'll take you to his rancho for steaks carved out of an Angus that died when you pulled in the drive. Then he'll spend the meal telling you what's wrong with America while his mistress rubs your thigh. You had breakfast yet?"

He cracked open the bottle. I waved him off, but he still poured a glass for himself and took a swallow.

"He will test you," Daniel said. "Reto Poirier's an existential threat to these guys. He's charismatic. Like Gandhi. Like King. That makes the rest of us imperialists and bigots."

"You're comfortable with that?"

"I do my job."

"You're wondering if I'm going to complicate that," I said, prodding.

His reaction was unexpected.

"Mr. Ambassador"—Daniel grinned—"I don't think you'll be a variable at all." He held up the bottle, quizzically. "Seriously, say the word, and this is yours to enjoy. Hinkley was a gin guy. Never go gin. And this . . . I just got a case of the stuff."

I shook my head and bit back my personal certainty that both he and Scoggins had a pool expecting me to regularly be shit-faced before noon as part of a pattern I'd established years ago in West Virginia. A pattern that had left me insensate to worlds of fresh pain, even as it numbed any sense of right, wrong, or responsibility as I traded with the second-most corrupt individual I knew to keep the Hope Scholarship alive. That was Elise's name for it. It was a testament to her optimism about our future together. Now that children were going to college because of it, the term "Hope" had very real meaning for a new generation.

But that's not the sort of dialogue you launch with a spy nursing a drink in your office while your hands shake. I rose to leave.

"Suit yourself." Daniel put the bottle under his arm and picked up his hat from the sofa, heading me off before I could leave. He paused at the door and looked at me. "Word from the wise?"

"What's that?" I asked.

"Tibideau's the artful dodger. He can sense a liar."
Then Daniel paused, self-correcting. "No. It's more
complicated than that. He's like the opposite of a poly-
graph. He can sense honesty. And he won't react well
to that. Some creatures don't tolerate light. He's one of
them."

I walked to the wet bar. My hands flexed on the
counter. The upended glass tumblers were stacked with
precision. Light from the window behind my desk shone
from the mirror and refracted in golds and blues and
emerald hues among the bottles. Daniel watched me
with interest.

"When my wife died, I promised her I wouldn't
throw everything away," I said. "I swore I wouldn't
surrender to grief. If I could lie to the best part of my
life as she lay dying, do you think I'll have any trouble
here?"

Daniel was silent. Appraising.

"Just tell me what I have to say."

Daniel nodded. He stepped back in and put the
scotch down. He took off his hat again. "It's going
to sound something like this: The full weight of the
government . . ."

". . . of the United States supports your efforts against
the terrorist, Reto Poirier," I said.

"Good. Good!" General Tibideau de Rosas roared.
"Music!"

The string quartet at the edge of the open patio resumed playing. The assembled host of military officers, men, and women that were part of the machine that kept Tibideau in power resumed their evening.

"So, Ambassador, what think you?" Tibideau asked. His hands gestured wide at the mansion nestled in the foothills not far from the military airstrip where I'd arrived in Malagar. I could see the valley and the distant airfield. Behind me, torches guttered and bloomed, illuminating a new wall being built to secure the rear of the estate from the slow rise of the hill behind us.

"This place," Tibideau said, "it is nothing. A shadow of my residence in Quixto. This is . . . What is it, Armando?"

Armando de Rosas was nearby with a clutch of Malagayan officers that were, like him, in dress uniform. They sported sidearms in leather Sam Browne belts. Armando unbuckled the flap on his weapon's holster as he looked over. "A refuge, Papa."

"A refuge." Tibideau nodded. "A place to shelter from the worries of the day."

Workmen on a scaffold lathed cement atop the wall. Waiters and servers carried boxes that clinked with glass and handed them up to the workmen. They upended empty beer and wine bottles into the fresh cement.

Beside me, Tibideau's mistress placed her hand on my thigh. She kept her eyes focused serenely on the general while her nails slid across the fabric of my slacks with a gentleness and duration that could not have been accidental.

"A bright smile. A pretty face." Tibideau winked at me. "These are things that should greet a working man, eh?"

I rose from my seat at the table. "General, I couldn't agree more."

The explosions startled me. Screams rose from the dance floor. I turned to see workmen diving from the scaffold and glass flying in gouts as bottles exploded atop the wall. Armando fired his 9 mm like the ticking of a brutal clock. Other officers joined him. They leveled their weapons, and soon, there was a cacophony of gunshots.

"Do not let the noise frighten," Tibideau said. "This is celebration, and now the top of the wall will be sharp."

"You're worried about trespassers, General?" I asked.

"A man must protect what is his. Do you not find this to be true, both for men and for nations?"

"They must protect what it is right to protect."

Tibideau thought about it for a moment. I could see that his mistress now had both hands under the table, massaging something unseen in the general's lap.

"See!" Tibideau shouted, finally reaching something of an internal decision and pointing at me with both hands. "He is a diplomat after all! His lips move, and I understand nothing he says!"

CHAPTER XIV

INTO DARKNESS

RETO POIRIER AWOKE TO THE murmur of voices outside the room where they slept. He was the last one to rise. He rose and moved past the black tarp. The rest of the group sat with two young villagers he did not know. A duffel bag lay at their feet. Laurent spoke with them, low and intent. He beckoned Reto.

"Los Generales destroyed their village," he said.

One of the men pointed in the direction of their village. "They hang the men from trees. They cut off their ears like they were swine! My father. His brother. They died this way."

"The women and children?" Reto asked.

Laurent shook his head.

"Gone," whispered the other villager. "Gone. We searched. They are never coming back."

The first man upended the duffel bag. The dim light from a candle burning on a table nearby flickered across the metal and wood of Lee-Enfield rifles.

"That is why we brought these."

Tibideau rolled his neck as his mistress massaged his back. I stood beside the table and watched Armando and the officers pick off bottles. An official with state enterprises had spread aerial photos across the table, showing a selection of factory sites. Elsewhere, the party continued, and the string quartet valiantly played on despite the off-rhythm and staccato interruption of gunfire.

"Here," Tibideau said, tapping locations on the images. "These are the best sites."

The official circled them in marker, then slipped them back into a folder and vanished.

"We do not have the same problems as your country," Tibideau said to me. "No poorly taught youth chain themselves to trees. Factories like this feed our poor."

"How were they fed before this?" I asked.

The mistress looked at me sideways but kept massaging the shoulders of a man old enough to be her grandfather.

"Poorly." Tibideau grunted as she found a knot and worked the soreness with her thumb. "But these are matters of economy. I am not an economist, Ambassador! Give me war! That I understand. Not schoolteachers who throw dirt in my eye!"

"Reto Poirier," I ventured.

"A heretic! You know this? They worship false idols carved in his image. Not the Saints and Madonna as they should! They call upon filth such as this." From a pocket, Tibideau produced a wooden figure of a man bowed in prayer.

"Perhaps he wants to protect what is his," I said, remembering the child with a similar figure and bandages in place of her hands.

"Oh, no." He gestured, and the mistress changed the area of her massage. "What is his? The trees we clear? The cement we pour? The machines we place inside factories?"

"Children," I said, knowing I shouldn't have said it.

"What?"

"The children who work there."

"They work hard, no? Because they are young. They are swift. Little hands for work that demands detail. They are paid adequately. This too, I know. Perhaps, too much."

"*Mi hermana* do this," the mistress said. "I know what she make."

"Well?" Tibideau prompted.

"One. Just one."

"One?" I asked. "Your sister makes one dollar an hour?"

She smiled brightly, as though I were teasing her. "No. *Por dia.*"

Tibideau relaxed. "Ah, as long as it is by the day, then. Tell me, is your sister as beautiful as you?"

"Not anymore." She wrapped her arms around him and kissed him on the cheek. "Now I am most beautiful."

Tibideau wrestled her onto his lap. Then he noticed I was staring at something on the figurine. "Ambassador? Has a piece of wood taken your tongue?"

"Blood." I put the figure down on the table. "There's blood there."

"Tell our friends in Washington we take care of Reto Poirier just so," Tibideau said, and he took the figure and gouged the red stain from the wood with a knife.

At the fence, Armando fired off fifteen rounds from his magazine. Glass rose in flickering gouts.

"Just so," Tibideau said and nodded. He set the figurine down as though all was now right with the world.

Reto knelt with his group, including the two new villagers. Each of them had a rifle before them. He let dirt from the floor sift through his fingers.

"When I was a teacher," Reto said, "it was enough for me to say, try. Attempt your best, and someday, you will awaken that which is most like God within your breast. From that day, the world will breathe beneath your feet, and every dawn will blind your new eyes with the beauty it holds."

The dirt sifted away.

"To try is no longer enough. Los Generales have colored the soil with blood. And I . . . I am no longer a teacher."

He touched a Lee-Enfield rifle.

"But I will not foul the earth with more blood."

He pushed the heavy weapon away and looked at each of the men and women around him.

"I am a warrior with empty hands. And if the ground is red, then I will not walk upon it. I will lay down my hatred and my fear and stand in God's hands." Reto rose to his feet. "Who will stand with me?"

Maya was the first. Slowly, Reto's daughter slid her weapon away and stood beside him. Then others. Shallah slid his rifle forward and rose, the loose overhanging folds of his shirt concealing the .45 that was snugged hard between his belt and his spine.

Tibideau danced out on the patio with his mistress. I skirted the edge of a crowd of military officers and other guests who cheered their general as he swayed with the girl. I found Daniel at the bar.

"You got kids, Jack?" he asked with an eye toward an entrance to the house. Five very young women gathered there. As officers approached, one—sometimes two—would take the man's hand and lead him into the house.

"No."

"Long time ago, my wife left me with our baby girl in her arms. I got resources and all this fucking tradecraft, and I can't find her." He looked down at the glass he held, then back across the patio of swaying celebrants and at the wall beyond, where the occasional gunshot still rang out, followed by the crack of fracturing glass. "I look at all those little girls and wonder what mine would look like. How is that? I mean, how does somebody you love just vanish like that?"

"In my case, they die," I said. "No offense."

Daniel looked at me, his glass at his lips. He lowered it without drinking. Then his eyes found neutral ground. "None taken."

One drunken officer grabbed a waiter's tray of full beers and placed three on top of the wall with the empties. From the dance floor, Tibideau saw that. The drunken officer aimed and fired a succession of five shots. The trio of beers exploded in slivers and foam.

Tibideau moved for him, shoving people out of his way.

Daniel and I watched as Tibideau slung the drunken officer to the ground and then stomped him with his boot. The music stopped playing. We could hear the man's cries, then a gurgling as blood filled his throat.

"Shouldn't have used a full bottle," Daniel murmured as he poured his drink onto the ground. "The old man hates waste."

In the secure communications room, Harold smiled as the new monitors glowed to life. He eased his fingers on an ergonomic keyboard.

"Ahhh," Harold said.

Watching Tibideau beat the officer to a senseless and gibbering heap diminished my appetite to see how the rest of the party would unfold. I took my leave of Daniel. Then I thanked General Tibideau de Rosas as he rinsed the officer's blood off his boots with a bottle of sparkling water.

I made my way around the side of the villa and back to the front. Drivers stood beside parked cars. The lights from the villa threw broad golden pools of illumination across the grounds and parked vehicles. Beyond the parked cars, a group of children played soccer with Riley. As I drew near, he kicked the ball to one of the children, then jogged over.

"Ready to go, Ambassador?" Riley asked, out of breath but grinning.

I nodded.

"We have some things we leave the kids when we come out on occasions like this," he said. "It's a goodwill investment. I can get them out and carry them over, and you can hand them out to the kids."

He swung open the back hatch of the Suburban and unzipped a duffel bag so I could see. Packaged food. Baseballs. Gloves. Soccer balls.

"Who was winning?" I asked.

"Oh, everybody but me," Riley said. "I'm not up to their level of play."

"I think these should come from you," I said. "Go on. Make 'em happy."

"Yes, sir." Riley grinned. He jogged back over to the children, duffel bag in his grip. He spun a soccer ball on one finger, balancing it easily as the children ringed in around him.

As he handed out the food, baseballs, and soccer balls, a shadow separated from the trees near where I leaned against the Suburban. A girl stood there. Her hands fluttered, and a glow stick dimly shone on a lanyard around her neck.

She beckoned to me.

"I don't have anything for you," I said.

She beckoned again. Her hand was missing two fingers.

She stepped back into the night. I could see the glow as she turned and made her way among the trees. I shot a look over at Riley. He was at the center of a mob of children.

Then I was in motion. Following her.

She was never very far ahead. The foliage at the edge of the forest gave way to a jungle path that was barely visible in the night. I ducked beneath branches as I moved behind her. The dim green light from the glow stick around her neck threw a pale aura above her frail shoulders and illuminated her dark hair. She was five paces ahead and slowed at a gentle curve in the path for me to catch up.

In the greater distance behind me, the tinny music from Tibideau's compound faded as we made our way down the trail. It was inaudible by the time we stepped from the cover of the jungle and onto a pristine new blacktop roadway.

To the right, the pavement led a curving path downhill, eventually, I assumed, to the main roads that converged on the seaport. To the left, it led to a gate secured with chains and a padlock. The girl walked uphill toward the locked gates. She walked in the middle of the road, as though there would be no traffic. As though there were no other people within miles and this place was hers to explore.

She turned, and I saw her as I first had, illuminated by the glow stick's spectral light. Her hand closed on the glow stick. Three fingers furled it to an incomplete darkness that rose as she pulled it from around her neck, her long hair rising with the string and then cascading back down onto her shoulders. The pale emerald light floated like a lightning bug into her pocket and was extinguished from sight.

Her hand rose again. Three fingers. Like an alien appendage, it beckoned. Then she turned and, with a certainty I wished I had, moved directly to a sign on the fence bordering the road. It showed a hand touching wire surrounded by lightning bolts. In Spanish, the black lettering warned: *Peligro! Cerco electrico!*

Before I could say a word, she lifted an entire section of the electric fence and swung it wide enough for me to pass. Then she stepped through, walked to the roadway again, and uphill from the locked gate.

I followed. It wasn't a conscious choice. It certainly wasn't a well-planned and rational decision that carefully evaluated the priorities and potential ramifications of a United States ambassador breaking and entering a facility situated in a foreign land.

I have had fever dreams. Moments of delirium when drink and impotent rage galvanized my body in a sweating and frozen stillness even as, in my mind's eye, I strode forward with a machete to do battle with apparitions that rose from the gray recesses of guilt and the crimson portal of hell. Demons, they were, and past versions of myself. They leered in their recreation of the worst of all I imagined my failings to be. Inevitably, I would let the blunted and bloody machete fall from my grasp in those dreams, no closer to a dispatch of all that haunted me than my subconscious was to running out of specters to fling into the carnage. I would awaken exhausted and panting, with the sheets soaked in sweat.

This carried all the potential of a fever dream.

The fence tore at my new coat as I slipped through the gap. On the other side, I stepped back onto the roadway. A halo of light rose from something just up the slope. She was a silhouette at the top of the hill, looking back at me with an unmoving patience. I could not see her face. But then a sliver of the moon broke through the overcast and shone upon us. She tilted her head, and I saw her expression change as she examined me in the darkness. It was unmistakable. I had seen it a thousand times in the days that followed Elise's death.

Pity.

She turned and vanished as the clouds closed on the light of the moon. The last of its reflection flickered across the black of her hair, like the movement of quick-silver.

I topped the rise. Before me lay a series of five large hangars. They had the inverted U shape of Quonset huts and corrugated steel sides. Each was elevated on a platform to allow container trucks to back in for loading.

She was at the side of the nearest hangar, mounting the shadows of a stairway that led to a platform with a single side door as access. There were no windows. As I neared, I heard the hum of the electric transformers situated to my right behind a separate fenced enclosure topped with bright silver curls of razor wire. Power lines were strung from ten-foot posts inside the enclosure. The posts were placed every twenty yards to carry the wires to electrical boxes at each of the huts. As I closed the distance to the nearest, I could hear machinery thrumming. It was a discordant base note that reverberated through the night air, eclipsing the trill of electricity transformers and making distant the memory of the musicians at Tibideau's party.

She stood on the platform beside the door. I could feel the vibrations from within the building in the metal stairs as I made my way up. The sound that penetrated the Quonset hut's corrugated metal walls clacked and roared with the same deep kinetic force as a train passing on ancient steel rails within arm's length. Power and fury and speed all wrapped into soundwaves filled the air between us. As I reached the platform where she waited and I stood beside her, I realized how small she was.

She looked up at me, her hands fluttering as though they had a life of their own. As though they were capable of speech if I could but see it in their movements. Then, as my lips parted to give voice to my own thoughts, her hands stilled.

Gently, her hand touched mine.

All the words I had to say vanished, and I inhaled air that was inexplicably warmer here. The breath pained me, as though I had simultaneously become aware of the need to breathe and of the fact that I had not done so for a very long time.

She laid my palm against the windowless steel door . . . and stepped back.

It vibrated with the force of whatever was at work inside.

I opened the door. A blinding light flew outward, slashing bright and white into the night. Hot air pushed against me as I stepped into the space, burning my nostrils with the stink of sweat and chemicals and something else—something that had burned to a wicked and noxious essence. The immediate roar of machinery pounded my ears and assailed my senses. Instinctively, I closed the door behind me, preventing any more of the world's maladies from escaping from this particular box.

I stood inside the door.

A steel centipede flailed piston legs above a conveyor belt. Children in identical blue shirts and black shorts worked between the machine's oiled and glistening arms. Their little hands manipulated the rubber parts as the pistons stamped and formed them into heels and soles and liners.

To my left, near the double doors that led to the loading dock, an overseer sat facing away from me in a swivel chair with his feet up on the desk. He wore heavy over-ear protection that sat atop his bald pate. The three stooges played on an ancient television connected to a disk player. He peeled a melon with a knife, cutting away hunks as soon as they were revealed from the rind, scraping the seeds onto a paper plate, and placing the hunks into his mouth with the wet fingers of his left hand while his right continued carving.

I blinked against the bright lights. My throat burned. Steam, or smoke, rose from the assembly line that occupied the center of the space. Children darted from their work at the machine, jogging a few steps to open crates of rubber forms and then back to the machine. As I drew closer to the assembly line, I felt something adhere to my shoe. I looked down, then knelt, almost reverential.

I touched the red stain beneath my feet.

My fingers came away red. From where I knelt, I could see across the factory floor. There were bloodstains beneath each flailing piston arm.

Close by one spinning and flashing metal arm, a little boy watched me with one arm holding his other across the blue shirt with a logo I knew. One eye and half his scalp were bandaged in dirty white. He swayed as he watched me. His hair moved in the wind caused by the piston's speed.

I beckoned the child. My lips moved. I spoke, but there was no sound more powerful than the machine. My words were shredded as they hit the foul air. I raised both hands, beckoning again.

The boy didn't move. Parts slid by on the conveyor behind him.

I rose and moved closer. Slow. Aware how precarious and illogical the balance was between a universe of possible outcomes. The machine flailed hot and close. The little boy's eye closed. I couldn't tell if it was fatigue or something else, but he tottered so close to having his skull bashed.

I lunged . . .

And grabbed him up and away from harm. The children on either side of his position saw the movement. They looked. Then they, too, stepped back from the machine's flailing arms, watching me just as the boy in my arms was. Until his gaze fixed on something beyond me.

The overseer rammed me. Head down. Shoulder smashing into my ribs and arm. His momentum threw me into a crate. I dropped the boy as I slammed into the roughened wood and raised my forearm in time to block the knife he swung overhand. I never saw the left hook. It spun me past the crate and into the curved metal side of the hut. His left hand clenched my throat as both my hands grappled with his knife hand. I lunged to the side. The blade skittered against the dull gray steel at my back.

He kneed me in the stomach and grabbed my shirt, dragging me up again, his face contorted, the knife rising high. The steel reflected the white lights with a brilliance that promised it would peel flesh as surely and as effortlessly as a melon. My hands rose, futile in their attempt to postpone murder.

Riley hit him like a linebacker.

One moment, my life was on the way to a bad end. The next, a Marine had knocked my attacker off his feet and onto the bare cement floor five feet away. The knife skittered across the floor and was lost in a pile of discarded rubber parts that were improperly formed. Riley backed up to stand in front of me, his head swiveling, ready to take on all comers. Uniformed military officers I recognized from Tibideau's party rushed in to secure the overseer in cuffs they produced from hidden places in their uniform coats. They dragged the overseer away as Armando strode into the factory, shouting orders that could not be heard.

I walked over to the pile of refuse and picked up the knife. Someone had found the power to the machine and switched it off. It died with a whine that lasted until I'd walked outside into the cool darkness and the fetid stink had been purged from my lungs. My ears rang in the silence, but I heard the clang of boots on the metal stairs leading down from the open door. Riley tensed, and that was how I knew Armando was there.

". . . assure you, Ambassador," Armando was saying with a conviction that could have fooled someone else. "Such things will not be tolerated!" Then he turned back to the hut, and Riley was at my side, murmuring something about it being time to go. In the shadows of the jungle beyond the factory site's electric fencing, I thought I saw a faint green glow retreat into a greater darkness.

At the top of the road leading to the now open gate, I stopped. Riley halted beside me, silent. Patient. He looked with me as I turned back to the Quonset hut in time to see Armando gesture. The officers holding the overseer released him. The man slunk up the stairs, stood for a moment in the bright light from the open factory door, then vanished into that brightness. The door clanged shut, throwing the scene into darkness.

We returned to Tibideau's ranch. As Riley drove away from the parking area and the bright lights and music that still wafted from the party, children ran alongside the Suburban, their hands out, begging. Besides the knife in my hands, I had nothing to give them.

I closed my eyes.

When I opened them again, the children were gone.

CHAPTER XV

STAINS

THE COLD WATER HIT MY face, flowing down my chin. I could feel the tips of my fingers trembling against my cheeks, like a subtle vibrato. It wasn't from the cold. When I opened my eyes and looked up from the sink beside the bar in my office, I saw only glasses before the mirror. The bottles were gone. I had no idea what Harold had done with them. That was by design. There was a price to the sobriety I'd begun when I arrived in Malagar. With them gone, it was one less temptation.

I lowered my hands to the smooth white marble of the bar so that no one else would see them tremble. In the mirror, both Scoggins and Doc Cassidy watched me with very different expressions. The window overlooking the embassy grounds was covered by heavy drapes, blocking out the night.

"Blame the parents," Scoggins said. His shoulders moved slightly under his suspenders. The corner of his mouth was a faint upward curve as he watched droplets of water drip from my face and onto my shirt. "They're the ones that shove them into factories."

"Are you even human?" Cassidy glared at him.

"Wake up, Doc. It's the third world. Children are disposable income."

Scoggins stepped to me and pulled a slip of paper out from the leather portfolio he held. He placed it on the bar. Almost immediately, it darkened at one corner from a small spreading circle of water on the marble.

"This came while you were . . ." Scoggins paused, as though searching for a word. "Hell, I don't know what you were doing. Reto Poirier's pissing off the heads of industry. We're instructed to use every resource to end his sabotage, Ambassador. Every resource."

My right hand clenched involuntarily. I looked down at it, willing my fingers to slacken their grip on nothing. The tips were still red from blood on the factory floor. I wondered for a moment if the stain was something only I could see. Scoggins followed my gaze.

"Use soap," he said. "It comes off."

I opened the drapes covering the office window, and dialed, even though we were in the same time zone as Charleston. The phone picked up after the fifth ring, only it didn't direct me to voicemail. I recognized the voice of Sarah Everly's clerk. Perhaps my greater surprise was the presence of anyone in the courthouse at this hour. She didn't put me on hold. I was not so arrogant as to believe it was because of my new status as an ambassador to a country she likely didn't even know existed.

"Putting you through," the clerk said.

Electronic silence that wasn't really silence hummed in my ear at the edges of audibility. I opened my office curtains. The industrial sprawl beyond the embassy walls was only visible in the dim light of the sliver of moon that remained and from security lamps burning like white dots in the deeper night. Container trucks rumbled past the gates on their journey to the harbor.

"Hi, Jack," Sarah Everly said in my ear.

I startled. For just a second, it was as though the former district attorney were beside me.

"You're working late," I said.

"Yeah. The bad ones don't go home at five. They're just waking up and starting their day. At least, that's true for the ones who beat their wives to death with three feet of rebar. Apparently, it takes a little time to get their drink on."

I heard her cover the phone and speak to someone in the room with her. The word "warrant" was unmistakable. Then she uncovered the phone and was back.

"Is this about your new sobriety?" she asked. "I don't think I'll make a very good twelve-step mentor."

"I'm not using AA," I said. "And besides, I need a different kind of advice."

"I'm an officer of the court, Jack. Reveal anything crooked and I will use it against you. That said, what do you want to know?"

Light from the window caught the silver blade I'd taken from the overseer.

"I saw some things today," I said.

After she listened, there was a moment of silence. I'd been in her office enough times to envision what she was doing, the look on her face. Her lips pursed as she pushed her glasses on top of her head and rubbed the bridge of her nose, eyes closed in thought. Then her voice was in my ear again.

"This is what I'd do," she said.

I made notes on a pad of paper at my desk.

At the end of the call, Sarah said, "You know, two geeks from the State Department came to see me. They wanted to talk about you. Quite frankly, I was surprised you got the post. I told them you weren't ready."

"You know," I said, "you got a weird way of motivating people."

"Yeah, I get that a lot. Funny thing is, they shrugged it off, like serious character flaws were on their list of desired attributes. The little one—a bald guy with some kind of Texarkana mealymouthed accent—grinned and called you his third monkey."

"I don't—"

"See no evil," Sarah said. "Hear no evil . . ."

A Malagayan Huey rotored past my window, directly over the fence that marked the boundary of protected airspace for the embassy grounds. The side door was open, a GAU-21 locked in the forward position. A coil of brass cartridges fed to the barrel. The gunner leaned out the door and looked forward over the gun's sights.

"You hear me, Jack?"

"Yeah," I said. "What else?"

Sarah hesitated. "The mine cleanup fund has a forecast liability."

"That's nothing new."

"Jack, it's a half billion-dollar liability over the next twenty years, and the fund has a quarter of that. Feds are involved. Governor Habauch sees a future for himself in the United States Senate. He's going to do whatever it takes. Hope's on the table. Parents are scared. Some are restarting the campaign for a constitutional amendment to protect the scholarship."

Air left me as though I'd been kicked in the gut. I closed my eyes, but when I did, I was instantly transported to a hospital bedside and to the sound of my own voice, making promises while in the crushing embrace of a sorrow that blinded me to the forces corruption could bring to bear. I opened my eyes.

"What people?" I asked. "What people are starting the—"

"Me," she said. "My people."

"What can I do to help?"

"I couldn't ever prove it, but I think Stan Habauch pulled you down. Corrupted you while you were grieving. He made you whatever you see in the mirror right now. I bet you know where all his bodies lie."

"Fuck you."

"Is that as mad as you get? First-term Jackson Ford would have burned up this phone line. That man wouldn't have to ask me what to do. Steve Ricker's death let you run from your crimes. That doesn't set you free. You call me if you ever find who you used to be."

The call disconnected.

I looked down at the overseer's knife. Dimly, I imagined the noise of the factory. It rose in my memory as I walked out of the office and down the corridor, past the communications room, and to a waste chute handle. I opened the chute that went to incinerators housed in the bowels of the embassy's basement.

The knife flickered as I held it over the opening, then vanished when I released it into darkness.

***

Private Richard Riley stood in the embassy's ordnance room on the third floor at the end of the hall. Though the Marine barracks had a larger armory, this room contained gas masks on shelves and Kevlar vests. Shotguns and 40 mm riot guns were locked in racks with ammunition and flares.

Riley had a box open on an equipment table. Bubble wrap and colored tissue paper furled up and out of the interior. When I came in, he looked up from a birthday card that had been partially filled with careful block writing.

"Mr. Ambassador," Riley said. He stood at ease.

"Richard," I said. "Look, tonight, I didn't have a chance to . . ."

Riley spoke as my voice faltered. "It's my job, sir. You don't have to thank a man for doing his job."

"I do," I said. "I sure do." I moved closer to the box. A printed label lay on the table beside it. "I thought care packages were supposed to come to you."

"My mom's birthday is this Friday," Riley said. "This being my first deployment and all, I'm trying to do something nice for her, sir. I never missed her birthday before, but I'm already late. Even if I get it in the embassy mail pouch tomorrow, it's only fifty-fifty it'll get there in time."

"What're you sending her?"

Riley carefully lifted a conch shell from inside the box. "Big mother, isn't it? See, my mom lives on the beach. I cleaned it up, and in the card, I tell her whenever she starts to miss me, all she has to do is hold this, and she'll hear the waves on my shore." He grinned for a second, then thought better of it. "It's, ah . . . It's stupid, I know."

I met his gaze. "No, it's not. She'll like that. Sorry I interrupted you." I moved to the door, then hesitated before opening it. "Richard, why do you give things to the children?"

He looked up from the card, a question on his face, like I was giving him an unexpected test. "Well, I mean, we're Americans. We're supposed to," he said. "We're supposed to help. Right?"

I nodded. "Right." I swung the door open. "Good night, Richard."

"Night, sir."

And as the door swung shut, I could see him bending back over his box, painstakingly writing in a way that would convey affection and diminish the distance between loved ones half a world away.

The pounding on the door was relentless. It thundered into Harold's dreams, scattering the nightmare in which he was trapped in a first-floor visas approval window and the room was shrinking in around him, horrific, claustrophobic, and airless. The pounding shattered the room and his dreams. He startled awake, gasping for breath atop sweaty sheets. He blinked at the door. Even as Harold grinned about his escape from a place of stress and regret, he wondered if he was heading for a less desirable alternative.

"Fuck," Harold said to himself, immediately regretting his decision to sleep in the nude. "Can't be good."

He shrugged into the threadbare housecoat he'd picked up during his spectacularly brief tour at the embassy in Jakarta and staggered to the door, muttering as he tried to clinch the robe closed over his bulk. "I'm coming! Jeez. This is what I get for living on post."

He flung open the door.

Ambassador Jackson Ford stood there, a look like determination etched on the older man's face.

They were inside the secure communications room less than five minutes later, the keyboard under Harold's fingers and his mouth slack in surprise. He read the messages and looked at Ford.

"You sure you want to send all this?" he asked. "I mean, you don't want to edit the tone just a—"

"No." Ford finished scratching out a note on a pad he carried, as though he were a physician and the script on the sheet of paper could end all that ailed them, if only they could get it to the right pharmacist. "This goes first," he said.

Harold read it, his brow furrowing in confusion. "To . . . Centers for Disease Control. Somebody sick?"

CHAPTER XVI

GLOAMING

SLEEP ELUDED ME. I ROSE from the sofa predawn, put on sweats, and strode the embassy grounds, loosening up for a run that took me around the half-mile circuit of the outer wall. On my third lap, I saw Gaines and the Marines heading out. As they moved in a measured and silent cadence to the mast and unfurled the flag, I halted silently. Unseen at the perimeter of the grounds, I stood in the humid air, my hand respectfully over my heart, sweat burning in my eyes.

I reached the embassy front doors as Scoggins came down the stairs. He was reading from a white sheaf of pages as he came down and almost turned an ankle and fell the last six stairs. He grabbed the rail. That's when he saw me. He clutched the pages against his leather portfolio, the beginning of words on his lips, but they changed to a snarl as he fumbled the portfolio and it fell. Loose pages spun out of it and onto the marble floor. Foreign nationals already taking their positions at the visa windows looked up at the commotion as Scoggins recovered his footing and shouted at me.

"Are you insane?"

I walked up the stairs and past him without a word. He hurried down to the first floor and scooped up his portfolio, then darted up the stairs after me.

"Ford!" he shouted.

I was on the third-floor landing and headed for my office suite when he caught up. He huffed along beside me like a prizefighter sucking oxygen before the bout. He didn't flinch away as I stepped into the office and then past the door that was still broken wide open, revealing the untouched bed in what had been Hinkley's quarters. I walked to the closet and peeled off the sweatshirt and T-shirt I wore.

"You cite Los Generales for human rights violations?" He was breathless, his face contorted, the sheaf of messages clenched in one hand. Papers stuck out of his portfolio at odd angles.

"They condone child labor," I said.

"They provide employees!"

"They place children in harm's way. I'll tour the rest of the American holdings today and include or exempt them from the report."

I tried to move past him to the shower, but Scoggins blocked me with a hand to my chest. Rage flailed upward in me. I kept my hands carefully at my sides and stepped back from his palm.

He waved the messages in his hand. "You don't get it, do you? This is State's response to your little report." Then he read from a page: "Am-Embassy Malagar will adopt the following policy and implement same forthwith. The current government of Malagar is an ally of the United States and shall have the full cooperation and support of this embassy as regards the interests of US registered companies conducting business or manufacture within Malagar's territorial borders. Future reports should concern the viability of relocating American business to Malagar from high labor cost areas within the United States."

I stared at Scoggins. He looked up from the message as though the argument were over.

"Don't make this difficult," he said. Then he stormed away.

Daniel watched the sunrise from the balcony above the whorehouse. He looked at the glass of warm milk and scotch. The phone cradled against his ear gave off no warmth. Not from the mechanism and not from the voice that came from it.

"Jesus, Danny. You know what time it is?"

"I know what time it is in Bogotá."

Daniel heard muttered cursing. Not just from Al Nivens, but from a woman who sounded half-asleep.

"Get up, you ungrateful son of a bitch, and answer some questions," Daniel said into the phone. "I didn't ransom you just to get a Christmas card once a year."

Daniel grinned as he heard a click from the far end that could only be a light switch flicking on at the reporter's bedside. A louder but still half-asleep woman muttered, "Asshole. Get an office."

"Jeez. All right," said Al Nivens. "What do you want to know about Jack Ford?"

CHAPTER XVII

ALEXANDER

SCOGGINS WATCHED AMBASSADOR JACKSON FORD walk out of the embassy and climb into the waiting Suburban. He waited until the vehicle with Ford, Gaines, and the driver rolled past the front gates and the Marines at the gates sealed the egress.

Then he walked up to the third-floor communications room to send his message.

The sun was high and hot. It seared my neck as we walked. Gaines was at my side, his dress blues exchanged for the duty uniform. I'd asked him to stay in the Suburban with the Marine driving, but that hadn't gone over well. When I explained that I didn't want to seem intimidating by having two massive armed Marines flanking me where we were going, he grudgingly agreed to leave his sidearm in the Suburban, along with the Marine driving. But the gunnery sergeant was still not happy about it.

"Maybe you could also smile at these guys," I suggested as we approached the two guards controlling the locked gate straddling the roadway before a factory site.

He glared at me.

"Or not," I said as we continued to walk. "Your call."

Beyond the gates, rust-speckled steel cargo containers were arranged in rows around a single-story factory that hummed with activity. Children carried in bolts of cloth from some containers. Others carried out newly sewn blue jeans in bundles. They took the bundles into cargo containers, where the jeans were pinned to the container walls and children wearing bandannas over their faces sprayed the jeans with something that bleached the dark blues and blacks to fading colors. Smaller bandanna-wearing children worked at the legs of the jeans with pliers and blades, distressing the material until holes gaped.

"Ambassador, we can't be here without invitation," Gaines said.

At the locked gate, two guards in white shirts with blue pockets watched our approach. Their pockets had corporate logos. Sweat dampened the collar around my neck. I pulled the knot from my tie and slipped it from around my neck, flicking open my collar as I slipped the tie into a coat pocket.

"Ambassador . . ." Gaines began again.

I spoke over him in Spanish: "I'm Jackson Ford." I smiled broadly, as though the guards were old friends. "United States ambassador to Malagar."

One guard looked at the other and shrugged. Then he unlocked the gate and swung it wide.

"There, Gunnery Sergeant," I said, continuing through the open gate without breaking stride. "Invitation."

We visited eight sites, all of them embedded in the supply chain of American multinational corporations. In the back of the Suburban, I looked at the photos I'd taken, each digital image left me with a visceral type of regret.

In one, a child grabbed rubber shoe soles as they dropped steaming from a press. He couldn't have been older than twelve. He applied the scorching hot rubber soles to shoe uppers in a mounting machine. His hands were seared pink from burns.

In another, dozens of girls and boys looked upward at the lens from their work. The image didn't convey the metallic cicada rhythm of their sewing machines. On the wall behind them, a poster showed a supermodel wearing the clothes they'd put together from precut pieces.

In another image, I'd captured a different jean distressing operation. This one fitted jeans over hard plastic forms that were like upside-down torsos with truncated calves pointing skyward. Taller boys slid jeans over the forms. Then they sprayed the jeans with chemicals using four-gallon backpack sprayers. Smaller boys slid the wet jeans off the forms and rolled them up, carrying them away to a place where they would let the chemicals burn through the color and erode the stability of the fabric. The atmosphere was caustic. The boys' eyes were red-rimmed, their faces wan.

I closed my eyes. The scent of old bleach was still on me. No one in the Suburban spoke as we jounced on a rutted lane that led to the blacktop that would carry us back to the embassy.

"Mr. Ambassador, hang on." Gaines' voice opened my eyes. It wasn't what he said, so much as how he said it. Then the driver braked so hard I felt the creak of the seat belt locking. My weight crushed against the restraint across my lap and sternum.

Up ahead, two Ford F-150 trucks swerved from screens of trees and into a roadblock facing our path. Soldiers jumped over the sides of the olive-painted beds, brandishing rifles at us. An officer stepped from the cab of one truck and strode into the center of the road, waving his arms for us to stop.

"Get us out of here," Gaines said. "Back it up."

The Marine slewed the Suburban into reverse. The Malagayan officer ran toward us, one hand producing a sidearm. Through the Suburban's bulletproof glass, I heard a popping like fireworks as he discharged his pistol into the air.

We executed a reverse bootleg, spinning off-road and throwing dust and gravel as the Marine rotated the wheel and braked hard. Then we were barreling down the road in the opposite direction, gaining speed. Twice more, the officer's weapon produced a flat crack behind us. I looked out the window at the roadblock fading into the distance and could see the other soldiers firing too. Their rifles discharged into the air—a more guttural bark of sound transmitted through the steel and ballistic glass that protected us.

Ahead, at the right side of the roadway, trees shivered.

Something massive rose from where it had lurked in a narrow copse. A tree trunk snapped in a spray of wood splinters, and sixty feet of timber and branches fell almost to the road's edge. The tank ground across the ruined trunk and onto the roadway. As it did so, the pine's canopy shed needles in a fine green rain as fifty-five tons of steel roared along, smashing branches.

The tank ramped over the edge of the road and onto the asphalt, straddling both lanes. The turret spun the rifled cannon muzzle toward us.

"Mr. Ambassador," said Gaines. "We can't get past that Crusader."

"Let's see what they want," I said as though there were other options I'd already weighed and dismissed.

The Marine pulled to the side of the road. In moments, soldiers flung all the doors open and dragged us out. A boot hit me in the small of the back as I stumbled down from the vehicle and fell into the grass. There were shouts. Gaines' voice rose, and the soldier that kicked me hit the ground, his upper lip stained with his own blood. Gaines flung the man's rifle toward the trees.

Four soldiers converged on Gaines, aiming their rifles at his center mass, shouting while the officer watched it unfold. More soldiers forced the Marine driver around the front of the vehicle and onto his knees. He bled from a gash on his forehead.

Then Daniel was there, moving like a ghost, speaking in Spanish in a calm and conciliatory manner. He used the soldiers' names, and I realized he was reading them from their uniforms. He deftly inserted himself between the rifles and Gaines, one hand out to hold the gunnery sergeant back, while slowly, with the precision of a surgeon, his other hand moved the muzzle of each rifle. I waited where I was, fearing any movement I made would upset this delicate ballet. Daniel moved their muzzles off Gaines and onto himself. He spoke in Spanish. It was low and unintelligible to me.

After a few seconds, the soldiers swung their rifle barrels away from Daniel and stood at rest, their weapons pointing toward the sky.

For a moment, there was silence.

Armando walked over to the soldier Gaines had punched and then thrown to the ground. In Spanish, he yelled for the man to get his fucking gun and return to the trucks. He watched the soldier run to where Gaines had flung his weapon. Then he turned to me and spoke in English.

"Ambassador," Armando said, "what are you doing?"

"I'm in a new country," I said. "Seemed like a nice day to explore it."

Armando moved closer. "Sightseeing?" He walked to the Suburban. "That is why you are here?"

"You've never been a tourist, Colonel?"

"In America, yes." He leaned into the back and pulled out my camera. He flicked through the digital display. "But I do not go to the ghettos. I do not take my camera to the ghettos."

"Souvenirs," I said. "I like remembering the people I meet."

Armando looked up at me. "My father, he is a fine host, is he not?"

"He is a fine host." I nodded. "What has that got—"

"Why did you not taste his wine?" Armando asked. "I understood that you enjoy wine. Beer. Liquor. You are quite fond of all of it. This is true? But, at his party, you took nothing. It was quite rude of you, as a guest."

"I've lost my taste for it."

"You know," Armando said, "my father, he say to me, 'Armando, do not deal with sober men. A sober man cannot bend, see, and so he breaks.'"

My spine was on fire. I could feel the adrenaline rush bottoming out. Soon, I would be trembling. "I'm not a sober man."

"No," he agreed. "I think you are a man who wishes for a bigger glass."

He gestured. A soldier put a bag inside the Suburban.

"Drink," Armando said. Then he gestured again, and the soldiers slung their rifles and turned their backs on us. The tank reversed from the roadway, leaving tread scars where it had chewed across the pavement. Daniel paused as he walked past me.

"I have a job to do," Daniel said. "Don't make me choose."

Then he, too, was gone, getting into one of the olive drab truck cabs as soldiers loaded into the beds. Armando climbed into a cab with my camera around his neck.

Gaines helped the Marine to his feet.

"You all right?" I asked.

"Good to go, sir," the Marine responded, though he was clearly not good to go.

"Let's get you back to Doc Cassidy," I said. "Make sure you don't have a concussion."

We got back into the Suburban. Gaines drove this time while the Marine opened the first aid kit to apply gauze to his forehead.

In the back, I opened the sack the soldier had thrown onto the floorboard. I reached in and came out with unbundled hundred-dollar bills. They were soiled by mud and by use. I held them, staring. When I looked up, I met Gaines' eyes in the rearview mirror, and his face hardened before looking away from mine and the money in my hand.

Gaines pulled directly to the medical tent at the side of the embassy, and Cassidy and one of the foreign national nurses broke away from the tables. Doc Cassidy led us directly into the first-floor infirmary. It occupied one corner of the floor, with windows that gave a view of the flag mast and beyond that, the front gate. It held banks of medical equipment and two patient beds. Doc Cassidy kept me and Gaines in the infirmary as she cleaned and sutured the gash on the Marine's head. She murmured to the nurse, who angled the light to illuminate what became an intricate series of stitches.

"Who do you know at the Centers for Disease Control?" Cassidy asked me. She didn't look up from the careful row of sutures she was making to knit the Marine's lacerated scalp together. She wore magnification lenses over her glasses, like the half visor welders would don if they cared about their eyesight but didn't give a shit about flying sparks or the ejecta from liquefied metal.

The suture thread and needle she obtained from infirmary stores were so thin they appeared translucent when they caught the light. Her hands moved with a precision that could have belonged to a violinist. They were swift, certain, and in time, I'm sure the Marine would agree they qualified in some manner as a form of art.

"Well, Ambassador?" she prompted.

I couldn't tell if she was angry or focused. But I didn't want to be the one that distracted her. "Look, Doctor, now's not—"

"Someone at the CDC cabled their biohazard disposal protocol to Embassy Douala," she continued, ignoring me. "Eight hundred pages of federal regulations, with a note that their medicinals are about to go bad. I got a call from the old ass-grabber himself. Acted like he was doing this big favor for old time's sake. His voice was an octave too high."

She knotted the final suture as she spoke to the Marine. "I studied under some of the finest plastic surgeons in Los Angeles. You have a double seam of stitches using a technique I guarantee—I absolutely guarantee—will leave a minimal scar. You may be able to see it, but that's only because you lived it and you know it's there. No one else will notice. We good?"

The Marine nodded.

"Sharra is going to give you some medicine, and you're going to see me tomorrow to check in. Light duty until I say otherwise."

"Thank you, Doctor," Gaines said.

Cassidy turned to me as the nurse gave the Marine a vial of tablets.

"They're sending vaccines, Jack. They're dumping them," she said, emphasis on the word *dumping*, her eyes alight. "Every vial. After they get here, I'm gonna call the ass-grabber."

She grinned as she shucked off her surgical gloves and flicked off the light she'd used to care for the injured Marine. She was almost dancing. "The vaccines are inert." I heard a lilt in her voice that must have been similar to the inflection she'd used as a child when she found out her parents were taking her to the carnival. "They don't expire. You have a grand Friday, Ambassador."

Then she was gone with the nurse, back out to the tent to minister to the needs of those that surrounded her.

"Friday," I said, a realization dawning. I looked over to Gaines. For some reason, he was watching me.

Gunnery Sergeant Joseph Gaines walked down to the front gate of the embassy. Riley stood to attention at his post, watching an intermittent flow of container trucks and smaller cargo vehicles along the main road outside the embassy.

"Report," Gaines said.

"No traffic, Gunny! Post is secure!" Riley responded.

Gaines glared. Riley didn't flinch.

"Marine, there something you want to tell me?"

"No, Gunny!"

Gaines nodded. But his expression said he was not satisfied. "The ambassador wants you."

I watched Harold adjust a computer camera. His voice was a murmur into a microphone to test the audio.

"There," he said. "That looks better." Gaines entered with Riley.

"Sir," Riley said to me, "you wanted to see me?"

"Not me." I smiled, gesturing him over to the computer as Harold vacated the seat. Riley and Gaines came around to see the image of Riley's sister jog as she adjusted her own camera. Behind her was a background of balloons, family, children, and at least one dog.

"Sis?" Riley said as his sister waved on the screen. And suddenly, Riley wasn't a Marine anymore. He was a big sloppy kid. His sister moved from the seat and knelt beside the keyboard so Riley's mother could take her seat.

"Mom!" Riley said. "I . . . I didn't think I'd see you. I was standing post and thinking I wouldn't get to see you . . ." Riley looked up at me. "Sir," he said. "Thank you, sir."

I nodded. Then he looked back to the screen as his mother raised a conch shell to her ear.

I stopped beside Gaines on my way out. "Need you to find someone for me."

He tilted his head, not saying a word.

I said the name.

Gaines' face remained as hard and impassive as obsidian, yielding no sign of recognition other than through the knots that formed at the side of his jawline as he clenched his mouth into a fine line. After a moment, he nodded.

I walked away. Behind me, Gaines watched Riley touch the computer screen as though he could feel his mother's face.

In the corridor, I rounded the corner leading to my office. Daniel leaned against the wall. He joined stride with me as I walked to the office.

"You a student of history, Ambassador?" Daniel asked.

I ignored him, my stride not changing. He kept up. Lean. Effortless. He continued as though he had never intended on waiting for an answer.

"During his retreat through the Gedrosia desert, Alexander the Great lost a third of his army," Daniel said. "Thirst. Exhaustion. The path they took across the sand was strewn with the bodies of sixty thousand men."

I halted at the door to my quarters. Through the office window, I could see wind lift the flag. It furled and unfurled from the mast in the warmth of late afternoon sunlight.

"You have a point?" I asked.

"At the worst of it, his scouts found a trickle of water. Not enough for an army. Enough for one man. So they collected it in a helmet, and they brought it to Alexander. Their king. So that he would not perish. Do you know what he did, Jack?"

I turned my gaze from the flag to Daniel. "He stood before them all and poured it into the sand."

"If they could not drink, he would not drink," Daniel said, watching me intently.

"I'm nothing like Alexander." I entered my office, turning my back on Daniel.

"Mr. Ambassador, it's important you stay that way."

When I reached my desk and looked again at the door, Daniel was gone, but Gaines was there.

"I found him," Gaines said.

CHAPTER XVIII

THE HANGMAN'S NOOSE

MY CHEEK TWITCHED AS THE fly landed. It crawled toward my ear, one of ten thousand points of horror throttling my senses. Bile churned in my gut. I breathed through my mouth to avoid the worst of the stench. Open sewage congealed in a trough that ran on a slight downhill slope from each of the cells and into the corridor where I stood with Gaines. He had insisted on accompanying me, even though I warned him what came next was best taken in silence to our graves.

The guards generated a cacophony of shouts. Their batons clanged against the metal cell door before us. They wore thin bandannas over their faces and couldn't have been out of their teens. But these were already hard men, made cruel by their experiences and the environment that held them captive as much as it held the prisoners rotting within the cells. One guard rattled keys in a lock and turned the ancient bolt. The door creaked wide, and a gust of foul air rolled out over us. The guards ran into the cell, batons raised.

"No!" I shouted, darting past Gaines and into the cell with them. "No!" I was between the batons and the man sprawled on the floor before they could strike him. A guard lowered his baton and squared off with me, glaring as he tapped his baton across his palm like it had a rhythm all its own. I could see in the squint of his eyes that he was envisioning where he would strike me. In my peripheral vision, Gaines was suddenly within reach of the guard.

From the corridor behind us, the director of the prison made a sound like the clicking of teeth. The tapping baton hesitated. Then the guards responded like conditioned animals and filed into the corridor. The director stepped in and recoiled. He raised a yellowed kerchief to his face and snuffed to clear his nostrils of air fetid with shit and sickness.

I knelt beside the figure lying supine on the floor. His eyes blinked, focused on some distant space. His face was mottled by bruises. A jagged laceration creased his temple.

"This him?" I asked Gaines.

The gunnery sergeant nodded.

The director muttered in Spanish behind the cloth he held over his nose and mouth. His words were defenses against accusations I hadn't made. The abuse was self-inflicted, he said. The conditions seemed poor, but that was because the prisoner had not kept himself or this cell clean. He was an animal. They were all animals, unfit for human company.

I ignored the director and turned to the horribly beaten man lying in his own filth on a cement floor.

"I cannot save her," I said in Spanish. "I cannot bring her back."

His eyes didn't register me at first. They drifted from point to point where the darkness above my head had been partially dispelled by the slant of light from the flickering florescent tubes in the corridor.

"I am sorry," I said. "So I do this for her."

He looked up slowly at me.

I unslung Armando's sack of cash from about my shoulder and extended it to the director. He gripped it, but I refused to let go. He took one look at my face and nodded.

"He died tonight," the director said. "We buried him with the others."

I released the sack. The director vanished as I took Sergeant Beryl Allister's arm and placed it around my neck. His elbow settled loosely around my neck, and I could feel the blood, excrement, and filth caked on his skin. He moaned, his eyes rolling up into their sockets. He was too heavy to lift, and for a moment, I teetered with frustration in my inability to do more than wish him free of this place.

Then he rose.

Gaines gripped Beryl's other side. In the slant of light from the corridor, I saw the Marine's eyes on me.

I gritted my teeth, inhaled through my parted lips, and stepped into the corridor. Beryl moaned again, his eyes slitted with pain and against the light as his feet shuffled across the stained brown floor.

As we walked past cell doors, other inmates cried out in panic. They cried out for mercy. It became a chorus of shrieks from men and women and children.

I am certain that at the end of my days, there will not be drums or trumpets or a host of angels to sing my way upward to salvation. No. In my last aching and unrepentant moment of life, I'll hear the chorus of the damned. The voices from behind the other doors in that corridor. There were no inveterate criminals among them. No psychopaths aping the emotions they could only observe and never feel.

This was the corridor reserved for political prisoners. The director had called it *jaula de la inocencia*. The cage of innocence. They had never seen a court or conviction. Instead, they had run afoul of Los Generales. For that, they'd been introduced to a world of brutality and privation designed to inculcate a healthy respect for obedience in the survivors and the certainty that, in the hierarchy of entitlement to sustenance, warmth, shelter, and dignity, only creatures that gave homage to Los Generales would be allowed to taste a life without horror, violation, and pain.

Those voices will come to me again, as will the crash of the guards as they shouted and pounded their wooden batons against dented steel doors until the corridor boomed with their violence and the plaintive cries could no longer be heard over the music of hell.

As we carried Beryl past the prison's director, he did not look up from counting the familiar green notes from Armando's sack.

Daniel leaned over a planning table with Armando and other officers in a flight planning office at the Malagar military airport. Security lights illuminated the airfield. Through the glass overlooking the field, he could see crews completing their preflight checklists in the trio of Hueys that would carry them on the mission. On the table, the laptop screen flickered, and images began to resolve from the National Reconnaissance Office asset dedicated to tonight's pursuit. Daniel swiveled the laptop for Armando to view. Tibideau's son smiled.

"Isn't that beautiful? Somewhere above us, a Lacrosse-Vega satellite is firing pinpoint maneuvering jets to point it right where we need it," Daniel said. "Four hundred miles high. Big as a dump truck. It will see everything."

Armando gestured. An officer spoke into his radio. Outside, Armando's copilot completed the preflight checks, and the Huey's engine began a whine in synchronization with the slow movement of rotor blades. Armando gestured to the real-time images of Malagar as they appeared and then refreshed on the screen.

"Once Poirier attacks, we track him," Armando said. "We find him. We kill him."

Outside, the helicopter's engine whine vanished into the maelstrom of a constant roar. Armando tugged on flight gloves and gestured for an officer to take the computer on board the helicopter.

The director did not double-cross us. There were no alarms. Guards at the three checkpoints we transited opened gates and averted their gazes as though there wasn't a lacerated and beaten semblance of a grieving father shouldered between Gaines and me. Without a word, Gaines drove us to a two-story walled compound near the docks. While I waited in the back of the Suburban with a semi-conscious Beryl Allister, Gaines pulled a bell on a rope outside the compound's tall stucco walls.

As though they'd been waiting there, three nuns exited a side gate. With a grim efficiency, they took Beryl from the Suburban. I didn't have Armando's cash anymore. I certainly hadn't set aside any of his bribe for future use. That, somehow, would have felt like acceptance. Like surrender.

All I had was the remnant of my first Department of State pay. It was an advance intended to help me handle incidentals before I arrived at my new post. I fumbled the bills from my wallet as the last nun paused at the open side door. Beryl was already gone into the grounds of the convent. I extended my hand to her but couldn't speak. I couldn't get the stink of the place we'd been out of my lungs. I held the cash out in a fist clenched so tightly my palm and fingers were a ghastly white. As she looked at me with the darkness enveloping us, I tried again to say something so that she might understand, but the words caught in my throat and came out with a sound much like a sob.

She came to me. A diminutive woman, dark-skinned and ancient. Without a word, she stepped past my fist with the paltry collection of crumpled bills and extended her hand. She laid one hand over my heart. There was warmth in her touch. Solidity, even though she was old beyond my ability to judge age. She removed her hand and placed it over her own heart. Then she moved through the side door and was gone from my sight without a sound.

Gaines was back in the driver's seat. The Suburban idled.

I opened the front passenger door and got in without a word.

We drove back to the embassy in silence, our headlights throwing a golden illumination over the empty roadway.

When I reached my office, it was empty. No Scoggins. No Harold. Nothing. I didn't realize what I was doing until after I opened each of the cabinets and storage doors at the bar. I stopped as I grabbed a bottle filled with clear fluid.

It was sparkling water. My hand shook as I struggled for control.

I put the bottle that was not vodka back where I found it.

In the master suite bathroom, I threw up until there was nothing left but bile. Then I showered. Hot water rinsed away the filth of the prison. But it couldn't scald the stench out of my memory or the cumulative effects of removing alcohol from my system. My legs trembled. My stomach clenched. I stepped from the shower and sank, dripping, to my knees. I was contemplating curling up on the cool of the bathroom's marble floor when I heard someone in my outer office.

I slipped on a shirt and slacks. When I opened the door of my quarters, the table in my office was set for two. There were crystal glasses. Domed silver plate covers kept something unseen warm.

Doc Cassidy sipped sparkling water from a crystal goblet. She looked at the expression on my face and my still wet, slicked back hair, and she half smiled in the way a parent does when their child has suffered a series of losses and mistakes that are wholly of their own origin despite having acted with the best of intentions. I wondered how much of my emotional scar tissue was visible to the physician's eyes.

"I can leave," Cassidy said, "but you still have to eat."

High above them, the Lacrosse-Vega satellite aimed its synthetic aperture radar at a series of locations selected by Armando as the Huey sped through the night. The radar penetrated through stratus and cumulus in the ocean of atmosphere, hit the ground, and returned, resolving into a series of pinpricks of yellow light representing human body heat as Reto Poirier's guerillas fled the red and white illumination of something that burned brightly.

"Burning transformer." Daniel pointed to the tri-color heat source on the screen Armando held. His voice crackled in headsets he, Armando, and the two officers in the Huey wore. "This group is who you're looking for."

"They are moving southeast," Armando said. His finger traced a circle around the half-dozen pinpricks of yellow. "Pilot, new heading."

The pilot veered the helicopter in a new direction. In the far distance, bright light blossomed above the trees as secondary explosions rocked the transformer at the factory site. Daniel looked down as the Huey jinked like a park ride, veering above soldiers who leapt down from trucks and moved into the forest in a blocking maneuver that would force Reto Poirier into a noose.

"Twelve years in LA with a plastic surgery practice," Doc Cassidy said. "People railed in my office because of blemishes only they could see. I catered to vanity far too long."

"Realizing that must have set you free," I said. My food went largely untouched on the plate. She had noticed but hadn't said a word. I liked that.

"It sent me careening into a succession of places just like this. Third worlds. Dead ends. Every so often, the woman I was looks toward Sunset Boulevard, and she whispers, 'Go home.'"

"What do you say?" I asked. She had my full attention. After all, we all have that little voice inside.

"I treated the little girl that Hinkley . . ." She turned away. "After Gaines got her out, I tried to treat her. Some wounds are beyond my skill. We called local authorities. They sent her home. No support. No aftercare. Just a warning not to talk about it. Next day, she rode a bus to the harbor, filled her pockets with stones, and walked into the sea. The mother lost it when they found out. She fled to family in Venezuela. Her father, he got reassigned to a one-man station in the jungle on the border with Brazil. Nothing but poachers, disease, and venomous things. Perfect place for someone to disappear. When the vaccines ran out, I was leaving this place."

"But they didn't. Run out."

"It's been a long time since I've had an ambassador give me hope, much less a reason to stay."

I believe that guilty men make their own ghosts. That visions and haunts and the chain-dragging Marleys the living encounter are the byproduct of memories we assemble in the abyssal depths of our gray matter. These memories are at once so offensive and so traumatic that our conscious minds can neither acknowledge nor wholly ostracize them from our waking lives. They rise from the depths of what we've done and who we once were at moments that may seem random but in actuality are the response to some deeper tectonic shift. Memories are our ghosts.

Out of the depths and in the midst of my dinner with a woman who had devoted much of her life to caring for others, I lost the thread of what she was saying. I saw her face. Doc Cassidy was smiling. Then my eyes darted to the office window, open on the night that roamed beyond the embassy walls, and for a scintilla of time, I was in the back of a limousine with Charleston motorcycle police escorts gunning their Harleys outside my tinted window through intersections, sirens whooping, parting the waters of opposing traffic so that I might hurtle faster toward a deal with one particular devil.

"Hey, Jack," memory whispered, *"you think the girls found peace?"*

I rose from the table. Cassidy startled, then seemed to realize I was signaling an end to it all. Conversation. Camaraderie. Confessions.

"You're right," she said and sheepishly nodded. "It'll be a big day tomorrow."

She folded her napkin before rising. As she opened the office door, I called to her.

"Doctor," I said without looking at her, but I knew she paused, attentive to what I had to share. "You shouldn't hang expectations on me."

She closed the door without saying a word.

They'd been running for hours. Behind them and on both sides, gunshots rang out in the otherwise eerily silent jungle. The night animals were still. Instincts warned the nocturnal creatures that this was an evening they should shelter in place. For the rest of this night, they were no longer the apex predators in this small part of the ecosystem.

Ahead, Reto saw a dim flickering of light as the trail neared what he knew as a massive industrial slum. They had made it out of the hills and were entering the low-lands. He paused at the edge of the foliage. Beyond, dimly lit shanty streets led to a maze of structures. High overhead, a helicopter circled, then turned back toward them.

Reto beckoned. The party darted out of the jungle overgrowth and down a deserted street. They vanished down an alley as the Huey rotored loud and low directly overhead.

CHAPTER XIX

MAYA

My run was a series of predawn laps around the inner perimeter of the embassy's security wall. It wasn't for my self-improvement. Nor was it to distract myself from the way my hands trembled or the way my breath smelled like bile and the sour leavings in an old brewer's barrel. Nor was it because I feared the small quiet moments, when a voice said it was okay to tilt a glass and let something warm and amber hit my stomach and infuse my bloodstream with the stuff that could reset human expectations for euphoria and numbness.

I was running because of the dream.

In the dream, Elise rose and turned to wake me. She did it the way she used to. Bending low, close to my face, her fingers caressing my cheek. My love was a lark. The smile of dawn was her most auspicious time of day. When we were working on the legislation we hoped would become a perpetual testament to our desire to help children, she would rise and shower and dress, then awaken me with the gentlest caress. I would feign sleep, as though I were a child and nothing could drag me from the world of dreams. But she would draw closer. I would smell the scent of jasmine. I would feel the warmth of her breath as her lips touched me and she whispered sweet things. Then she would kiss me.

Last night, Elise woke me. I lay in a reverie on the sofa in my office. It was a twilight sleep. I knew where I was. I knew that I was dreaming.

And still, I smelled jasmine.

In the dream, I knew—somehow, I just knew—that she was there. In my dream, I opened my eyes, and she knelt beside me, a sad smile on her lips.

She wore white, and I thought at first that it was her wedding gown. The love of my life leaned close and went to speak, but then she turned, as though she could hear something I could not. I watched her, unable to move.

As she turned back to me, I realized in horror where I had seen that gown.

Her lips parted as she drew near, something urgent in her motion. Her lips brushed my cheek, and the air filled with a growing mechanical vibration, and I almost heard her whisper . . .

But the sound became a roar. A tumult. A scream that sucked all other sound away. It was the pneumatic sizzling clamor of machines from the factory where the boy with a bandaged scalp had tottered between steel arms flailing in the open air. The sound consumed every sense as Elise and her warning were yanked away into a crucible that produced only darkness.

I awoke gasping, drenched in sweat, on the sofa in my office, with the memory of my wife receding from me in her funeral gown.

In the dead of night, I donned a T-shirt and sweats and trudged past the Marine on sentry duty and outside the embassy. In the cool of the night air, amid the sounds of insects, I ran in the soft grass along the embassy's security wall, moving from one pool of pale golden light to the next beneath the high security lamps inset in the twelve-foot wall. I exerted myself without counting the laps, running until my head no longer throbbed with the insane cacophony of machine noises and I could no longer feel the warmth of her breath on my cheek. Finally exhausted, I stumbled up past the barracks, where even the three Marines that would raise the flag over the embassy were still not up; past the vehicle pool, where two Humvees, the Suburban, and a small flatbed truck were parked; and then into the embassy, past a different young Marine who only momentarily reacted with surprise to see me before he allowed me into the building.

When I returned to my office, a Malagayan helicopter rotored past outside.

I moved through the darkness to the unoccupied bedroom and into the shower.

Shallah sat by the doorway to the hovel where Reto Poirier and the rest of the small group had taken shelter. He glanced back at the sleeping forms huddled across the floor in the dim interior. A breeze curled the edges of the sheet hanging across the doorway, and as it did, Shallah could see that the sky in the distance held clouds flecked crimson and pink. He got to his feet, stretched, and then moved the sheet just enough to step outside onto the rutted lane.

At the far end of the roadway, smoke trickled upward into sky as someone out of sight coaxed a fire to life. He walked to the far side of the street, where a partial wall stood isolated from any other structure. He pulled the heavy .45 from his pants and placed it out of sight atop the wall, then unbuttoned and relieved himself.

He heard them as he finished, one hand against the wall, the wet spray of his urine sluicing down into rivulets caused by rain and the biological needs of other residents in this part of the shantytown. He buttoned his pants and turned, looking down the street again.

From a hovel down the lane came angry voices. Then a crash and the thud of something solid striking flesh and bone. There was the sound of splintering wood and of other things being broken. A woman wailed inside the structure as two soldiers stepped out onto the street and turned toward Shallah, their rifles held ready in both hands, their eyes darkened by fatigue. One wore a helmet that was too large. The other wore a black bandanna. Both were boys Shallah's age. As they advanced, they raised their rifles into a careful aim on the center of his chest. He raised his hands and stepped back until his bare feet were caked in mud, the acrid scent of urine was strong around him, and the knuckles of his hands and flat of his back met the rough blocks of the wall.

The boy with the bandanna said something Shallah didn't hear. Shallah's eyes went wide as the boy wearing a helmet used the muzzle of his rifle to swing back the sheet covering the hovel Shallah was supposed to be standing watch over.

Reto Poirier stepped through the sheet, as though the rifle had revealed him.

The soldier stumbled and fell backward, yelling. Then both soldiers were shouting and backing away, and the only person in the world looking at Shallah was Reto Poirier.

Shallah lunged for his .45.

"No!" Reto shouted. "Shallah!"

The schoolteacher's voice was lost in the boom of Shallah's .45. The ancient pistol bucked in his grip, and the world became veiled in a gray smoke that seemed to slow the movements of all before him.

The soldier with the bandanna hiccupped a rope of blood from his torn throat. As he fell, rolling in the dirt, his rifle clattered to the ground beside him like a forgotten appendage.

The soldier with the helmet fumbled his rifle up and aimed at Shallah, the muzzle blooming with bright flame as pure and yellow as the noon sun.

Something shoved Shallah hard against the wall.

Reto fought as the other rebels and Maya tore at him, dragging him back into the hovel. His hands stretched toward Shallah, as though he could pull the boy with him.

Then the wall erupted all around Shallah. Brick fragments and red dust plumed outward from a dozen places. The young soldier in the helmet arched his back, and puffs of visceral matter erupted from his chest and arms. Something knocked his helmet flying.

Reto vanished into the hovel, the faces of the rest of the group vanishing with him as they turned to flee.

At the base of the street, a troop of soldiers fired their weapons in a fusillade that sounded like thunder. The world resumed its normal rhythm as Shallah felt the .45 leave his grasp and his legs lost the ability to keep him standing. Something shoved him again, hard, and a red mist filled the space before him as he fell to the dirt, his face turned away from the soldiers running up the dirt track toward him.

The last sight he saw was the bright red streak his torso had made as he slid down the wall.

Laurent dragged Reto away, hefting the smaller man off his feet and against his chest. The cloth covering the doorway tore in Reto's grip, and Reto pleaded for his friend to let him go.

"You can't save him," he hissed in Reto's ears. "Save the rest!"

Bullets zipped and hummed through the shack's frail wooden structure. Splinters exploded from the crate walls. Maya pulled her father's arm with all her might.

Reto had one last glimpse. Shallah lay with his back to them, a massive red hole where the first two thoracic vertebra should have been. Then Laurent shoved his friend across the shack and out the other doorway. There, the rest of the group were already fleeing down the muddy track between other hovels. They rounded a bend as shouts rose from close behind them, followed by staccato gunfire and the hum of rounds into the structures they passed. People screamed inside one as bullets scythed through it. On the path ahead, a rebel arched his back and wailed, high and horrible, before he pitched forward into overgrowth and was gone from their sight.

Maya stumbled on the path. Reto caught his daughter and kept her moving. As they ran, they glimpsed faces cowering inside the frail shacks.

Daniel was at the rear of the pack of soldiers Armando led in pursuit. Armando stepped off the trail, leveled his sidearm, and fired twice into the underbrush. Then he waved Daniel to take the path ahead.

"You pursue them!" Armando shouted. "I cut them off!"

Armando led a group of soldiers down a different path.

Reto led Laurent, Maya, and another rebel down from the trail and into an intersection with the main roadway.

As the rebel darted into the road, there was a shout—a single crisp and clear command. Then there was a volley like a thunderclap.

Without a word, the rebel pitched sideways into the roadway, facedown.

Reto dragged Maya to the side of a structure beside the road. Laurent huddled beside them, saying something, urgently, that faltered as Reto raised his hand from Maya. His fingers were wet and red.

"Maya?" Reto said.

Reto looked to Maya. One arm was held close to her body. Her breathing was labored. He gently moved her arm. Her stomach was wet with blood. A frayed circle in her shirt showed the passage of a bullet.

All was still for a pallid moment. Laurent crouched at their side. The dead rebel lay in mud. The only path to safety lay past him, past the guns that were aimed and waiting. Reto lifted Maya into his arms, his face agonized.

"A doctor," Reto said, turning to go back.

Laurent's hand stopped him. "That is not the way. You must go across." Laurent stood, large as a bear. His hand on Reto's shoulder turning him toward the street ahead where soldiers lay in wait for more rebels. The machete snicked free from the sheath on Laurent's belt. "I will buy your passage." He touched his forehead to Reto's, then smiled at Maya. "You will make it across. Be ready, my friend."

Laurent ran into the street, angling directly for the soldiers that stood aiming down the lane. Armando was turned, organizing soldiers into another firing line as they leapt from the back of a truck that lurched to a stop.

"Reto Poirier!" Laurent yelled. He sprinted toward them. The soldiers looked at Laurent, hesitant. They were teenagers in ill-fitting uniforms with rifles that wavered in their aim.

"Take him!" Armando yelled as he turned from the truck. "What are you waiting for?"

Laurent's ragged clothes flapped like a cape. His machete was uplifted toward the sky.

"RETO POIRIER!"

"Shoot him!" Armando struck one of the soldiers with the butt of his pistol. He kicked another.

A soldier fired.

He missed. But others fired then. Laurent staggered but kept going directly toward them. A man as big as a bear. A swarthy face and dark skin, clothed in rags. Filthy. But the machete in his hand was silver and clean and bright.

Reto Poirier reached the opposite side of the road. He paused, looking at Laurent's shambling gait toward dozens of pointed gun muzzles and the officer screaming at the children in uniform.

"My friend," Reto said.

Then he ran, Maya in his arms.

Behind him, the soldiers released another fusillade.

Laurent was barely alive by the time he staggered to their line. A teenage soldier flinched back as the machete swung down. Laurent stumbled to his knees, the tip of the machete penetrating the dirt. Laurent leaned on it as though it were a crutch. His bloody hand reached out, as though the soldier was one of his own lost children.

Daniel reached the intersection in time to see Armando stride up to the wounded rebel and place the muzzle of his pistol hard against the base of Laurent's head.

Daniel turned away. The street echoed with the flat crack of a single shot.

When he looked back again, a red mist hung in the air. Armando stepped past Laurent's body, hitting and kicking the soldiers into pursuit.

Reto staggered through an industrial part of the slum. Concrete structures rose in flat one-story monotony around him. All the streets were asphalt. He ran down the middle of the street, murmuring to his daughter that she would be all right. They were going to find help for her. In his arms, her eyes were wide open, looking up at him.

Behind him, there were shouts and gunfire.

A bullet shattered the glass in a parked utility van as Reto ran past it.

Ahead, he saw walls topped by the bright curls of concertina wire. Movement caught his eye as a red-white-and-blue flag rose to the top of a steel-gray pole that towered above the embassy walls.

When I came out of the shower, cleansed of the sweat from my run, wearing slacks and a crisp white shirt, I felt better. Dawn threw a hint of rose light through the window. I moved to the window with a necktie in hand. At the mast, Gaines and two Marines hoisted the embassy flag to the top and tied it off. In the distance, fireworks crackled, as though in celebration of the flag raising.

Gaines gestured the two other Marines into motion. One jogged for the barracks, the other into the embassy. Gaines moved at a run down the embassy's long drive to the post where two Marines secured massive iron gates that controlled the egress and entrance to the embassy from the main roadway. At the roadway, locals lined up to apply for visas in the United States turned as one toward the direction of the sound.

As I watched, the sound of fireworks came again—a crackle that would have been at home on any Fourth of July—as the flag rippled in a breeze.

But this wasn't a holiday.

I was in motion as the line outside the gate disintegrated, and men, women, and their children fled in a direction opposite the gunfire.

Daniel kept pace with Armando. They ran toward gunfire, pacing with the squad of soldiers that had witnessed Armando's alleyway execution of Reto Poirier's lieutenant, Laurent Veldago. Veldago's blood was even now congealing into the soil, and the airborne mist of brain matter and blood spray had no doubt left a substantial DNA trace on Armando. That would have been useful in a land with an operational justice system.

Veldago had not fired his weapon. He'd had an opportunity to provide covering fire that would have killed a few of the new recruits Armando had levied for the operation. Likely, that would have gotten Reto Poirier across the road. But instead, he'd run at them headlong. It had been a distraction. Worse—a sacrificial rush toward oblivion.

Daniel recognized where they were.

"Armando," he said. "We're nearing the embassy."

Beside him, Armando jogged along, his eyes tracking the intermittent droplets of blood that marked the pavement. If he heard Daniel, he didn't respond.

Daniel remembered dead men swinging among trees, their ankles bound by ropes, their contorted faces flushed with blood from hanging upside down. Fires from burning huts glistened on the wet red smears where someone had razored their ears away in a trophy-taking mutilation of the dead—or of the dying.

They neared an intersection, where the leading element of the squad was crouched, their rifles aimed at something on the cross street. A soldier at the intersection whistled and waved to Daniel and Armando. Some of the other soldiers leaned into their rifles. Yellow muzzle flashes plumed as they fired.

"They have him!" Armando ran to them.

Daniel ran as well. The soldiers fired in the direction of the embassy. In the distance, an alarm began its wail.

High on the embassy roof, the alarm wailed. The rising and falling whine reverberated across the embassy's grounds. Marines at duty stations sealed the main gates at the embassy's drive and at the side entrance. More Marines ran from the barracks with weapons, helmets, and body armor.

Gaines was with the two Marine guards posted at the end of the embassy's driveway. He stood at the pedestrian gate.

Reto Poirier shambled toward the pedestrian gate. In his arms, he held a girl that couldn't have been more than ten. Long black hair shrouded her face, and her arms were draped across her stomach. Her shirt was smeared a deep arterial red that was, at once, the color of exsanguination and regret.

"Gunny," one of the Marines called. "Open the gate?"

"Hold your ground!" Gaines yelled. To the other Marine: "Find the ambassador!"

"Asylum!" Poirier called out to the Marines, his eyes looking past Gaines, addressing the flag and the building beyond them. "I request asylum. Please!"

In the far distance, soldiers darted into the street from intersections. Some took positions behind cover and aimed their rifles at Poirier, Gaines, and the Marines.

"Shoot him!" Armando cuffed the soldier and then moved his rage to the next crouching nearby. "Shoot him! Now!"

"No!" Daniel grabbed the soldier's rifle barrel, thrusting it upward as he fired. Other soldiers swung their weapons into aim on his chest. Daniel raised his hands and walked backward. "Armando!" He kept his empty hands high. He was in front of Armando and the soldiers now, a half-dozen gun muzzles aimed at his center mass. "Marines are in the line of fire!"

"Maybe I do not care."

"Maybe you check with Daddy before you break something he can't fix."

Armando jerked a rifle from a soldier's grip and moved in close to Daniel. "You do as you're told. You were told to kill this man or to bring him here, to me. Why must I chase this terrorist? Maybe you should do your fucking job, Danielo." He thrust the rifle toward Daniel.

Daniel kept his hands open, palms out and just above his shoulders. His eyes narrowed.

"Just as well," Armando said. "You are better, I think, with the knife."

Two hundred yards away, Reto Poirier was almost to the embassy gate.

"Do not worry. I will try not to kill any of your Marines," Armando said, swinging the rifle into aim. "But if I do, America has shown the world that your people tolerate great wrongs as long as there is profit." His index finger edged to the trigger. "That is what we are to you," Armando whispered as he exhaled. "Profit."

"Ambassador!" A Marine beckoned me from halfway down the embassy drive. "To the gate!"

I ran beside him to the gate. A man clung to the bars with a girl in his arms, begging. Somehow, Scoggins and Doc Cassidy had both gotten there before me. Scoggins was shouting at the man.

"She's wounded!" Cassidy said. "We've got to bring her in!"

"No fucking way! Gaines, you do not open this gate!" Scoggins extended one arm toward the man and girl, pointing. "This man and anyone with him is a known terrorist!" Scoggins snapped his fingers until the man looked at him. "Hey! You! You're Reto Poirier. Aren't you?"

The man nodded, once. Grim.

"They're going to arrest you and put you in a cell. Best thing you can do is back the fuck up and hope your own people show you some goddamn mercy."

Reto Poirier saw me coming. He shouted to me. "Please! She is injured! Help her!" He rattled the bars. "Please!"

Doc Cassidy and Scoggins turned.

"Jack!" Cassidy yelled.

"You piece of shit! Get back in the road!" Scoggins yelled at Reto over Cassidy.

Gaines put a hand on Scoggins' chest and moved him firmly from the gate. Reto Poirier shifted his grip on the gate, shifting his body to face me.

And a bullet exploded through his right arm. The rifle round was fast and unforgiving. It ripped through his flesh, throwing blood into the air. The round ricocheted from the black iron of a vertical bar in the gate with a flicker of sparks. Reto staggered, clinging to the bars. The Marines brought up their weapons, calling out the location of the shooter. Scoggins crouched and ran low for cover behind the security wall at the end of the drive.

"Get her in here!" I said.

Gaines flung the gate open. Riley darted out and took the girl from Reto. In a heartbeat, Riley was running for the infirmary with the girl in his arms, Doc Cassidy leading the way.

Reto stood just outside the gate, his arm bleeding.

The gate was still open between us. Gaines held it open, intentionally. He would not move to close it on the wounded man until I directed him to do so.

Reto swayed. He made no move to enter, but his eyes followed his daughter. The expression on his face registered relief. A part of me wondered how he could escape the inevitability of his demise at the hands of a regime with little tolerance for villagers that refused to live in third world versions of company towns. His mouth moved in a single soundless word I would later learn was his daughter's name: "Maya."

Then he turned, facing the soldiers that stood with their rifles raised a hundred yards away.

A plume of light flickered from the muzzle of a rifle. I saw it at the edge of my vision as I grabbed Reto, jerking him off balance and backward. As we fell, there was a crack like thunder as a round snapped through air that should have been occupied by our bodies. Gaines slammed the gate and secured it. Then he helped me lift Reto Poirier to his feet.

CHAPTER XX

REFUGEES

GAINES AND I HELPED POIRIER into the embassy's infirmary. He moved under his own power, one hand applying direct pressure against the wound on his right arm. When we entered, Doc Cassidy was already at work on Maya. Riley assisted while Harold huffed around, putting sterile packs on a tray stand.

"Harold," Cassidy said, "I need plasma from the cold unit."

"How much?" he asked, the door to the cold unit open before him. The cold vapored upward into the air.

"All of it."

Reto moved close to his daughter. Cassidy scissored Maya's shirt, cutting to reveal the wound. Maya's eyes suddenly fluttered open, then went wide.

"Hold on! Hold on! Everything's going to be all right," Riley said, trying to calm her while holding her gently on the examination bed. She jerked loose. Soundless, she screamed. Her hands struck at Riley.

Then Reto was there, and her hands moved on his face. She calmed, and Cassidy was able to resume work.

"She was born mute," Reto said to us, almost as an afterthought. "The rest, she lost to machines."

Doc Cassidy worked around Reto, ministering to Maya's wound. I turned, leaving her with Riley and Harold.

In the corridor outside the infirmary, Gaines stood alert, his gaze on the far end of the hall. Daniel stood there, his 9 mm in a clenched fist. After a moment, he holstered his weapon and walked away.

Soldiers formed an armed cordon around the embassy's grounds. Just outside the main gates, Armando de Rosas deployed more soldiers as they arrived on trucks. Inside the embassy's walls, two Marines were on duty at the main embassy gate, another two at the side gate, and two more were on roving security.

Sunset left the world dark outside. Reflected in my office window, I could see Harold, Doc Cassidy, and Scoggins behind me.

". . . wound was through and through," Doc Cassidy was saying. "She lost a lot of blood, but I've got her stabilized."

"What about Poirier?" I asked.

"Could have been worse. The bone's intact. The muscle will heal. A foot to the left, he'd be dead or paralyzed."

Scoggins pounded his knuckles against the marble of the bar. He pointed a finger toward me. "Get 'em out of here. Did he request asylum? 'Cause I'm sick of every fucking armchair lawyer thinking they can get asylum at an embassy. He has to ask for asylum while he's standing on US soil, and that's not here."

"He's in danger," Harold said.

"We're all in danger because of him!" Scoggins said. "Get him out! The law's on our side. If he wants asylum, he can swim a river for it like everybody else."

"He's on the grounds," Harold said. "It's not about asylum, Ambassador. It's about human rights now."

Scoggins shook his head. "You're grasping at straws."

"The US is a signatory to the International Covenant on Civil and Political Rights," Harold said. "I've lived through this in Jakarta. We have to consider what happens if we hand them over."

"They'll receive justice," said Scoggins.

"They'll be murdered," said Doc Cassidy.

"If there's a risk they'll be killed or even injured, we'll be held accountable," said Harold. "The concept isn't asylum, though they got a case for it if they get to the US. This is about refuge. We've got a process for—"

"No," Scoggins said, pacing.

"Ambassador, you can refer Poirier and his daughter to the Refugees Admissions Program," Harold said.

"Homeland Security will send an investigator to decide if they can enter the US as refugees. It protects them in a way that's kinda like asylum. The hard part's negotiating with the host government for travel to the US."

"This is insane! Look, Ford, in the heat of the moment, you made a mistake," Scoggins said. "Poirier had a screaming little girl in his arms and a bunch of guys with guns chasing him. You couldn't tell he was the bad guy. It was a mistake. Fix it."

"She doesn't scream," I said.

"What?" Scoggins asked.

"She can't scream," I said. "She can't speak. She's mute."

"A trait I wish more of us had." Doc Cassidy glared at Scoggins.

"Harold—" I began.

"I don't care if she's goddamn Helen Keller! Turn 'em over!" Scoggins said.

I moved close to him. "Don't interrupt me."

Scoggins winced and looked away. I turned to Harold.

"Harold, please send an alert to State. Let them know I've given shelter to Reto Poirier and his daughter inside the embassy. We'll care for them here pending the Department of Homeland Security's examination of their case for entry."

"Love to, boss." Harold's eyes flicked to Scoggins. "You should know somebody's already been on the phone."

"They had every right to know the compromising position you've placed this embassy in," Scoggins said.

"Fine," I said. "Harold, fill in the blanks for them. How long will a decision take?"

"What I seen?" Harold said. "Investigator can be here inside twenty-four hours."

"Mr. Ambassador." Gaines stood in the doorway. He extended a document that bore the seal of the nation of Malagar. "They're waiting for your reply at the gate."

Reto stood beside Maya's bed, her hand in his. His head was bowed. As I approached, I recognized the prayer he said and waited for it to conclude.

"Men died so that we might live," he said to me as I moved beside him. Then he made the sign of the cross. "I pray for their salvation."

"You should pray for your own," I said. "Los Generales demand your surrender. Both of you."

Reto went to the window, looking across the grounds. The two Marines at the gate faced off against a cluster of Malagayan soldiers with bayonets fixed at the ends of their rifles. He pointed to the gate. "What do you see when you look beyond the walls of this place?"

"An army."

"I see little boys," he said. "Children given weapons when they should be given knowledge."

"It's hard for me to mourn their lost youth when those guns are pointed at us." I noticed Maya looking at me. A part of me relented. "I've requested refugee status for you and your daughter. An investigator will consider your situation. You'll both be safe here while that happens. I promise that."

Reto's smile was wan. "You promise. Does the wolf now protect the lamb?"

Gaines stepped out onto the flat roof of the embassy. He strode to the edge of the building, beyond a one-foot brick parapet, for a view of the soldiers standing in parade-rest lines at both gates. He raised his field glasses, scanning past the detachments of soldiers to a view of a distant side street.

A military truck rolled up as he watched, and men in civilian clothes climbed down from the back.

I stood at the front door of the embassy on the ground floor, looking out through the glass, the written demand from Los Generales in my hand.

Daniel stepped in front of me, blocking the door.

"What do you want?" I asked.

"The world's coming to an end, Jack."

"He'll have a chance to make himself heard before it ends."

"You're making mistakes here."

"People have told me that before."

"There are no distractions this time," Daniel said. "No dying wives you can use as an excuse—"

I hit him hard. The heel of my hand caught him in the sternum. The force slammed him into glass, and the doors quivered with the impact.

He looked at me a little differently.

"She was never an excuse," I said.

Daniel straightened, then exhaled like he was letting go of something. But he didn't move out of my way. "Scoggins will betray you," he said. "The Department of State will abandon you. Inevitably . . . Inevitably, Doc Cassidy will falter, and Harold will fail."

"What about you, Daniel? Which way does the wind blow?"

"Against you."

"How old would your daughter be?"

Daniel's eyes narrowed, and he moved close. Behind him, the glass door swung open, and a Marine looked at us.

"Ambassador?" He shot a look at Daniel, then back to me. Daniel's left hand unclenched from a fist.

"Yes?"

"You're needed at the main gate, sir."

The Marine swung the door wide and stepped aside for me to pass through.

At the main gate, Gaines faced off through the bars with Armando. The tall gunnery sergeant stood at the center of the gate, glaring at Armando and the double line of soldiers at parade rest behind him, their rifles grounded at a forward angle with bayonets fixed. There were easily thirty soldiers in that dual lane of rifles.

In contrast, Gaines had posted only one Marine at each end of the gate. They wore combat kits, ballistic plates, and had their rifles slung, muzzles down. They were positioned one step from the cover the cement security wall could provide against rounds or bayonets.

The dictator's son smiled brightly when he saw me. He wore his colonel's uniform. Somewhere in the time since the troops first ringed like a gauntlet around our walls, he had found time to change.

As I approached, he took off mirrored sunglasses and gestured to the reinforced iron bars and welded sheets of steel plate on the gate between us.

"Ambassador," he said, "you know the trouble with gates? They sometimes keep friends out."

"Show your friendship, then, Colonel," I said. "Call off the troops."

He laughed as though I'd said something amusing. Then he shook his head and moved close to the bars. One hand caressed the metal as he spoke. "I love America. I've been, you know. Twice. The music. Hip hop, eh? The Mets. But mostly this . . ." He tugged a money clip from his pocket and edged out a new hundred-dollar bill from the folded greenbacks. "Black and green. These should be the colors of your flag. The color of business. Poirier is bad for business."

"I've granted them refuge," I said.

"You do not have to give it, not to one such as this. Human filth that interferes with commerce. With our progress." Armando smiled again, broadly. "Let us in. We will remove the garbage."

"No." I stepped back.

"Your gates are not strong enough!" Armando yelled at me. "Your walls are not high enough!"

I stood watching as Armando spat, then crumpled a hundred-dollar bill from his money clip. He flicked it through the bars to Gaines' feet. The big Marine picked it up.

"Marine." Armando smiled like he'd found an entrance. "You open up, eh? Maybe I throw some more like this down. For you. For them."

Armando gripped the gate with one hand, leering up at Gaines. Gaines held up the cash before folding it into his fist. Then he clenched his massive hands over the one Armando had on the gate. Armando winced.

"Don't litter my property," Gaines said.

When Gaines released him, Armando stepped back, and the crumpled bill was back in Armando's fist.

"This is a five-acre compound. Outer perimeter is precast concrete with rebar reinforcement," Lieutenant Colonel Jeremy Quinn said, tracing the outer wall protecting the embassy in Malagar on one of the three monitors at his station in the Department of State Operations Center. Beside him, Watch Officer Ben Crisswell and two junior Department of State analysts listened. "There are two gates. North egress for pedestrian access. Main gate for vehicle and pedestrians. I don't see any bollards on the main road or barricades beyond the wall. They're vulnerable to IEDs in vehicles."

"Just like Lebanon," Crisswell said.

"What's the building security?" Quinn asked.

"Metal shutters around the first floor of the embassy. Same was planned for the barracks and emergency generator station, but they're not in place yet," Crisswell said.

"Anything from the DSS security liaison?"

"He's in Brasília with the RSO. We briefed them, but OPSEC is running through the center here because we've got better comms." Crisswell took a tablet from one of the junior analysts and read. "The deputy's screaming they're locked down and a military presence is forming."

"We have ten Marines in the security contingent, plus their NCO. That's not a lot of bodies for a 2,000-foot perimeter over five acres." Quinn turned to a screen as it refreshed. "We're getting real-time imagery now. This is the main gate."

Quinn magnified the image, pointing out ranks of soldiers arrayed in two lines opposite the Marines. Then he panned to the streets beyond the embassy and pointed out trucks with mounted machine guns overlooking the Americans guarding the gate. "Technicals with mounted automatic weapons. That's a concern."

"Maybe this is just a show of force," Crisswell said. "More of a Baghdad than a Teheran."

"Hold one," Quinn said. He switched the view and the backdrop went dark, with the exception of heat signatures. The embassy security wall radiated a faint glow from the heat it had absorbed during the day. The cooler vegetation and grounds became mottled areas of green and dark gray. Marines and the soldiers opposing them at the main gate became red human silhouettes. Truck engines became red blobs, exuding heat into the air.

At five points around the perimeter, clusters of red human forms gathered near the wall.

"Well . . . shit," Criswell said. "That's a lot of guys."

Quinn moved in closer on one of the groups as they advanced on the embassy walls. "They're in position to breach." His hand moved to the alert phone.

"Are those ladders?" Crisswell asked, but Quinn was already speaking into the receiver.

"This is Military Attaché SecState. Inform Admiral Haas the crisis room is active for Am-Embassy Malagar."

On the first floor of the embassy, Marines moved from window to window, manually rolling down steel shutters behind the glass and securing the shutters to anchor points cemented into the floor. Two Marines posted at the open glass main doors to the embassy.

"Exterior shutters are tactical steel," Gaines said. "We fortify here. Ground floor. Staff and wounded barricade inside the comm room on the third floor. It's a vault. One-inch steel plate welded in a box behind the ceiling, walls, and floor."

"What's the worst case?" I asked.

Gaines looked at me without a sign of either mirth or malice. "We all die."

Captain Enrique Ivers read the orders. Outside the bridge, the Atlantic was placid. A Seahawk settled on the deck of the Marine amphibious assault ship, newly returned from a training mission to detect subsurface threats.

"What do you think?" Ivers handed their new orders to his executive officer, Maria Holdener.

"Diplomats," his XO said, like the word was a curse. She bent to the chart table and plotted the course that would carry them on a detour from their planned port call in Argentina. "At best speed, twenty-one, sir."

"Thank you, XO," Ivers said. "Comm, send acknowledgement. State can tell the ambassador we'll be on station in twenty-one hours."

CHAPTER XXI

DRY WELLS

"WHO ELSE KNOWS?" THE PRESIDENT paced, his back to the television screens filling the wall of the White House conference room. He glared at Matthew Pope, who opened a valise and took out a folder that held a single sheet of paper.

"None of the networks, Mr. President." Pope put the folder on the table. "But this is an election year. If we don't handle this aggressively—quickly—it will get out. Our worst case is mainstream picks it up, followed by opposition ads. Human rights. Child trafficking. Sex trafficking. Slum builder. All the old gripes will come back, and our sponsors will evaporate. By August, we'll be sitting here with nothing better to do than watch three months of the other guy's campaign ads."

"Goddamnit, Pope, we turn a dying child into the streets, and we can pack our bags now!"

"You think a public hearing will yield a different outcome?" Pope asked. "Poirier's a reformer fighting tyrants. Your tyrants. The moment we see our mess on those screens, we're done."

"Solve this thing," the president said. He turned his back on the kaleidoscopic blur of wildfires, lanes of refugees, and storm waters encroaching from the sea on the news feeds.

Pope stopped the president with a hand as he tried to pass. "I've done a lot already. This is different."

"What have you done, you arrogant little—"

"Paid off your interns and whores," he said. "Boys and girls. Yeah, I kept track. Plus the other stuff."

Pope flipped open the folder to show the single typed sheet under the presidential seal. The president clenched his fists as he read the page.

"Like when I ruined a decorated Army veteran just because her husband wanted to challenge you in a party primary. A. Party. Primary. Remember that? You weren't going to lose that thing, but because you were afraid, we opened up everything that happened to a bronze star POW while she was in captivity. She committed suicide. He dropped out. You got the primary. Remember that political assassination?"

Pope slid a Montblanc from his pocket and examined the black lacquer, the gold highlights. Rainbows of reflected color slid across the barrel as carnage and sorrow unfolded on the televisions. "This time, I expect top cover." He uncapped the fountain pen. "I have somebody reliable in place. Just have to send the message."

"Reto Poirier and the girl go away," the president said.

Pope laid the uncapped fountain pen on top of the page. "Oh, yes," Pope said. "But I'm not gonna twist in the wind waiting for a presidential pardon if it goes sideways."

"What about Ford?" the president asked.

"Langley will do a lot of sketchy things, but they won't kill a sitting US ambassador. I've got a different plan for him." Pope inclined his head to the page under the president's thumb. "As soon as I have your . . . authorization."

The president gripped the pen tightly. The ink smudged beneath his fist as he scrawled his signature across the page. He let the pen clatter back to the tabletop, pushed the paper to Pope, stood, and left. The corridor light illuminated the conference room for just a moment before the door closed again and Pope was alone with screens that showed despair.

"That's my boy," Pope said. Then he picked up the page between two fingertips and blew on the ink of the president's signature until it no longer glistened wet and new.

Atop the roof, Daniel directed his attention to the embassy walls opposite the main and side gates. Somewhere in the darkness, soldiers were pulling back to their staging areas. Armando had guaranteed there would not be any attempted incursions until he needed the distraction.

Daniel had given up smoking years ago, but there was, it seemed, always a need for fire, so he kept his old Zippo fueled and in his pocket. He held it and nursed a flickering light onto the slip of paper Scoggins had brought him. The fire consumed it in an arc that sent fragments of ash fluttering away in the breeze.

He let it burn to his fingertips.

It was after sunset when Harold came into my office and placed a Department of State cable on my desk. Scoggins stepped in behind him. The cable confirmed that an investigator from the Department of Homeland Security would be arriving tomorrow to conduct the initial refugee case review.

"You really think they're going to go through with this?" Scoggins asked. "Every time Poirier shuts down a factory, the president hears about it."

"One of the men outside put a bullet through a little girl," I said.

"Sad, huh?" Scoggins said. "You ever catch the evening news in Miami, Jack?"

The lights flickered several times before coming back on with a dimmer hue.

"Auxiliary power," Harold said. "They just pulled us off the main grid. May I?"

I nodded, and he picked up the phone from my desk and listened. He shook his head.

Harold walked with me as we exited the grim facade of the fortified embassy. Shutters hulked gray and resolute behind each pane of glass on the main floor. Ahead of us, the driveway was illuminated, but the lights didn't reach up to clearly show the flag I could hear moving in the breeze and rattling hoist ropes against the hollow metal flagpole. Gaines had not lowered it this evening. The rules for display of the flag during normal operations are simple: if the embassy has a light source that can make it visible throughout the night, it can stay on the mast. Our embassy was one of three that did not have spotlights capable of this. Each evening, Marines lowered it, folded it, and stored it until dawn.

That was normal operations. We left that cadence when I accepted a bleeding child and her father into our care. During times of crisis, the Marines leave the flag aloft. The alternative is allowing adversaries to whisper that the Americans have struck their colors.

Symbolic move, I thought. Let it fly.

"Auxiliary generators can carry us seventy-two hours," Harold was saying. "More if we prime 'em with gas from the embassy vehicles."

"Communications?" I asked.

"Long as we have power, we've got the satellite links. That's it."

Gaines met us halfway down the drive, joining our stride. From a distance, I could hear the call and response of chants in Spanish. Just past the line of soldiers outside the gate, there was a mob of men that waved Malagar's flag. As we approached, a man touched a torch to an Uncle Sam effigy.

"See anything unusual about our civilian protesters?" Gaines asked.

I looked closely at the crowd of men. "They've got the same barber."

"Those are officers leading the chants and lighting the fires," Gaines said. "This is the way it went in Teheran."

Armando stood at the gate, looking unperturbed by the chanting and arson behind him. Not a single soldier in the line behind him was faced toward the mob.

"You asked to see me, Colonel," I said.

Armando inclined his head slightly, then unfolded a document and read: "Ambassador Ford, until the criminal Reto Poirier is turned over to our authority, Los Generales cannot guarantee the protection of US property or the reliability of local services. Popular feeling runs high. We cannot expose our men to violence for the sake of protecting those who would harbor criminals."

He looked up from the document, then smiled and gestured. In neat lines, the soldiers double-timed between lanes that opened in the mob and away into the night. After Armando and the soldiers left, the mob surged up to the gates and the embassy walls. Their chants filled the air. They beat the bars and the walls with sticks and batons in an angry rhythm. Bonfires they'd set along the road and in the waste piles of nearby buildings threw light and burning embers high into the sky amid sulfurous columns of smoke.

Pope found the president as he walked the corridor to the pressroom. The night air was illuminated by lights on the White House grounds. The president slowed his walk, and Secret Service stood aside in a discreet presence as Pope spoke.

"At our request, locals shut down the phones and power," Pope said. "DTS is monitoring the sat links. So far, Ford's kept it private."

"What's our angle once we get Ford back?" the president asked.

"Federal charges for corruption and bribery during his term as governor," Pope said. "The Bureau's doing the paperwork now."

"Who's the new man?"

"You'll recognize the name." Pope handed the president a dossier.

The president halted before the double doors to the press briefing room. He opened the file and just as quickly closed it and handed it back to Pope. "Well. Definitely got a handle there, don't we?"

Then he opened the doors and walked into the press briefing room, where cameras whirred and the men and women of the White House press corps came to their feet, shouting questions.

Chapter XXII

WHEN YOUR PAIN IS OVER

"They're sending someone from Homeland to make a refugee determination," Gaines said. "Our primary security plan is to shelter in place until morning, when the investigator will arrive."

It was 2:00 a.m. Outside, the chants were still raucous. Blackout drapes had been drawn across my office window. Gaines had pointed out that it was not made of ballistic glass—one of many structural gaps in our security profile for the embassy. Scoggins, Harold, and Doc Scoggins gathered with me.

"They've been given safe passage by Los Generales," Scoggins said. "Airfield to embassy. Transportation will be Los Generales' responsibility. We're not allowed to leave the grounds. I'd say we've lost their trust. Gaines, wasn't there something more you need to discuss?"

"Mr. Ambassador," Gaines said, glaring at Scoggins. "I received orders to maintain a security posture using nonlethal defenses. And then only if protestors enter the grounds and pose a threat to you and the other US citizens. Sentries are carrying shotguns with rubber pellets, CS, and flash-bangs."

"What if some of those guys come over the wall?" Harold asked.

"We should see it coming," Gaines said. "The Marine sentry station on the first floor still has camera feeds from the entire perimeter. That early warning will allow us to repel incursion. Including me, we have eleven Marines. Two are deployed at the main gate, two at the side gate, one on the first floor, one as security for Poirier and his daughter. I have two teams of two with CS and plasticuffs to respond to anyone that comes over the wall. I'll coordinate our forces and will move to support where needed.

"If we're forced to fall back to the main building, we bunker behind the blast shields and await rescue. USS Wasp is on station as early as noon tomorrow. Wasp is a Marine amphibious assault vessel, and she has far more than what it takes to relieve our position. No matter how dire our circumstances here may seem, the Wasp is our salvation."

"That's encouraging," I said. "Reinforcements. A hearing for our guests."

"Yeah, congratulations, Ambassador," Scoggins said. "You've subverted the local system of justice, harbored a terrorist, and brought shame to the annals of American diplomacy."

I looked to the broken doors that led to the ambassador's quarters. Gaines followed my look, and for a moment, his eyes were far away. I wondered if he was reliving things. The screams of a child. The crash of his boot shattering a door.

Scoggins looked coldly at me. Sniffed. "We about done here?" he said.

Five hours later, I stood at the front of the embassy with Doc Cassidy. The ring of protestors had chanted all night. There was a militaristic rhythm to the chanting. Every two hours, sections of the mob moved off the line as though they were an organized military unit retiring from the field, and a new group in civilian clothing took up their sticks and began pounding on the walls and gates. Others in the back waved Malagayan flags on tall poles that could be seen over the gates. They heaped kindling and tires in the green space between the walls and the roadway and ignited them in bonfires that threw wicked orange light on their angry faces and plumed columns of blackness upward into the heavens.

Others in the mob attacked the row of cinder block structures across from the embassy, pounding walls into piles of fist-sized rubble that men collected on tarps and dragged to places where others could pick them up and throw them at the Marine sentries whenever they came into view.

It had gone that way all night. Marines manned the two gates and kept up two-man roving patrols across the rest of the five-acre compound. Their helmets and armor prevented the worst of injuries, but there were cuts and bruises and one concussion that kept Doc Cassidy busy.

Gaines told me that, from his perspective on the rooftop of the embassy, he could see military trucks and tents established down side roads where cook fires indicated the men were having hot chow after their shifts berating America and flinging stones.

"They're organized, and they're here to stay," Gaines had said to me.

Now Gaines and another Marine jogged down the drive to support the two Marines at the front gate. The protestors gripped the bars and swayed the massive iron barricade, trying to wrench it free of anchors holding it in place. Gaines and the other Marines yelled in English and in Spanish, warning them back.

Stones flew.

"They're targets," Doc Cassidy said of the Marines. "Call them back."

"I knew a caretaker at the West Virginia Governor's Mansion," I said. "He spent six years in a North Vietnamese prison camp."

A jagged piece of cinder block struck one of the Marines on the side of his helmet. He went down.

"His captors would bring an American flag before the assembled camp and force prisoners to urinate on it. To defecate on it," I said. "Anyone who refused had their legs broken with cinder blocks."

Gaines moved to the fallen Marine, extending his hand as more jagged rocks sliced through the air, striking their armor and helmets. He hefted the fallen Marine from the ground and gestured back to the embassy, where Doc Cassidy could look him over for injuries.

"That old man could barely walk," I said, my voice almost a whisper, my thoughts thousands of miles away. "You can't tell a man his duty. You can't tell him what's right. The good ones already know."

The bleeding Marine waved away Gaines' concern and turned to stand his post, facing the screaming faces opposite him at the gate.

I found Reto in the infirmary at the small sink. He wiped his face and neck with a hand cloth and rinsed it. Behind him, Maya slept on a bed, an IV bag dangling from a post next to her. He met my gaze in the mirror over the sink. A hint of predawn light limned the spaces outside the shuttered windows—a rose glow that promised a fine new day.

"We have guest quarters," I said.

Reto looked at me, then at the Marine posted beside the infirmary door.

"You could clean up. Be comfortable. The investigators arrive today."

"And what will they investigate?" he asked. "I have destroyed American property. I have disrupted the operation of American companies. I came here because I was not prepared to let my daughter die. But you must know, I do not fear death."

"Then you don't understand dying," I said.

I looked at Maya. Her eyes were closed. White bandages crisscrossed her abdomen. Her hands moved, as though even in the depths of her sedation, she saw danger and sought to warn the rest of us.

"When your pain's over, hers has just begun."

CHAPTER XXIII

SPEAK OF THE DEVIL

THE GULFSTREAM THREW SMOKE WHEN its tires touched the tarmac. It sped down the runway, the nose hanging briefly in the air, as though undecided about leaving flight and enduring the vulnerability that winged things have when they succumb to gravity. Then it gently arced down, and the nose wheel puffed a thin gray veil of smoke that was instantly shredded by the passage of the machine. Reversers angled upward from the twin Rolls-Royce engine nacelles at the tail as it decelerated and made the turn from the runway to the taxiway and thence to the tarmac where Armando waited.

Armando stood with the vehicle at his back. He wore mirrored aviator sunglasses that caught the light and flared it back into the sky, as did the double row of gold and silver medals on his dress uniform. Behind him, the driver stood beside the armored town car.

He worked his tongue around his teeth, trying to loosen the shard of gristle from the steak he'd had for lunch at a meal with his father and a representative of two of their most combative industrial concerns. Conglomerates that measured productivity in increments that shattered time down to hundredths of seconds and parsed costs to tenths of an American cent.

He hadn't been able to enjoy the filet mignon. Their conversation was a blunt threat. Either Reto Poirier left the safe haven of the American embassy and Armando's father neutralized what they called an existential threat to their outsourcing strategy in Malagar or they would depart for opportunities in Cambodia and the Dominican Republic. It was important, they said, that their brands not become the object of discussion or scrutiny from any government or news source.

The Gulfstream eased to a halt, and the pale blue Department of State livery separated as the forward passenger door swung open, the stairs distending and arcing to a halt just above the ground. Behind him, Armando heard the driver open the passenger door for the man that would descend the Gulfstream's steps.

The State Department ops center was a murmur of voices. Wall monitors tracked the current hot spot, showing flooding and wreckage from a tsunami that had swept across Indonesia's shores following an underwater earthquake. In a separate huddle, the South American watch standers focused on screens that provided what was, for all practical impacts, a sideshow. They viewed real-time updates indicating the Gulfstream had just landed at the military airport in Malagar.

"He's on the ground," said an analyst. "ETA to the embassy is less than five."

Ben Crisswell was the senior watch stander for State. He looked at the president's chief of staff, Matthew Pope, and mentally ran through the decisions that had relegated Am-Embassy Malagar to the sidelines for resources and had re-tasked Military Attaché SecState Lieutenant Colonel Jeremy Quinn to oversight of the security reinforcements bound for Lebanon.

"Send the message over my signature," Pope said to Crisswell.

"This is wrong," Crisswell said, surprised his voice was level given the magnitude of his statement and his audience. "What we're doing now is wrong."

Pope picked up a photo from the man's station. Crisswell's wife and children stood with him on a green lawn under sunlit skies.

"You got an opinion. I appreciate that," Pope said. "You're what, twenty, maybe twenty-five years with State? Got a pretty family. Nice house in Georgetown. Big mortgage, I bet." Pope put the photo back on the desk facedown. "Opinions won't pay that note."

Ben Crisswell typed.

I stopped by the infirmary. Riley was posted outside. Doc Cassidy met me at the door.

"Heard you spent the night in here," I said. "How're you, and how's our patient?"

Cassidy looked back over her shoulder. Maya was awake. Reto spoke with her, their fingers moving soundlessly. He leaned forward and kissed her forehead.

"She's stable," Cassidy said. "But I'm concerned."

"If she needs medicine or you need equipment, we can—"

"No. The antibiotics are doing what they're supposed to. She needs a safe place and continued rest. Can you guarantee that?"

"Where it's in my power," I said.

My reassurance had the opposite effect I'd hoped for. She frowned at me. "You know what's refreshing?"

"What?"

"When someone just says yes. No caveat. Not 'If I can' or 'If it's in my power' or 'We'll see.' Just yes."

"For somebody who works in medicine, you have a poor grasp on how little one person can control."

Riley was ramrod straight, eyes ahead.

"No, Ambassador," she replied. "As a physician, I've seen the miracles that can happen when someone makes a promise. Maybe that's because everybody is aware of how little one person can control. Maybe it's because people who actually make a commitment do more, try more, strive to not betray their promise."

"I'm going out front to welcome the Homeland Security delegation that'll consider their request for refuge," I said. "That was my promise. A fair hearing. They will receive that. If you find that somehow limited or frustrating, maybe you should go listen to popular opinion outside the walls. They're throwing rocks the size of baseballs. Twice, they bolted tear gas canisters onto rebar and held them through the front gate. They're a passionate bunch."

"You're assuming the system hasn't already been rigged against the girl and her father."

"Maybe in this country, but I've still got hope that that's not the way ours works." I sighed and changed my tone. "Come on, Doc. Why don't you walk out with me? We're all tired, and it'll do us good to see the cavalry roll in."

But she was gone as I was speaking, my request falling on deaf ears.

Outside, beyond the shutters and the glass and the distance, I could hear the chants and clatter of batons, bats, and poles against the outer wall. Belatedly, I realized that the anger of the mob was something she would have experienced as a sullen rhythm that drummed through the night.

"Keep 'em safe," I said to Riley.

"Yes, sir," the Marine said, and there was no doubt that he had made a promise.

Gaines stood at the center of the gate. A spray of stones rose from the back of the crush of military-aged men. Gaines raised the Plexiglas riot shield at an angle above his head. Stones caromed off, one leaving a thin white scar in the plastic from a ragged edge.

"Gate, Overwatch." The radio receiver in Gaines' ear picked up the transmission from the Marine he'd posted to the top of the embassy. "There's movement on the roadway. Sedan escorted by army vehicles."

As though in response, the mob before the gate began to move as poorly concealed detachments were yelled back by NCOs positioned in their midst. He could pick out the NCOs because they wore white earpieces just like the ones Gaines and his Marines had plugged into their mobile hand radios.

As the mob parted, a Malagayan Ford truck with four soldiers hunched in the back bed pulled up to the gate and then turned out again onto the roadway, clearing room for the black town car that pulled to the embassy gate. Armando stepped out of the Lincoln and moved through the reconvening mob. A NCO to the right of the embassy gate had started the chants again, and it spread. Soon, the voices were joined by the sound of batons and wood pounding against the security wall.

A smattering of rocks flew into the air and landed to Gaines' left, but he didn't move. His focus was on Armando as he opened the Lincoln's passenger door.

In the communications room, Harold read the page on the screen as he printed it, muttering under his breath. He snatched the page from the printer and hustled his girth around tables and out the door. Harold's muttered imprecations and vulgarities gained voice as he strode down the third-floor corridor, past empty rooms.

"Ambassador!" he yelled. "Ambassador Ford!"

Armando left the door open to the Lincoln and walked through the protestors to Gaines. He took off his sunglasses as he approached the gate. Gaines imagined the brass and medals on his uniform were polished by someone else.

Armando grinned. He gestured through the bars for Gaines to come conspiratorially close. Gaines didn't move.

"Come closer," said Armando.

"Do you have a message for the Ambassador?" asked Gaines.

"Oh, no," Armando said, innocent. "No message. You see . . ."

Then he gestured, and the mob moved away, and Gaines saw the white hair and slack jowls of Frederick Hinkley. He stepped out of the Lincoln, holding his suit coat over one arm while the other shifted the suspenders on his shoulders like a southern lawyer posturing before the jury he would ask to emancipate men who bombed synagogues.

"I have the ambassador," said Armando.

I heard it as I moved past the Marine at the main floor guard station. The heel of my hand pushed the glass doorway open, but before I could step into the sunlight, Harold was on the stairs, stumbling and catching himself on the rail, leaning to catch a glimpse of me.

"Jack!" he cried out, thundering onward, barely recovering from what would have been a wicked fall. "Jack!"

Harold had never used my first name.

I stepped back and let the door swing closed. Harold met me halfway across the embassy floor. The Marine watched us, his expression professionally neutral. Harold's own expression was a proprietary blend of frustration, horror, anger, and dismay.

Doc Cassidy walked toward us from the infirmary, probably alerted by Harold's shouts.

Harold didn't say a word. He just raised a hand and thrust the State Department cable at me.

I read it.

Twice.

"Jack?" Doc Cassidy said. "What's wrong?"

I crumpled the page and let it fall from my slack hands.

Behind me, Harold spoke in the tone the bereaved use when just outside the memorial room. "They didn't send an investigator," Harold said. "They sent his replacement."

Gaines' face was stone.

"Open the gate," Hinkley said to Gaines. "Come on. It'll be almost like old times." Hinkley smiled. With practiced ease, he slipped State Department credentials from a pocket and held them up before Gaines' line of sight. The two Marines posted at either side of Gaines listened while keeping their eyes on the mob.

"Open up, Gunny," Hinkley said, saliva wet across his teeth.

Gaines didn't look down at the white-haired old man. "I do not recognize you, sir," he said.

One of the Marines shot a sideways glance at Gaines.

"What?" Hinkley blinked. Then he pressed his credentials against the bars, his mouth set into a fine line. His nostrils flared. "If you know what's good for you—"

"Step away from the gate," Gaines said.

Armando laid both his hands on the bars of the pedestrian opening and shook it. The weight and girth of the structure was such that nothing moved.

"What is this?" Armando yelled. "Open the gate!"

"I do not know you, sir. As senior Marine NCO in charge of security for this embassy, it is my duty to refuse entry to anyone without proper authorization and all persons unknown to me."

"Goddamnit! Open the gate! Gaines!" Hinkley raged. "You open the goddamn gates before I reach through these bars and—"

Gaines stepped right up to the bars, within Hinkley's reach. "And what?"

Daniel leaned against the edge of my office window that overlooked the main gate. The cloth of the American flag behind my desk brushed his sleeve.

He spoke as I came in but didn't turn around, as though he'd decided I was not worthy of acknowledgement with eye contact. "Don't you get tired of it?" he asked.

Outside, men beat on the walls with sticks and crowbars. In several places, bonfires threw ash in black swirls that rose high into the air before drifting down on the embassy's grounds. It was a tumult of orchestrated anger.

"All the world's a beggar," Daniel said, "and we're the only guy in their path."

"That's not the way I see it."

"When was the last time you saw Japanese teams helping American earthquake victims? Did France send relief as New Orleans drown?" Daniel looked at the flag. He raised the cloth, his thumb touching the red and white bars as though he'd found arterial blood on a leaf and knew the wounded animal he tracked was near. "In Somalia, when was this anything more than a bright red target? Two World Wars and billions in aid, and what's the rest of the world done for us?"

"It's not about them," I said. "It's who we are. Wasn't there ever a time when you could look at someone suffering and say, with conviction, 'This must end'?"

Gaines was close, his armor plate carrier within easy reach of Hinkley's fingers.

"And what?" Gaines repeated.

Hinkley staggered back from the gate. Armando glared, slowly following as the American retreated toward the Lincoln's air conditioning, soft leather, and a window tint so dark it created a sunless space that seemed immune to the passage of time and the tribulations of memory or conscience.

Hinkley stumbled through the men that stood in his way. Enraged, he grabbed their shirts and pushed them aside. NCOs that saw him coming shouted men out of the way. The mob parted before him. Except for one.

By the time Hinkley recognized Beryl, the crowbar was already high and arcing down with a blurred finality.

I glared at Daniel. He let the folds of the flag slip from his fingers.

From outside the window came the flat crack of gunfire. A single shot. It halted the men striking the walls with sticks and chanting in a chorus of obscenities and blame. The sound of the shot rippled outward across the grounds.

At the gate, Gaines and the two Marine sentries were immobile. Like stone.

Soldiers leapt from the two trucks that had escorted the black Lincoln to the embassy's gate. From a distance, we could see the mob of men part as they hefted first one, then a second body by arms and legs. They carried each facedown to the bed of one of the trucks and threw them in.

Blood flowed onto the pavement from Hinkley's shattered skull. Flecks of pink brain matter rose like islands in the scarlet. Armando gestured, pistol still in his hand. A thin gray rivulet of smoke drooled upward from the barrel.

Soldiers dragged Beryl's body away first.

Gaines turned slightly as footsteps sounded behind him down the embassy driveway. Panting, Scoggins arrived at his side as soldiers dragged Hinkley through his own blood and brain matter and tossed him into a truck bed beside Beryl.

"Hey." Scoggins straightened his tie, oblivious to the stains on the roadway. "Is the new ambassador here yet?"

After the sun set, the protestors tripled the number of fires outside the walls. The glow illuminated the perimeter. Light from a massive fire built upon the blood-stained ground outside the main gate threw a rose hue across the windows and steel shutters the Marines had cranked down over the interior glass of the main floor. The chanting was an organized reverberation in the air.

I looked around at Doc Cassidy, Gaines, Harold, Scoggins, and Daniel. A Marine escorted Reto Poirier to where we stood. He looked at me.

"Mr. Poirier, I've been recalled, effective upon the arrival of the new ambassador," I said. "I felt you should know that."

Reto nodded, as though accepting the inevitability of seasons, solstices, and tides. "You have done what you can. I am grateful for that."

I turned away, unable to meet his gaze. After a moment, Doc Cassidy led him back to his daughter's bedside in the clinic. Outside, someone threw accelerant on the bonfire in front of the embassy gate. The conflagration whooshed through the gates and high into the air, spreading along the ground and into the grass.

"Fuck this," Scoggins said, and he headed to the third floor.

"Mr. Ambassador—" Gaines said.

"Don't call me that," I said.

"That's what you are, until relieved," Gaines snapped back. "Gates are secure, Mr. Ambassador. The night watch is set." With military precision, Gaines turned and left to make the first of a series of rounds I knew he would continue through the night.

Daniel looked at Harold and me. "We're inside the Alamo. There's no one coming. Best you can hope is to get the Americans out." Daniel walked outside, nodding to the Marine at the entry door as he moved past.

Harold and I watched him go.

"Harold," I said. "He's not going to get a hearing."

"No." The bitterness added a resonance to his voice. "Contrary to the laws of our land."

"Should make good copy," I said. "Don't you think?"

In the comm room on the third floor, Harold had the newest computer online. A satellite link was active. In a video inset on the screen, a white-haired man looked at me with an expression that said he knew me from somewhere but couldn't quite place me.

"Ambassador Ford," Harold said by way of introduction, "this is Joe Cumming, CNN Bureau Chief for South America."

"Mr. Cumming," I said, "thanks for taking my call."

I heard it before I finished speaking—static creeping into the audio.

"Your consular officer tells m—" Static. More pronounced. Then the image began to flicker and vanish.

Harold was at work on another computer. The image cleared for a moment, but Harold was sotto voce cursing at something I could not see and he apparently could not control. Cumming continued in the way people do when they see a tenuous connection fraying and about to snap.

"... interview ... interested in ... Can you ..."

The reporter vanished. A series of diagnostics boxes appeared on my computer. Joe Cumming was gone.

Pope waved as he exited the pressroom amid the flash and glare of lights. The hubbub of reporters faded as he walked down the corridor to where Tony Ball waited.

"Hinkley didn't make it," Ball said. "And Ford just tried an end run. Our people in communications caught it and shut down his DTS access, but some senior foreign service officers are starting to ask questions. Civil service. Not politicals. Going to be tough to distract them. We're running out of options."

"All right," Pope said. "Send it."

"Yes, sir," Ball said. Then he was gone.

"Five minutes," Pope said to himself. "And it's all over."

Night had fallen. Armando wore plainclothes. His attention was on his watch. As the second hand ticked toward twelve, he raised his hand, then gestured sharply toward the embassy, where a ring of protestors fanned bonfire flames and beat the gates and walls with sticks.

A stream of men darted past him with ladders and tarps, their voices raised in a battle cry. Gunfire sparkled upward from the mob with the *click-click-click* of silenced subsonic rounds in places where cameras hung. Black glass and lenses exploded.

From the ring of protestors already at the wall, a dozen torches and flaming Molotov cocktails arced into the sky. They flew over the wall, trailing embers in the night air. Where the Molotovs hit, light bloomed like strobes before glaring steadily as they exploded from broken glass and flowed into pools of flame. A fireball engulfed a Marine's leg at the gate, and he dropped to the ground, rolling while the other Marine threw a blanket on him to smother the fuel.

Alarms wailed across the grounds.

On the far side of the embassy, four camouflage-clad figures lowered themselves from a spot along the embassy wall between two sparking and shattered security cameras. They darted across the lawn, hugging the shadows. Two ran for the radio transmitter tower at the back of the Marine barracks. The other two ran for the generator shack situated beside the pad where the Humvees and ambassador's SUV were parked.

The metal shutters did not cover all of the window space. It was an inherent flaw in the security system that the winch mechanism required two inches of clearance from one shutter to the next.

In that gap, the Marine posted to the infirmary door could see the plumes of light from the firebombs. The alarm wailed, and radio calls clamored as elements of the mob appeared atop ladders facing the security wall.

Then there was a twin concussion. A blinding white flash. Glass exploded into the shutters, followed by a foul blast of air, and the building shook. Dust sifted from the ceiling above them. Sudden currents of hot night air brought in the scream of folding metal girders as the radio aerial crashed down across the barracks.

Lights flickered inside the embassy before switching over from generator to battery power on emergency backups. The alarm fell silent.

"Go," Reto said to the Marine guarding him and Maya. He thrust a fire extinguisher into the Marine's hands. Outside, in the aftermath of explosions and collapse, cries of men echoed along with the *WHOMPH* of a vehicle catching fire. "We will be safe. Go!"

The Marine ran out into the night, leaving Reto alone with Maya. Her eyes were wide. Dust hung in the air. Firelight from dozens of sources shone through the slats between the steel shutters and cast light across the darkened infirmary. The shadows in the corridor moved in a way that was both deep and sinister. They jerked as the light flared and flickered, macabre in their movements.

Except one.

That shadow moved, inexorably, toward them.

"I wondered when you would come," Reto said.

The shadow moved closer. It coalesced into Daniel. "You know me?"

"Men like you, you think yourself strong. You think you hold the devil in your hand." Reto's eyes took in the dim light that flickered along the blade in Daniel's hand. "But he holds you."

"This isn't about heaven or hell," Daniel said. "You're just another job, and then I go home."

"What home brings such comfort that you must kill a man to return there?"

Maya's hands were restless against Reto's arm. Afraid and in pain.

"There's a little bar close by. That's enough."

"Your choices will not leave you. When you are in that bar, amidst the company of lost men, the glass will feel like a knife in your hand."

"Shut up," Daniel said.

"He changes form but never lets go." Reto positioned himself between Daniel and Maya. Daniel was close now, sculpted in shadow and half-light. "You must be the one to let go."

Maya saw the knife. She struggled to sit up.

Daniel stopped, holding her gaze. She leaned against Reto, her arms reaching out as a feeble barricade between Daniel and Reto, as though she could push him back. Slowly, the white of her bandages began to darken with blood.

Daniel watched the stain spread. Watched Reto force his daughter's arms back down.

Reto Poirier turned his back on Daniel as his daughter's hands fluttered against him like butterflies. "I know," he said. "I love you too."

Then he turned and stepped away from her and into the open.

Maya sobbed. Hand to mouth. Tears streaking her face.

Daniel was gone.

Outside the embassy, Daniel crouched in glass that had been blown out by the charges used to destroy the embassy's generator shack and shortwave radio antenna. The Humvee closest to the generator shack burned brightly, the flames a dull roar in the night. The metal frame moaned and popped from the heat.

He looked down at the knife in his hand, and bile burned upward from his gut and into his throat. Violently, he stabbed downward, embedding the blade into the soil between the shards of glass glittering orange and yellow and white in the firelight. As though that gesture signaled the last tick of a clock, protestors retreated from atop the wall and back down their ladders, leaving Marines shouting in the night as they fought the spread of flames on the grounds and through the barracks.

Three times, crisis and despair have overwhelmed my senses. These were moments when my ability to record events lost coherence and instead became a frame-by-frame series of images that would later prove both difficult to summon and disjointed, as though they resided in a mental scrapbook with pages that were tattered and incomplete.

My mother's funeral.

The last day of my vigil at Elise's hospice bedside.

My exit from the press conference announcing Steve Ricker's death.

These are times when everything I saw and heard and felt and said was captured only in enough detail to hint at my presence in the moments they occurred. They unfolded before my eyes with a selective sensory clarity. Sound would be wholly absent from a memory that should be a cacophony of voices screaming in dispute, yet I would retain a visual image as vivid and as real as those that astronauts perceive of objects in space without the intervening haze of atmosphere.

I knew when I was in this state. Could feel it as I moved. Sensation fled from me. Perhaps that was the benefit. As I strobed from moment to moment, winking in and out of existence in a world of confusion and helplessness and loss, the camera of my mind closed its shutters on my culpability and the certainty of what was to come. It suspended pain.

No . . . There's a better word for it.

It suspended *grief.*

I departed the third-floor communications room without a word to Harold after the building concussed with explosions outside. Behind me, his voice called out.

"Ambassador, what do we do now?"

If I answered, I don't recall it.

I remember moving past the first-floor guard station, where a Marine surveyed the dwindling number of active security camera images. All showed men screaming outside what seemed to be an inadequate wall. Then I was outside, in the cool of the night air. I don't know how long I stood there on the embassy grounds near the motor pool, my back against the smooth black hide of a Suburban. My head tilted back, my eyes upward, looking at bottles that moved against the sky like constellations of light, their passage marked by lit rags trailing behind like incendiary comet tails.

I blinked, and the grounds were on fire. Doc Cassidy was by the gate, her medical bag open, tending to a burned Marine. The roaring in my ears drowned out the voices of Marines, but I could see them shouting and gesturing, just as I saw the symphony of rage from men that stood now atop the embassy wall, waving Malagar's flag on long white staffs and flinging rocks at the Marines. Two black-clad shapes darted away from the Marine barracks and past me. A Marine on the lawn spotted them and shook out a baton.

A burning Humvee lit the scene as though it were noon. The roaring in my ears had nothing to do with any coherent sound in the environment. It was, simply, a filler my mind had chosen to mask cries for help from the Marine trying to stop the two black-clad figures. It was a deafening sound the instinctive primordial creature within me knew as a warning. It was a banshee's scream. A portent of death. Smoke burned my lungs.

I levered away from the Suburban as the Marine went down. One of the assailants used a cattle prod on him, the electric flame at its tip embedded against the fold of the Marine's arm as he spasmed.

I ran. I had a crazy backward glance image, in which the radio antenna lay draped across the collapsed roof of the barracks and bright flames rose from the gutted generator shack, throwing sparkling light on the jagged edges of glass in the broken windows around the embassy's first floor. Then it was gone, and I was hurtling forward, my legs pumping faster than I could recall having run before. In madness, desperation, or in fear, I ran headlong into the oval of flames where a Molotov had splashed upon the earth. The fire wreathed me, clawing for my legs and arms and face. I felt the camera of my mind in motion. The shutter sliding to close my view and protect me from horrific things that were certain to come next. Things that were my fault. Things I once dared to believe I could influence. Now it was best, my mind had decided, to triage away the worst of the memories associated with the trauma of death.

"No."

I heard my own voice. It was a whisper. A plea, if not a prayer.

As I ran through fire, the roaring stopped.

I heard myself as I emerged from the flames, leaning into it. Yelling now, with every bit of what was left in my lungs.

My shoulder caught the black-clad man in the chest. Embers flew up and around us. I hit what felt like ballistic plate. The impact snapped his head forward and knocked him off his feet. We flew together another three feet, the cattle prod flipping out of his hand and landing in the grass. We both scrambled back up, but I was already in motion again, pivoting for the other black-clad figure dragging the Marine to throw him into the Molotov's pool of flames. He dropped his grip on the Marine and staggered back, reaching for a baton. In the firelight, his eyes widened.

The look on his sweat-streaked face was a testimony to fear as I walked steadily forward, smoke rising from me. Flames guttered along the soles of my shoes from burning accelerant that painted the leather. Embers flickered on my coat at the breast and along my sleeves, burning bright as coals, worming through threads and leaving lanes of black behind.

By now, I stood between them and the Marine.

I raised one arm and pointed.

Both turned and fled into darkness.

Chapter XXIV

INTO HELL IF SO ORDERED

Captain Enrique Ivers surveyed the flight deck from the bridge. In the hours before dawn, the Wasp had moored at a military pier across from the busy Malagayan commercial port. Cranes were already at work at a pair of terminals opposite their berth, lifting cargo containers from the docks and into the holds of bulk carriers. Clouds masked the dawn, but in the rose hue, he could make out increased activity as one of the container ships moved away from the terminal and tugboats marshaled the arrival of another.

Their own berth was a ghost town. The harbor pilot that had met them and the tugboat that had escorted them to the berth authorized by Malagar's maritime defense forces were long gone. The pier itself was vacant except for the Marines posted as sentries at the gangway.

"State wants us to convey instructions to the ambassador," Ivers said. He handed his executive officer the communique. Maria Holdener read the instructions.

Ivers raised binoculars and looked out across the long pier while she read. At the end, a pair of Malagayan military trucks pulled up with four soldiers in the bed of each. They flanked a Lincoln Town Car with tinted glass windows. The trio of vehicles idled there, as though waiting for something to happen.

"Embassy phone lines are dead, and their sat link's inop." Holdener looked up. "We can't even raise them by radio."

Ivers handed Holdener the binoculars. "I think our hosts want us to do this the old-fashioned way."

Gaines was not pleased. He spent the first minute of the briefing with me, Doc Cassidy, Scoggins, and Harold making it clear that the point of a defensive perimeter was to keep objects of value inside. That was me, Doc, Harold, and Scoggins, he warned. Objects of value.

"Stay in-fucking-side," Scoggins said, one finger pointed at me, his tone accusing.

"Wow. Personally, I think Gaines said it better," Harold said.

Scoggins snuffed like something in the air offended him. "Mock if you want." He shot a glance toward Doc Cassidy. "She dies, it's a footnote. Your death goes on a wall in the Truman Building lobby, on Wikipedia, and in the news. Hauling you out in a bag isn't worth the problems it creates. Shelter in place. I did."

"The comm room is our shelter," Harold said. He'd spent the remainder of the night in a fruitless effort to regain communications access after DTS severed our satellite connection. "Didn't see you in there. Where, exactly, did you shelter?"

"My quarters, between the toilet and the tub," Scoggins said. "There's extra protection there. Plus access to water."

"Yeah," said Harold. "Bet it's easier to clean up after you—"

"Doctor," Gaines interrupted. "Today and tonight, let us bring casualties to you in the infirmary. You've got better resources there, and you can monitor the little girl. There are fewer threats inside the embassy, both to you and our wounded. To be clear, you have my gratitude and my respect for the way you put yourself out there last night. But if something happens to you, our wounded will suffer. That little girl will suffer. You concur with the plan?"

"Yes." Doc Cassidy nodded, her mouth a fine line.

"Mr. Ambassador," Gaines said. "Last night, we lost auxiliary power from the generator and two vehicles. And we lost a lot of equipment stored in the barracks. It was either destroyed in the fires or is in an area that'll require heavy equipment to gain access. Most of our security cams on the wall were disabled last night, but that's not much of a problem considering batteries have died for the system. I've got roving patrols and a watch on the roof, but we're stretched thin. The Wasp should be in the harbor soon, if it's not already there, but we have no means of broadcasting our situation."

"Harold?" I asked.

"I tried like hell." There were bags under Harold's eyes. "I'm sorry. We've got the local security radios for the Marines for the next twenty-four hours—maybe longer if they ration the batteries—but the handsets don't have range for the harbor. Embassy emergency lights are on batteries that'll start to fail soon. I expect sometime tonight, they'll give up the ghost."

"Give him up," Scoggins said.

"Not going to happen." Doc Cassidy glared at him.

Scoggins didn't flinch from her gaze. "You know I'm right. All this is because we've got a criminal on the first floor. Turn him and the girl over and all this goes away. Am I the only one who sees this nightmare is the product of Ford's bad choices? I mean, Daniel's not even here. The man has a keen sense of self-preservation. I bet he's already out of the country." He pointed another finger at me. "You were recalled, Ford. I don't even know why we're having this conversation. Gunny! Come on. We're going to open the gates."

Gaines' posture made it clear he wasn't going anywhere.

"Mr. Ambassador." Gaines looked pointedly at me. "What are your instructions?"

"You have faith the Wasp will make contact with us?" I asked.

"Yes, sir," Gaines affirmed. "They most certainly will."

"Then we wait to hear from them."

Contact us they did. Armando delivered Captain Enrique Ivers to the gates in the same Lincoln that had brought Frederick Hinkley. Gaines briefed Ivers as they walked inside the damaged embassy. I met him in my office. We stood at the window, overlooking the soldiers pretending to be protestors.

"This is some kinda mess you got here, Ambassador," Captain Ivers said.

Smoke rose from six points around the wall where protestors stoked bonfires. Gaines had spotted military trucks bringing in the kindling. Though Malagayan army tents and their chow hall had been moved out of direct line of sight from the embassy, there was little doubt that they were still out there. After Gaines alerted me, I was able to discern the movement of groups of men among the protestors. They rotated their time on the wall in six-hour shifts, each unit chanting or hurling rocks or pounding against the security walls like it was their day job until the signal came for them to fade back and make way for a new group of incognito soldiers.

None of that seemed to register with Captain Ivers. He looked out my office window at the car that had brought him to the embassy. Without subtlety, they'd positioned his door beside the bloodstains that marked the death of two men. His escort of Malagayan soldiers kept that area clear of protestors.

I dropped the printed instructions the Department of State had forwarded via the Wasp facedown on my desk. When I didn't say anything, Ivers looked over at me.

"What about Poirier?" I asked.

"That man's not in my orders."

"I will not abandon him."

"Ambassador, when you pull out of here, bring your personnel, your coded material, and the flag. Everything and everyone else stays behind."

"Has the embassy been closed?"

"My orders didn't include that word." Ivers shook his head. "They said evacuate, and that is what I intend to do. At eighteen hundred hours, local authorities will convoy your people to the Wasp. Be ready."

"Captain, we have obligations here."

"Ambassador, I've got a helicopter platform sitting in that harbor with a contingent of Marines that'll rappel into the mouth of hell if so ordered. The fact that none of 'em are landing here tells me your obligations aren't as critical as you might think."

"You ever surrender a man and his daughter to their executioners, Captain?"

"Goddamnit," Ivers said. "You have no means of communication, relief, or resupply. You are outgunned, sir." He looked from me back to the stain on the road where Hinkley had bled out. "There's already blood from one American on that road. Move your people before somebody else gets killed."

Ivers stopped by Gaines on his way out. "Local authorities wouldn't agree to any of my Marines coming on shore," he said. "Your orders are to protect embassy staff during the evac. I expect to see you and your Marines on the dock."

"Yes, sir," Gaines said.

Ivers looked back at me. "Eighteen hundred hours, sir. Do not be late."

Chapter XXV

EIGHTEEN HUNDRED HOURS

THE ORDERS FROM THE DEPARTMENT of State were un-
equivocal. Destroy documents and computer equipment. Render any Marine protection detail items mili-
tarily unuseful. Shutter the buildings.

Come home.

It was unspoken that, in the course of time, a new
ambassador and staff would be assigned to Malagar—
people that would not repeat my mistakes.

Los Generales would not allow us to drive out in embassy vehicles. The mob was unusually silent as soldiers
backed a two-and-a-half-ton military truck to the embassy gate and lowered the tailgate. Malagayan soldiers
formed a cordon on both sides of the truck. They were
ostensibly keeping the mob of protestors at bay, but
their backs were to the mob. They faced Gaines as he

opened the pedestrian gate, and the Marines, Harold, and Scoggins loaded the truck with luggage and equipment. The mob jeered as they loaded.

Armando stood among the mob. The medals were gone now. He wore military fatigues with a sidearm on one hip and baton on the other. As Gaines supervised the loading, Armando took the baton from its belt loop and began tapping it rhythmically against the gate. The armed Malagayan soldiers joined him first. Where they stood in line facing the Americans, they dropped their rifle butts into the roadway in time with Armando's rhythm. The mob caught onto what Armando was doing at the gate. A NCO dressed in civilian clothing gestured, and the men around him harvested tools and crowbars and axe handles from a cache just beyond our view. They moved to the gate and walls alongside Armando and joined his rhythm.

And so it went. Group by group. All the way around the outer ring of the embassy. Shouting gave way to silence, save for the rhythmic and constant crash against the outer barriers of the embassy. Every other second, like the ticking of a clock, a thousand hands raised and struck with a thousand blunt objects while mute faces glared at the truck where Harold, Scoggins, and Marines loaded for an exit.

"You know," I said, "what seems like a long time ago, I was a governor. It was a beautiful state. A wild sort of place. Like here."

I watched with Reto Poirier from between the shutters. The gap was wide enough to allow in light. The sound resonated across the open space of the embassy grounds and vibrated if you reached between the metal shutters and laid your fingers on the remaining shards of security glass.

"Like here, there was a time when prosecutors and angry politicians circled my administration," I said. "I thought my life was over. I had a friend. I believed he could make it all go away. I believed he could fix everything. All I had to do was ask."

Behind us, Maya slept, sedated. Doc Cassidy had changed her bandages and re-sutured the wound she'd somehow torn open. I looked at her. Then at Reto.

"Ambassador, is that what you ask of me?" he asked. "You want me to make all this go away?"

"No," I said. "I was asking if you believe in second chances."

Doc Cassidy waited for me just outside the infirmary. I realized she had purposely waited where Reto Poirier and his daughter could not hear our conversation. She pressed a slip of paper into my hand.

"What's this?" I asked.

"You took an oath," she said.

"To support and defend the Constitution of the United States against all enemies, foreign and domestic," I said. "Doc, our nation is calling us home."

"Jack, she's going to bleed if we move her."

"We're not moving her."

"Oh, sorry," she said. "She's going to bleed the moment those goons drag her into the street, which shouldn't present much of a long-term health problem after they put a bullet through her eye."

I raised the paper. "What is this?"

"My resignation," she said. Then she walked into the infirmary.

I looked at the signed page. In concise and legible lettering, she had scrawled words from an ancient oath: *I will do no harm or injustice to them.*

Scoggins jogged halfway up the drive. He stopped just before the flag mast and waved when he saw me step through the embassy's glass front doors.

"Let's go! Let's go!" Scoggins yelled. His voice was a frail thing. It was carried away in parts between the tremendous crash of wood and steel against the gate and eighteen-inch-thick reinforced concrete security fence. He turned and jogged back down the embassy drive and through the pedestrian gate. He leapt into the back of the military truck, slinging luggage toward the front as he progressed, the first one to enter the truck's confines.

Gaines, Riley, and a third Marine walked up from the gate. They wore dress blues and white gloves. With precise motions and commands that were audible only to the three of them, they lowered the flag and folded it. Gaines turned and faced me as the other Marines returned to the truck.

"Mr. Ambassador, the truck is loaded. Dr. Cassidy has elected to remain and provide medical care during the transition. She informed me that she has resigned her foreign service commission. As such, she falls outside my orders for protection."

I looked at Armando. At the sea of angry faces creating a tumult of noise.

"You can't stay here, sir." Gaines put his hand on my arm, without force, as though his touch would be enough to give me the momentum to leave the embassy.

"Take your hand off me," I said.

He looked at me as though struck. His hand fell to his side. "I have my orders, sir."

I nodded.

Gaines drew the sidearm from the black polished holster at his hip. He flipped it, offering the 9 mm to me butt-first.

"Good luck," I said as I reached past the weapon and took the triangle-folded cloth from his grip.

Gaines clanged the pedestrian gate shut as he stepped through, then tossed the locking key through the bars and up the embassy drive. He climbed into the back of the truck with the Marines, Harold, and Scoggins. As he looked back at me, the truck slowly lurched away.

The Malagayan soldiers evaporated into the mob as the truck turned onto the roadway heading for the harbor. Armando stood at the center of the gate, flanked on either side by a screaming mob. He smiled at me and gripped the gate with both hands as though he had the strength to rend steel. Around him, others threw fuel on the bonfires. Black smoke rose over towers of flame. A thousand men pounded rocks, sticks, and weapons against the embassy walls.

Gaines swayed at the back of the truck as it rolled through the stadium noise of the mob. There were places on the security wall where the mob had hammered the cement away in chunks, exposing the crisscross veins of rebar that reinforced the eighteen-inch width at its core.

"Gunny—" Riley started.

"Stow it, Marine," Gaines said.

Reto covered Maya's ears with his hands. Dr. Cassidy stood with them. Maya flinched with every cacophonous blow against the wall.

"I can give her something," Doc Cassidy said to Reto.

"No," he said. "It is fear. A fear of something that sounds like anger. But there is only one out there who is angry. The rest—they are children. They do as they are told."

Reto moved to the shutter that blocked their view of the flagstaff and front gate. He knelt and fumbled with the locking key that held the metal shutter anchored to the floor.

"What are you doing?" Doc Cassidy said.

"I am letting in the light," Reto said.

"They'll see us."

"They will see we are not afraid."

Armando gestured, and men on both sides of him gripped the gate. They began to shove and pull. A NCO among them shouted the rhythm.

Shove.

Pull.

Shove.

Pull.

The gate swayed. Gradually at first, then with a rippling rhythm that made the iron moan.

There are times in life when the uncertainty and crisis that swirls like a storm will suddenly and without reason abate. One such moment came to me when I was circled by walls surrounded by hordes waiting for the bloodshed that would culminate all their destructive efforts. In between the crash of their fists and tools against bars and walls, there was a singular green moment of reverie. It was a moment in the rhythm of chaos in which time dilated, became longer and broader than it should have otherwise been. Or perhaps my mind, overwhelmed by the enormity of forces outside the walls and fully grasping the futility of any single thing I could do, refused to process the sensory information that assaulted me.

In that moment, there was a certain calm. A peace that washed over me.

A breeze touched my face. I heard the soft clatter of the rope and flag attachments against the mast's gray steel.

Then it was gone. Impacts roared against the wall. The forces at the end of the embassy drive swayed the gate, and the fixtures moaned against their hinges and posts.

My hands tore at triangle-folded cloth.

Reto rose from his knees, forcing the shutter upward. Through the glass, the tops of the gates at the roadway were visible, swaying back and forth. Flames leapt from the opposite side of the walls, throwing palls of smoke toward gray skies. The mob was chanting again.

But the embassy was on a slight slope. The driveway descended to the roadway below, and the angle did not permit them to see the men at the gate, who hammered the security walls down to the steel core.

There was only one person they could see.

"Jack," Doc Cassidy said.

They watched as Jackson Ford hoisted the flag.

A Marine at the tailgate saw it first. He pointed, shouting, and was joined immediately by the others. Gaines looked.

The flag caught the air and rippled as it reached the top of the mast. Red, white, and blue, tethered to a steel ramrod that stood against the dull gray backdrop of sky. Palls of black smoke drifted through the air in ragged columns.

The Marines were a chorus. A roar of protest.

"We will follow orders!" Gaines shouted over them. "Our mission is to get embassy personnel to the harbor! Is that clear? *Is that clear?*"

Marine voices affirmed and fell silent. Riley was the last to say it.

"Semper fi, Gunny," he said, almost a whisper.

Gaines glared at the young faces swaying with the motion of the truck. From the shadows of the far back of the truck, Scoggins shoved his way past Marines in order to see. He flinched as they passed a bonfire and the heat licked across the open space at the tailgate. Ash swept into the back of the open truck.

Then Scoggins saw the flag.

"You should have shredded that." Scoggins scowled up at Gaines. He coughed, then spat out the back of the truck. Spittle hung in a thin line from his lip. "At least they'll have something to drape his coffin." Scoggins turned and walked unsteadily back to the front of the truck.

The truck turned onto a road that would take them to the harbor, and the flag passed out of sight.

The flag crested the pole, cracking and flowing in the wind. The lanyard moved as though it tethered something alive.

The mob wrenched the gate back and forth. Armando's voice rose above the groans of steel. He shouted commands that were echoed by the mob of soldiers not dressed as soldiers. Metal screamed. A billowing cloud of black smoke from bonfires on the far wall rose and caught the wind, hazing the air high above me. Golden embers winked and flared out in the drifting smoke.

My hands trembled.

Then it came to me from a memory of a faraway place.

I blinked as I whispered the words.

"For society." I secured the lanyard to the flagpole.

"For the victims," I said louder, in Castilian Spanish.

In that moment, my hands stilled.

I walked down the embassy drive and retrieved the key Gaines had thrown. I faced the gate. Armando shouted, his words lost in the clatter of blows and the screech of steel. I watched them with something like peace, awaiting the inevitable failure of metal as it yielded to the fury of human hands.

That's when the rhythm broke.

It began as a series of shouts from the roadway. The clatter of tools against the walls faltered. Then the mob at the gate turned. Cries of surprise and pain rose. A phalanx of hands shoved aside the mob. Armando turned from the gate with a look of surprise. Then he was shouting amid a crowd of rising voices and gesturing commands as I ran down the embassy driveway.

In the mob, fists swung. A man raised a baton.

And Gaines snapped the baton from him and slammed him onto the roadway before the gate.

"MOVE, MOVE, MOVE!" Gaines shouted.

Behind him, eight Marines ringed in around Harold. They stiff-armed the mob back. One swung an axe handle and caught a Marine in the shoulder. Another Marine hooked the assailant with a left. Then he head-butted a second, sending the man reeling back with a spray of scarlet across his lower face. As the Marine's fists lashed, I saw it was Riley. Harold helped the fallen Marine to his feet, and they shoved and fought their way to the gate.

"Ambassador!" Harold yelled. "Hurry up! It's getting tight out here!"

I worked the lock on the pedestrian gate and flung it wide.

Harold stumbled through, followed by the Marines.

Gaines was the last on the other side of the pedestrian gate. There were four men on the ground before him. The crowd was an angry semicircle at the length of Gaines' reach. Armando was among them, pistol in his hand.

"Gunnery Sergeant Gaines," I said. "Ready to join us?"

Gaines swept his utility cover from the ground. "Am now, Ambassador," he said and put it back on. Then he stepped through the gate.

I slammed it. The locking mechanism clicked. Harold helped the injured Marine to the front of the embassy. Doc Cassidy opened the doors, her med kit in hand.

"You're disobeying orders," I said as Gaines stood beside me.

"My orders are to protect embassy personnel," Gaines said. "That's you, sir."

Then he organized his men into sentry positions.

Executive Officer Holdener motioned to Captain Ivers. "Embassy personnel have arrived, Captain." She extended binoculars. "Sir, you should see this."

Ivers took the binoculars. The direction of her gaze pointed to the end of the military pier. Ivers raised the glasses. "The hell . . ." he said.

Beside him, Holdener murmured into a radio. Through the lenses, he saw two embassy Marines flanking a civilian. The civilian wore red suspenders and wrestled with a pile of personal luggage. A Marine captain from the Wasp spoke to one of the embassy Marines, then raised a radio to his lips. Ivers' XO copied the report.

"Captain de la Hoya reports we have one foreign service officer and two members of the protection detail." Holdener looked at him, her finger against her radio earpiece. "Sir, the Marines request permission to return to the embassy."

Daniel watched the USS Wasp from a waterfront bar on the opposite side of the harbor. The two-and-a-half-ton truck threw exhaust from a smokestack pipe just behind the cab as it rolled away from the pier. He changed the focus on his binoculars. The blur of three figures came into sharp relief.

The barkeeper put down his drink.

Daniel put US dollars on the tray. Then added more. "You got a phone?" he asked.

CHAPTER XXVI

NO ONE DIES

ARMANDO CALLED IN THE OFFICERS and NCOs from the units stationed along the embassy's exterior wall. Throughout the day, trucks had delivered fresh men, ladders, and a message from his father. With the approach of night, the only reliable light was from the bonfires that surrounded the embassy. Dim slits of battery-powered emergency lighting was visible inside the embassy, but all along the walls, the security lighting was dark.

"Tonight," Armando said.

"We need a game plan," I said to Doc Cassidy and Harold.

"You mean you didn't have one when you opted to stay here?" Harold asked.

"I did not. But I've got every faith that the elected leaders of the United States government will do the right thing . . ."

Doc Cassidy rolled her eyes.

". . . as soon as we show them it's in their best interests to do the right thing."

"The Wasp is our closest resource," Gaines said.

"Captain Ivers refused to take Reto and his daughter," Doc Cassidy said. "To Ford's point, we've got to change their orders."

"Can't help you there, sir," Gaines said. "You should know, we also spiked all the weapons we'd use to defend the building with lethal force. My Marines are down to tear gas and batons."

"Harold?" I asked.

"We destroyed the DoD receiver and all our IT, except for a new laptop I hadn't unboxed. Los Generales still have internet, landline, and cell towers down. We're on a technology tier equivalent to camping. Not like rich guy-white glove-fine china-safari in Africa camping. I mean the kind where you get dropped off with a knife and no clothes camping."

"Somebody once told me it's a big sky," I said.

Harold tilted his head at me. "Yeah? I know that guy."

"What if you didn't want Niagara Falls?"

"You mean no DoD receiver," Harold said. "Not even a US sat. Something commercial, right?"

"Don't take long," I said.

Gaines faced the Marines. One had his arm in a sling after having his shoulder dislocated. Others bore cuts and bruises. They wore fatigues and were armed with batons and tear gas canisters.

"Ambassador's orders," Gaines said to them. "No one dies tonight. Understand me? No one."

Pope and Christine Harper sat with the president. The Oval Office seemed an inappropriate place to have this conversation, but Pope had torn fifteen minutes out of the president's schedule to update him on the situation.

"There's no other way," Christine Harper said. "But when we trend the reaction of voters to news like this—"

"Stop." The president held up a hand, his frustration growing. "You already fucking polled for reactions to this?"

"It's part of . . ." Harper faltered under his glare.

"Pope, you said this was handled," the president said. "It doesn't sound like that."

"Mr. President, we're just . . ." Pope chose his words carefully. "Moving the knife to a different hand."

"I don't like—"

"At this stage, it doesn't matter what the fuck you like. Put 'em in Arlington. Give them medals," Pope said. "If it's not their funeral, it's yours."

Ivers spoke into a radio phone that patched the Department of State Operations Center to the Wasp's Combat Information Center.

"Mr. Crisswell, you don't understand," Ivers said. "I thought I made this clear to the military attaché for State."

"Yes, Captain," Crisswell answered. "Colonel Quinn has briefed your estimate to our team. You're to stand by for further orders."

"My current orders are to get everybody from the embassy on this ship," Ivers said. "Far as I'm concerned, the embassy is out of contact, and we cannot rely on the locals to get our people here safely."

"Stay on your ship, Captain," said a new voice.

"Who is this?" Ivers demanded.

"Anthony Ball, and I'm speaking for the president."

"Well, Mr. Ball, does he know the situation down here?"

"He is adequately informed."

"I doubt that," Ivers said, "so I'm going to make this clear to you. There are over a thousand violent protestors surrounding twelve embassy personnel and two foreign nationals. Either we support this post or they're going to roll over it tonight."

"Captain Ivers, you're not our only asset. Our intel reports all Americans are clear of the building. The post itself is inconsequential compared to the damage that would be caused by allowing you to land Marines in a facility that's abandoned."

"Where are the personnel, because I've only got three?"

"They're at a safe house maintained by the Malagar foreign ministry," Ball said. "Trust me, Captain, everyone is accounted for."

"That's bullshit," said Ivers.

"Say again, Wasp. Your transmission broke up." After a moment of silence, Ball said, "Yeah. That's what I thought. We'll contact you if you're needed, Captain. Out."

Ivers racked the phone and looked at his XO.

"You going upstairs?" Holdener asked.

"High as I can climb."

Admiral Haas waited at the end of the West Colonnade, face expressionless. The navy dress whites were a stark contrast against skin as dark and weathered as the olivine basalts on Mauna Kea's slopes. Pope excused himself from the clutch of lobbyists, nodding for Christine Harper to lead them onward to their accommodations for the night.

"Admiral Haas." Pope shook a cigarette out from a silver case. "Don't get to see you over here in the big house. You must enjoy working in the fields."

"What're you doing in Malagar?" Haas said. His eyes glinted as Pope ignited the tip and breathed smoke upward.

"That situation's under control."

"I got a captain on station tells me you'd like him to stand by while an embassy burns. I got an attaché in the crisis room tells me you're holding the ball."

"Some men take orders better than others." Pope shot him a smile of manufactured empathy. "Not your fault. What you should know—from me to you—is it's an empty building."

"Prove it."

Pope shrugged. "Come on."

They entered the West Wing and turned into the Situation Room. Pope knocked, perfunctory. The room was in movie theater darkness, illuminated only by the light from the television screens that populated stories of nightmare, trauma, and loss from across the globe. A single man sat before the screens, hunched forward in his chair.

"You don't have to take my word for it." Pope nodded for Haas to enter and then closed the door.

The president looked up at them.

The pad beside the barracks was cratered from the satchel charge that had blown out the generator room. The blast had partially collapsed the barracks wall. Secondary fires scorched Gaines' office before Marines had put them out. One of the Humvees was blackened wreckage. The other was lopsided; the two tires closest to the burned-out Humvee were blown.

Riley ran panting to the vehicle and released enough winch cable to bring it around to the driver's side door where he hooked it to the window frame. He cranked the Humvee and shifted into gear while another Marine leapt into the driver's seat of the Suburban.

They accelerated off the pad in different directions, the Suburban beelining for the side gate where the mob pounded at the concrete barriers around the steel entry door. The black Suburban threw sparks as the Marine slewed it hard against the compound's wall. Plastic and glass sparkled as the mirror exploded on contact. The Marine came to an abrupt halt, with the big SUV jammed hard against the wall and the portal, providing extra layers to block any efforts to force open that gate.

Riley fought the steering wheel and slewed the wobbling Humvee around the flagpole, the rubber from blown tires shredding and slapping the pavement. He flicked on the forward lights and the headlights, and a search beam pinpointed the main gate with a white glare that momentarily halted the rhythm of the men, who were now rocking in a way that torqued the steel interlocking mechanism at the center of the gate. Riley raised the bandanna over his lower face as Marines at the gate dropped a tear gas canister just before the center lock on the embassy side. The mob couldn't reach the canister. They fell back as it sprayed a dirty white plume of noxious smoke into the air.

A Marine waved Riley forward until the front of the Humvee touched the gate at the center. Members of the mob were already returning, most coughing through rags and bandannas, but in the glittering light of the bonfires, Riley saw a cohort of fifty men jogging toward the gate with crowbars and axe handles. They wore army-green T-shirts, fatigue pants, tan boots, and bug-eyed gas masks with side-mounted filters.

Riley leapt out into the smoke and climbed the front hood. A Marine tossed him the winch cable. Riley looped the cable around the two iron bars that marked where the left and right sections came together. He dropped the winch cable to the Marine on the ground.

"Ready!" Riley shouted, his voice hoarse from the gas.

An axe handle lashed through the bars and struck the Marine in the side of the face. He staggered back. The winch cable clattered to the ground. Hands gripped the gate and began to sway it again, smashing the center into the Humvee with each push.

Riley leapt to the ground. He threw his shoulder against the axe handle as it stabbed between the bars again, then wrenched it sideways and twisted it from hands on the opposite side. The air was difficult to breathe. His vision blurred in the smoke. Hands pulled the winch cable toward the other side of the fence as Riley knelt beside the injured Marine. A gash jagged the side of the Marine's face. He waved Riley off and struggled back to his feet.

"Winch," the Marine said with bloody teeth.

"It's gonna be fine," Riley said. He reached into the Humvee and triggered the winch. It began a tug of war that would be a losing battle for those on the other side. "I'm gonna have that back, one way or another."

The gates halted their sway. The winch cranked the gates firmly against the Humvee's brush guard. The hook lodged against a lower bar with tension so tight that the men opposite could not pull it free.

But they still tried. All along the gate, they pushed. Then they pulled. The movement continued to stress the attachment anchors where the gate met the security walls, but the Humvee acted as an additional anchor, impeding the sway that would ultimately tear the gate down.

"On the wall!" the wounded Marine yelled, pointing.

A man wearing a gas mask stepped onto the wall at the left of the gate. He fumbled something that sparked. Then a rag tied to the neck of a gasoline-filled jar ignited, throwing light across his fatigues and his mask. The clear glass eye ports flashed orange, reflecting the flame as his arm cocked back.

Riley and the Marine dove away from the Humvee as the Molotov exploded to a greater flame, covering the windshield and hood of the vehicle. Liquid fire dripped down the sides and ran under the fence past the sputtering tear gas canister. Dimly, Riley was aware of the similar arc of a dozen flaming lights from points all around the embassy. Where they touched the ground, they blossomed into gouts of brilliance.

The man on the wall above ignited another Molotov bottle. He looked at Riley and the Marine as his arm rocked back to throw.

CHAPTER XXVII

THE STAND

PHOOM!

It was a familiar sound. Like a mallet striking the taut membrane of a drum.

Like a switch, it eliminated all other sound. Riley lost the angry cries of the mob, the tumult of blunt objects against the walls, and the groan of the gate. He could not hear the liquid roar and crackle of flame spilling to the ground beside him from the burning Humvee. The wounded Marine closer to the gate gestured as though he'd suddenly inhabited a world of molasses. His hand slowly rose, his mouth opening wide in what would become a shout of warning—a cry, perhaps—for Riley to run. To save himself.

All of it receded into a dull silence.

Rocks seemed to twist slowly in the air high above the wall. A jagged chunk of cement mutely struck the ground near Riley's hand, and the impact threw a puff of white dust and fragments. High over the wall, someone hurled a burning two-by-four as though it were an Olympic hammer. It spiraled, the rotation whipping flames from the burning half of the board into a flat blur that clawed the sky.

Atop the wall, a soldier raised a lit Molotov. The man's arm was high and poised to throw. The corked bottle of detergent and gasoline glittered as it reflected the fluttering and dripping brilliance of the burning rag tied around the bottle neck. The light from the bonfires, the rag, and the flaming Humvee cast ethereal and hellish glows across the black respirator he wore. Riley knew, in that expanded moment of time, that he did not have a weapon that could stop the release of the thing that would engulf him in flames. That even though rocks hung in the air, there was not an eternity between him and the soldier's intent.

Then he saw it. It streaked faster than anything else in the sky. The trajectory was low and flat and from a point that must have been near the embassy's flagpole. It trailed a thin gray haze of smoke.

The 40 mm tear gas round hit the soldier. It concussed the man's chest, and he yelled from under the mask as he flailed backward and fell on the other side of the wall. With a roar, sound came back to Riley as a brilliant flame erupted where the man landed, followed by screams. Riley rolled to his feet and helped the injured Marine up and away from the gate. In the firelight from the Humvee, he saw Gaines aiming a single barrel tear gas launcher as he strode toward them.

PHOOM!

Gas hissed upward from where the shell landed on the left side of the gate. Gaines cracked the launcher as he walked toward them, ejecting a smoking shell and thunking in a fresh round. Smooth.

"Fall back!" Gaines yelled.

PHOOM!

Another shell came down at the right side of the gate. The faces vanished from the bars. But they were replaced by the inhuman silhouettes of men who wore gas masks. As Riley staggered away from the gate with his arm around the injured Marine, the mob climbed ladders and spilled over the wall in a dozen other places around the perimeter. Gaines' voice seemed to boom across acres.

"FALL BACK!"

I followed Harold up the third-floor stairwell to the embassy's roof. It was a single gray flight that ascended under the dim flicker of failing emergency lights. Harold moved fast for a man of his girth. He hit the metal door at the top and flung it wide, motioning for me to follow him across the roof. It was a flat feature, with only a foot-high brick crenellation at the edge. The satellite was poised on support arms at the far end of the roof, near the embassy's air conditioning handlers. Harold was talking about azimuth and elevation. A book he'd referenced back in the communications room provided him with coordinates for geostationary satellites visible from our location. From that, he'd selected two that seemed to offer the best chances of connection.

He handed me a wrench and pointed to a series of bolts on the satellite dish's support arms. "Loosen those. We're going to change where this points. While you do that, I'll hook up batteries I stole—sorry, *repurposed* from stuff that isn't important anymore. This is going to power our send/receipt of signals from either a French satellite or something Russian in low orbit. Can't tell which we'll hit."

"I thought you destroyed all the equipment," I said.

"We did. Except for that new laptop I hadn't imaged yet." He gestured to the computer he had under one arm. "This is our shot to reach out to somebody that cares."

Out in the night, firebombs landed along the perimeter of the embassy's security wall. They blossomed like bright flowers. Ladders protruded above the walls, and then ladders and ropes lowered onto the embassy's grounds. Men began to tumble over the walls.

Daniel stood in the humidity. Behind him, a line of cabs queued for travelers coming out of Malagar's civilian airport terminal. The roar of an arriving turboprop aircraft slowed to stillness from a pad on the far side of the one-story building that housed security, gates, and luggage claim.

For a moment, he thought about the wisdom of his decisions. About the people he'd left behind at the embassy and the moment when their fate had been in his hands.

He shrugged the thought away as he shouldered his pack and walked into the terminal. If their fate had ever been in his hands, it certainly wasn't now.

Harold pounded keys like Elton John. The laptop's speakers emitted a humming and static.

"That's it!" Harold said. "Lock it down!"

I tightened the bolts, securing the dish on a new azimuth and elevation. When I came out from behind the dish, I heard the distant *whup-whup-whup* of rotor blades.

The embassy grounds were dotted by liquid pools of flame from Molotovs that had been flung over the walls. Men ran past the flames illuminating the grounds. They carried axe handles, crowbars, lengths of rebar, and batons. Some paused their run to throw rocks at barracks and embassy windows. The sound of breaking glass punctuated the chaos of the night.

Behind me, Harold muttered a litany of progress. He adopted a bad French accent, letting me know he had located the French satellite hanging overhead.

The embassy's front gate warped as the mob pushed and pulled it. Fire from the burning Humvee illuminated the scene. The center locking mechanism snapped with a sound like a gunshot. Now only the metal cable hitched to the Humvee's winch held the two sections of gate together. But the ends connected to the security wall moved. Dust sifted as bolts worked their way free from anchors deep in the cement.

"My leetle Helios," Harold said. "Orbit to me, you big ugly French beech. We make'a the cheese. We make'a the wine—"

The static was replaced by a sound of electronic modulation.

"We make'a the love," Harold said. "Come on . . . Comm link . . . up. Mr. Ambassador, who you wanna call?"

A jar exploded in a wave of combusting fluid and flying glass ten yards from Gaines. The liquid fire spattered like napalm all the way to his boot as the last Marine darted past him and inside the glass double doors at the front of the building. Gaines reloaded and fired again, arcing the tear gas shell down among a cluster of men pulling and pushing the front gate. The gate screamed as it tore free from the concrete and steel posts that had secured it to the embassy walls. It collapsed forward onto the burning Humvee and across the drive like a bird with wings slumped in repose after a long flight. Men surged through on both sides.

Gaines fired his last three tear gas rounds, sending them into low arcs that bounced the noxious fumes directly into the forward pack of men surging through the gate and up the driveway. Many in the mob recoiled, but more than he had time to count surged through the billowing gray clouds of smoke. The black gas masks they wore leered at him with glassine eyes and features made macabre and hellish by firelight.

"Gunny!" Riley yelled behind Gaines.

He glanced back and saw that the young Marine held the glass doors wide for him. Then Gaines heard something else. He looked in the direction Riley pointed, to the east, toward a telltale sound that grew to a roar.

A UH-1Y Super Huey helicopter hovered over the gate. It bore the livery of the Malagayan defense forces. The rotor wash flattened the gray tear gas into flows that dissipated without effect on the men that were now running past the mast where the flag whipped in the tormented air. The door gunner leaned out the Huey's open side door, aiming the GAU-21 at Gaines, then upward, to the roof of the embassy.

The helicopter swung in low over the sprawl of industrial sheds surrounding the embassy, nose tilted slightly down, rotor wash blasting the bonfires and slicks of incendiary fluids burning in its path. The fires cast the machine's belly in a crimson hue and illuminated the helmet and face of the door gunner as he leaned outward, traversing his weapon.

"Harold!" I yelled. "We have company!"

The door gunner never once pointed his weapon at the mob. He aimed it at the front of the building. He aimed it at the embassy Marines.

"Holy shit!" Harold yelled as he looked up from the laptop. "That was fast! I didn't even make a call yet!"

"We've got to go!" I yelled.

The helicopter rose from its position just above a trio of gas shells exhausting themselves to no effect in the downwash while men surged through the breached gate and up the driveway. I turned from the edge of the roof and ran to Harold as the helicopter climbed from its position level with the second floor to a height that allowed the door gunner to traverse his weapon toward us on the roof. It was a change in interest and a portent that had all the significance of a dragon's head rising to perceive new prey.

Harold had put down the laptop and was standing up. He waved one arm.

"Hey!" he shouted at the helicopter. Then his eyes widened as he saw the Malagayan flag on the door of the Huey. The gunner raised the muzzle of his weapon toward us.

"It's not ours, Harold!" I yelled, pulling him toward the rooftop access door. Wind whipped us as the helicopter rotored past just fifteen feet over our heads, circled the perimeter of the embassy, out over the grounds, and then came back again, sideways.

As we dove through the stairwell door, the *BRRRR-RRTTTT* of the door gunner's weapon rang out. Tracers flicked past us, shredding the satellite dish, equipment, and laptop Harold had used to create a lifeline to the outside world.

Captain Ivers looked out over the Wasp's flight deck. On the deck, a Seahawk sat fully crewed, her rotors idling, the wind whipping the incandescent green-and-orange sleeves of the deck crew. The pilots were waiting for a decision Ivers had been expressly advised there was no need to make.

Ivers raised his field binoculars again, but the optics and night weren't sufficient to detect what had been revealed to the tactical action officer in a satellite feed of the area.

"Sir," his XO said, "TAO pulled fresh imagery. There are fires on the embassy grounds. The main gate appears to have been compromised. There are people on the grounds. No way we can tell who they are, but they're focusing their mayhem on the embassy. That's where the ambassador would shelter."

"Fires," Ivers said. "Mayhem. XO, you ever stand by while Americans died?"

"Never, sir."

"Me neither," Ivers said. "OOD, send it."

The officer of the deck murmured into a radio.

On the flight deck, the Seahawk crew waved all clear, and the Seahawk powered upward into the night sky.

Harold sobbed against the stairwell wall. The door to the roof flayed open from the downwash of the Huey as it thundered past. The gun run had shredded the roof and the supports for the satellite dish and had exploded the brick crenellation.

"You dirty, deceitful—" Harold screamed upward at the open door. The helicopter hovered directly over the roof now, blasting grit and foul exhaust into the stairwell where we stood. The entire structure vibrated with the force of the vortex.

I put my hand on Harold's arm and pulled him down the stairs and into the third-floor corridor. Together, we forced the door shut behind us. After a moment, the roar of the helicopter rotor blades diminished and was replaced by the sounds of shattering glass and the first-floor shutters taking a pounding from stones, steel, and batons.

Harold blinked at me. "I couldn't . . ." he said. It was an apology.

"Hey," I said, "it's okay."

We found Reto, Maya, and Doc Cassidy in the Post Communications Center. The room had been cleared. The server racks and tables of equipment had been moved into the hallway. Inside, most of Doc Cassidy's infirmary equipment was arrayed on tables that had once held monitors or printers. The floor had been cleared and prepped with blankets, towels, and pillows scavenged from the barracks. It had been transformed into a triage space. There was only one gurney in the room. Maya was on it, her eyes closed. Reto stood at her side.

A Marine sat in one of the chairs. Doc Cassidy cleaned the gash on his forehead and laid out the implements she would need to stitch the laceration.

"Not tonight, Doc," the Marine said, looking at the suture thread. "You gotta get me back in there."

She nodded and applied a butterfly bandage to the wound. "Good to go."

"Thanks Doc," he said.

I stopped him. "Where can we help?"

The Marine looked at me as though delivering bad news. "Mr. Ambassador, Gunny expects you to shelter here with the other civilians in the comm center. With your permission, sir?"

I nodded, and he darted into the corridor and was gone.

"Doc?" I asked.

"I'm good, Jack," she said. "I've got supplies. Reto and Maya are protected. For now, this works."

"You need anything from me?" I asked.

"Regime change," she said. "Spread democracy. Increase literacy. Think you can do something about hunger?"

"So that's a no?" I asked.

"For now." She smiled.

"Hey," I said to Harold, "this isn't an order, but I'm gonna go downstairs. Love to have your company."

"Ambassador, you had me at 'This isn't an order.'"

We descended to the second floor. It was a deserted space that consisted of offices and meeting spaces. Some of the office windows had been shattered by rocks. The illumination was dim. It flickered as wall-mounted security lights exhausted their batteries.

We made our way down the stairs to the first floor, where eight Marines and Gaines stood with batons to defend far too many shutters. The wall-mounted emergency lights flickered here too. The air was acrid with tendrils of tear gas and smoke. Thick grains of tempered security glass glittered on the floor. It crunched underfoot like shards of ice. The shutters bulged and leapt in places as hands and blunt objects struck the hinged sheets of metal. Between the two-inch gaps, the silhouettes of men moved in a frenzy of blows, and axe handles, batons, lengths of rebar, or crowbars lashed out when Marines ventured too close to the gaps. The shutters danced against the floor-mounted restraints. They were held in place by two security pins. Already, several floor restraints were tearing up from the cement that secured them in the floor.

The air on the first floor was oppressive and hot. My eyes watered. The cacophony of sound from metal on metal was as loud as a discordant set of drums. It was impossible to hear and daunting to think. The pressure changed as the Malagayan Huey hovered low outside the front of the building. Air whistled through the gaps. Then the Huey was gone, and there was silence for just a moment. A reprieve in the assault.

"Wounded to the vault!" Gaines bellowed. "The rest of you, on your stations!"

No one left. Wounded Marines spaced across the floor, each one facing a half-dozen shutters.

Outside, a voice rose, calling out a cadence. In response, the shutters shook again and again. It became a call and response that battered the metal barriers like a rising storm.

"Sir, Malagar military ATC picked up the Seahawk," the XO said. "They're claiming embassy airspace as sovereign territory."

"ETA?" Ivers asked.

"Twenty seconds, sir. Recall the bird?"

"Hell no."

Reto held Maya's hand. He smiled at her. The lights flickered, but she didn't flinch. Her hands moved against his own. Signing.

"My place is with you," Reto said.

Her hands moved, signing to him, insistent. Reto nodded. Her hands moved again, then released his.

"Doctor," Reto said. "Look after her."

He kissed Maya's forehead and slipped out the door.

A Marine cried out as a crowbar lashed through the gap between two shutters and caught him in the ribs. He went to one knee. The shutter facing him vibrated from the unmistakable fury of sledgehammer blows. They were aimed high, near to the upper winch mechanism of the shutter's rolling box. Dust sifted down, and one corner of the shutter's upper winch moved. The Marine leaned on a nearby reception desk and tried to drag the desk against the shutter to reinforce it.

"Harold!" I yelled, pointing. He followed me. We joined the injured Marine and hefted the desk onto its side, then slid it into place. It was wider than the shutter. In addition to the sledgehammer blows, we could feel the smaller impacts as rebar and other objects slammed against the desk's surface through the gap.

Nearby, Riley staggered back as the anchors on one of his shutters failed. Hands forced it upward three feet. Men in olive T-shirts and camouflage pants leaned in the opening, wearing gas masks. I ran for Riley as he fought to drag the shutter back down.

One of the soldiers stepped onto the first floor. I swung with my right. Back in the day, I knew my way around a speed bag. I hooked him in the ear, and he fell backward, roaring with pain. Hands grabbed me, and the soldiers tore at my arms and clothes. They got a grip and pulled me toward the opening as the shutter shrieked higher. I freed one arm from a grip on my wrist and lashed out, knocking the gas mask from one soldier's face. His anger was clear as he raised a knife.

Riley lunged between us as the blade swung. He grabbed me, and we both tumbled back into the embassy.

Soldiers surged through the gap with us.

Reto waded into the fray with fists like bludgeons. Then Gaines was there too, swinging his baton. He pulled a flash-bang and flicked it outside into the darkness. Reto threw a man after it, and Gaines front-kicked another man out of the embassy, all as Harold wrenched the shutter back down like he was dropping the curtain at the conclusion of an act.

When the flash-bang went off, I didn't hear a thing. But I did see Riley. He was on his back, his hands pressed hard against his side. Blood seeped between his fingers.

The thunder of a helicopter roared into the first floor. Air sieved between the gaps in the shutters. Smoke and tear gas fled the space.

"That's one of ours!" Gaines yelled. "Seahawk!"

Bright searchlights flashed over the shutters. Slanting beams of incandescent light sliced through the gaps and across the people and walls as the American gunship hovered, rotor winds fanning a dozen fires.

"Wasp, this is Eagle," the pilot said. "We're on site."

He spun the Seahawk around the perimeter of the embassy, rising to clear the burned shell of the generator shack, the splay of broken radio antenna across the grounds, and the low one-story barracks.

"The ground is hostile," the pilot said. "Numerous fires. Shutters are down over the embassy's ground-floor windows. They're trying to force—"

There was a garble of voices and static in his earpiece as his crew chief spoke into the comm. It was a warning. Suddenly, an olive-green UH-1Y Super Huey cut across their path, dangerously close. The Huey's door gunner swiveled the GAU-21 up toward their faces.

"Wasp, be advised, our skies just got crowded."

Reto and I helped Riley to his feet. He winced when we pulled him off the ground, but to Gaines, he said, "Good to go, Gunny."

"No, you're not. Get to the doc," Gaines said. "We got this."

Reto and I carried Riley up the two flights of stairs. Inside the Post Communications Center, Doc Cassidy motioned for us to lay Riley on a blanket on the floor not far from Maya's gurney. Cassidy cut away his blood-soaked tunic.

"Looks worse than it is. Right, Doc?" Riley said.

"Just a scratch," Cassidy said. "A really, really deep scratch."

Riley winced as Doc Cassidy probed the wound. He saw Maya watching from her gurney. "Hey, Mr. Poirier," Riley said, "might not want her to see this."

Maya's hands moved.

"She says you are very brave," Reto said.

Riley laughed, then winced. "Kid, I like you."

Lights flashed across the corridor outside. They had to be from the sweep of a searchlight's beam. The bass thrumming of rotors reverberated in the air. Doc Cassidy saw my look.

"We're good here, Ambassador," she said.

I patted Riley on the shoulder and rose, then moved into the hallway as the search beam swept past and was gone. I darted into my office. The broken window framed a night sky in which the Seahawk darted past.

"There's only one," I said.

Reto stood beside me, looking into the night.

"It's a recon flight, not reinforcements," I said. "They may not even be sure we're here."

I turned from Reto and walked into the semi-darkness of the third floor.

Admiral Haas stood. He had not been invited by the president to take a seat. The president's eyes scanned the news network channels while he spoke to Haas.

"Admiral, what kind of man would I be if I put your people in harm's way?" He didn't wait for an answer. "I have been assured by the Malagar foreign ministry that our staff are in their good hands." He looked briefly at Haas, then back to the screens. "Any hardship they face is from having one olive in their two-olive martinis or having to smoke Honduran cigars."

Pope stepped between Haas and the president.

"That sufficient, Admiral?" Pope asked. "We done here?"

Reto watched Ambassador Ford vanish into the shadows of the third-floor corridor. From the first floor, he heard the continuing clatter of blows against the steel security shutters and occasionally, the shouts of men. The acrid scent of tear gas wafted upward. Reto walked down the stairs to the second floor on his way to rejoin the Marines.

The sound of shattering glass stopped him.

Reto edged into the office. The window overlooking the embassy grounds from the second-floor office was broken. He closed the door behind him. A Huey flashed past, followed by the American helicopter. Wind roared through the room, buffeting the vertical blinds that had been drawn wide. Broken glass littered the floor, and jagged remnants of glass still protruded from the frame. A ladder's rungs clattered against the windowsill, then creaked under the weight of someone climbing.

The door was open to the third-floor ordnance room. The Marines had destroyed the weapons that had once been stored there. Useless rifles and shotguns were propped against the far wall. Broken parts littered the armorer's table next to the tools that had been used to render them safe. I flung open drawers and doors, looking for . . .

They were inside a locked cage.

I darted back into the hallway and located the fire hose reel and axe recessed behind a plastic door. I flung it open and unlocked the axe from the clips that held it in place, then moved back into the ordnance room.

On my third swing, the axe-head struck the seam between the wire mesh cage door and thin metal frame. It gave, denting the frame. I flipped the axe and swung with the pick. It struck directly on the lock mechanism, springing the door wide.

I dropped the axe and took what I needed.

A soldier hesitated as he climbed over the lip of the windowsill and stepped into the second-floor office. Reto stood in the shadows along the wall, waiting. The man was dressed in civilian clothes. He removed an army-issued .45 from his waistband and eased it up toward the closed door as he reached for the knob.

The Seahawk pilot jockeyed his airframe as the Huey thundered past.

"Nothing on the roof," his copilot said.

"Keep looking," the pilot said into his mic.

Turbulence rocked the helo as he tracked the presence of the Huey and obstacles while his crew searched.

"I got guys with small arms on the embassy grounds," his crew chief said from the rear cabin. "Looks like civilian and local military."

The radio came over his headset. "Eagle, can you confirm?" It was Captain Ivers' voice. "Are there Americans in the building?"

"Negative Wasp!" the pilot responded. "We cannot confirm!"

I shoved the roof access door. It swung wide, and I stumbled out. Before me, the night was alive with lights. Fires from incendiaries still burned on the embassy grounds, and the mob had apparently delegated people to remain behind and stoke the bonfires that roared in a broad circle around the embassy's compromised security wall. The diesel in the burning Humvee at the gate had added to the combustion, and black palls of smoke rose fitfully. They were tormented by the Huey and the American helicopter that jockeyed for position. The American helicopter directed a searchlight to the ground. It played across the broken face of the embassy.

"Up here," I said to myself as I knelt, flicked the cap off one of two flares, and revealed the striker. "Shine it up here."

I struck the igniter with the striker in a smooth outward stroke that produced a shower of bright red sparks and a 2,500-degree flame. The hellish glow revealed the shattered satellite antenna and holes the Huey's machine gunner had punched into the roof. Some of those scars were nearby my feet.

"Come on," I said. "Can't ignore this."

I held a second flare up until the igniter caught. Then I waved the flares toward the American helicopter as each geysered red light.

Captain Ivers and every other Sailor in the Wasp's CIC listened intently.

"Flares!" The radio captured and broadcast the pilot's excitement. "Flares on the rooftop!" Then there was a garble of static.

"The slick's spotted him!" the pilot said. "They're coming around!"

"Patch me through to Admiral Haas," Ivers said.

The Huey's door gunner swung his weapon around. It was a long slow arc, like watching a circus motorcyclist ride his bike in a massive steel ball cage from the vertical through forty-five degrees, then sixty-five, then ninety degrees. I ran toward the American helo even as the Huey arced upward in a turn that, for a moment, held the gunner sitting faceup to the sky and the flight crew on a horizontal ninety-degree incline that would have received a nod from any self-respecting, thrill-seeking daredevil.

The Huey's turn dropped them between me and the Americans. The door gunner swung his weapon into aim at me. We were close enough for me to see the grim set of the gunner's jaw. The red flares I held glittered in his night vision goggles.

Reto smashed into the soldier from behind, grabbed him by the neck and his belt, and slung him over a desk and into a far wall. The man struck the drywall, breaking through and revealing a stud. His .45 had fallen to the far side of the room. He rolled away from the wall, stunned.

Then Reto was upon him, pounding his face with his fists in a fury and with the certainty that this soldier had crept into their midst to murder his daughter and to murder him.

I threw the flares.

With all my might, I flung the first one directly at the door gunner. It spun end over end toward him, bathing his face in a rose glow. Then the rotor wash and gravity had their way, and it arced down past the side of the building and to the ground below.

By then, I had already thrown the second flare. It spun across the roof with commanding rose beauty before bouncing to a halt near the junk that had once been our hope of summoning aid. Before it reached the ruin of the satellite dish and the shards of Harold's laptop, I was already running in the opposite direction.

Machine gun fire exploded into the roof. It tormented the place where I'd been, then tracked toward the collapsed satellite dish.

Reto raised his fist.

Outside the shattered office window, a flare fell from the sky. It threw bright red light across the floor, the walls, and the soldier as it slipped past.

And in that moment, Reto realized the soldier he'd beaten until blood scrawled his lips and nostrils—the man he'd intended to kill—was neither a soldier nor a man.

He lowered his fist.

Beneath him, the fifteen-year-old boy wept and tried to hold up both his hands, pleading in a voice that Reto could only now hear as the roaring in his ears subsided and the rage that fueled him sank back into the depths whence it had come.

The roof shuddered under me, and rounds exploded splinters from the roof and brickwork at the edge of the building where I'd thrown the second flare. It was my hope that the gunner's night vision had been dazzled, and that even now, he was firing blindly at the incandescence of the flare.

Hunched and stumbling, I staggered toward the open stairwell door when the gunner traversed. Bright lanes of tracers shot past me, deconstructing the metal door and flipping it away over the far side of the roof before the target shifted to the stairwell's alcove. I stumbled backward, tripping over a ruined section of roof where tarpaper and plywood had been blown to splinters. The metal stairs rang, and bullets ricocheted as they hit the girders supporting the structure. Then there was silence, and the wind roared as the Huey turned slightly. I lurched into a run across a roof ruined by machine gun fire, knowing the gunner was looking for me.

The boy scrambled down the ladder in the rotor wash of the Huey overhead. He looked up when he hit the ground.

Reto stood in the window, watching him. With one smooth movement, Reto's arm swept the ladder aside, and it clattered to the ground. Then he was gone, and high above them both, the Malagayan Huey's door gunner opened fire. Expended brass fell from the sky, clattering against the embassy's driveway. The boy blinked. His face was leaden, his nostrils filled with blood. When he closed his eyes, he could still see Reto's fist rising above him, overlaid now with bright white afterimages of machine gun tracers, which lashed out in streaks of hot light purer and whiter than anything he had known in his life.

The boy turned and ran, leaping over coils of rope someone had cut from the embassy's flagpole and the torn cloth that had fallen from the mast.

I ran. There was no plan. No risk mitigation. No carefully erected safety net meant to ensure I would remain alive and in relatively good form after the escape.

I ran.

The gunner would have me soon. There was no way back down into the building. I'd seen the warped and holed metal stairwell door backflip off the edge of the building, along with most of the stairwell exit structure. The stairs themselves had collapsed in a screeching cry of shredding metal as either their integrity or the building around them gave way under the heavy weapons fire.

I ran across the tortured and uneven spaces in the roof without any more thought than of making it to the edge and jumping to the ground from three stories up. My goal was to deny the gunner the vicarious thrill of seeing my form explode like the bricks and technology and everything else he had mauled.

Then I saw it.

As the air warped behind me in the downdraft from the Huey's massive rotor blades and rounds boomed past at supersonic speeds, I leapt toward what had become only a slightly better plan than a swan dive from the roof.

I dove for a hole in the roof that had been shorn from the gunner's fire.

I threw up an arm to protect my eyes as the ragged ends of joists and plywood sagged and then failed before I became a part of a rain of debris and splintered wood.

The Seahawk pilot and copilot watched with horror as the Huey gunner pummeled the hole in the embassy roofline.

"Goddamn!" the copilot swore. "They took him down!"

"Evasive!" the pilot yelled as the Huey spun above the embassy, and for a second, the Huey gunner stared at them from behind his smoking weapon.

Reto ran to the third floor. The corridor was full of smoke and dust. Coughing, he shouldered open rooms, searching. In the ambassador's office, he forced open a door and found the way blocked by caved-in roofing timber. The thunder of helicopters echoed from outside.

Gaines pressed his shoulder against a shutter as the locks tore free from their cement anchors. Hands from outside fought to force it farther upward. He waved Marines to another entrance that was torn partially open by the concerted blows of a pickaxe.

"West side!" Gaines shouted. "Go!"

But he knew they were too few. A shutter shrieked upward on the far side of the main floor. There were no

BRIAN C. BAKER

Marines there to stem the crowd of hands that fought to raise the metal barrier.

Then something moved through the dark. A flickering emergency light caught the red paint of a fire extinguisher in the hands of a very big man.

"Get back, you fuckers!" Harold roared. "This window's closed!"

He triggered the extinguisher before the first three were able to get inside. The foam made them fall away, screaming, their eyes and nostrils congealed in white. Another group of men tried to take their place.

Harold charged, hosing them until the foam was gone, then shoving the extinguisher into the chest of the first in the group. The impact forced them back. They toppled outside and then stumbled away, fleeing. Before a new group of soldiers could enter, Harold hefted his bulk into the shutter. It squealed back down to the ground. He sat against it, panting, and wore a slight smile. Harold raised a hand to Gaines when he saw him watching him.

"Always wanted to say that!" Harold yelled.

Beside Harold, another shutter danced as the mob switched to that one. The sledgehammer blows thrummed high against the mechanism that held the shutter in place. One end of it tore away from the wall as they watched. Then the shutter under Gaines began to leap and bounce again, and dust sieved down on him from the wall above as sledgehammers pounded at the supports.

"Fall back!" Gaines yelled.

The Marines began to withdraw. Orderly. One of them helped Harold to his feet and steered him to the stairs.

Gaines took up a position at the top of the stairs on the second floor. The Marines stood with him in a line like a phalanx.

Across the main floor, shutters creaked and fell in three different places. Then in five. Then more. Men with hammers and with other tools set foot in the litter of battle and congregated at the foot of the stairs, looking up at Gaines and the Marines.

"Deploy gas!" Gaines called.

The Marines on either side of him dropped tear gas canisters into the huddle of men downstairs. Gray clouds of noxious smoke billowed upward, and the men below them stumbled back, blinded and coughing.

Reto found him atop a pile of rubble. Jackson Ford lay sprawled, his head against a broken joist. As he pulled away debris to reach him, Reto Poirier felt certain he was trying to reach a dead man.

The captain's voice came across clearly on the briefing room's conference bridge device. At the center of the table, the light blinked green, indicating the phone's microphone was active in the room where Pope and the president sat and where Admiral Haas stood.

"Admiral," Captain Ivers said, "I have a team ready to fly."

Pope leaned forward and muted the microphone. The conference bridge device blinked red. "He witnessed local authorities exercising their right to quell a riot."

"With automatic weapons?" Admiral Haas challenged.

"Who are we to judge?" Pope said.

"Mr. President," Haas said, "they sighted flares."

"Everybody has flares," said Pope.

"They're firing at something. It can't be their own."

The president looked up at Haas sharply. "Tell me, Admiral, why can't it be their own?"

A mob of fifteen men rushed up the stairs and hit the line of Marines. A few tried to vault high and over. The Marines dragged them back down and pushed them onto the ones coming behind. Gaines put a boot into one man's chest. The man flailed backward and disappeared into the haze billowing across the first floor. The rush of fifteen retreated. The next group was larger, and among them were Malagayan soldiers wearing gas masks and carrying batons. They closed on Gaines and the Marines, swinging.

Maya climbed down from her gurney. She moved slowly, one hand across her bandaged stomach, the other holding a pillow. In the distance, there were shouts and gunfire. Tremendous explosions boomed from the roof above them, and the building shook as though it trembled in a giant's hands. From outside came the sounds of wood splintering and important things breaking.

Maya placed her pillow on the floor and sat down beside Riley. She took the semi-conscious Marine's hand in her own.

His eyes opened. "Hey, kiddo. Shouldn't you be up there?"

Doc Cassidy helped a wounded Marine stagger past them. A bloodstained baton fell from his grip and rolled toward them as Cassidy laid him down on blankets and prepared to provide aid.

"Okay." Riley looked at Maya. "I promise. We're gonna be okay."

There are places we go to when our bodies are so shocked or torn they can no longer cope with conscious thought. For me, this is not a place of darkness or seclusion. It is not a dream of the abyss into which we must all, at some point, descend.

I fell away from the thud of helicopter blades and the *whip-crack* of supersonic heavy caliber rounds, and splintering wood slammed against my face and head as though it had a vendetta against me for its destruction. When a ceiling joist struck my temple, the roar of destruction and violence was transformed into a different place.

The park never changed. It was a grassy hill. Sunlit and green. The lawn was newly mowed. I could smell the scent of the grass and a faint citrus odor, as though someone had just split a watermelon and the ripe red flesh was laid bare on a table under the sun. The shadow of a cloud scudded across the grass, folding and changing as it passed. It reached out to merge with the pool of shade thrown by a mature oak at the base of the hill before changing again and disappearing beyond the trees that served as a boundary in this part of my mind.

She was in the oak's shade. I could never see her face. I trod the gentle downhill slope, feeling the grass beneath my bare feet, in the same way I had walked toward her a thousand times in dreams and drunken hallucinations and waking fantasies. I could hear their laughter. Hers and our child's. Our child cooed in a swing that Elise pushed. I saw our baby's arms flailing and heard the burble of excitement.

Elise never had the option to become a mother. Her battles required a decision. Either parenthood or survival. Being who she was, she made me part of that choice. One particularly bad night, the woman I loved suggested there was still time for me to move on. That I could find someone who could be all the things a woman might become: a friend, lover, partner . . . and mother.

I'd stilled my rage. Anger was not what she needed to hear.

There would always be time for adoption, I'd reasoned. There were so many children in need.

And I also had a need. I didn't want anyone but Elise. No matter the cost.

In that place, I strode toward my wife and the child we never had. Sunlight dappled the shade over them. Laughter rose as I neared. The day was warm, and in this place—while I knew it was only a fantasy sustaining me through injury, shock, and the possible end of my mortal coil—I was closer to reaching them than any other time.

Something struck me.

I staggered, never taking my eyes off Elise and our child. I trudged forward, as though I could reach them. Something roared in the distance. Like the tumult of a waterfall, hidden by trees. The din of the cataract rose.

Then something eclipsed the sun, and they were gone. In the space of a thought, they were gone. I opened my eyes and half sobbed, half choked back to consciousness as Reto Poirier leaned over me. He'd pulled me from the shambles of the bar and half my office and propped me in my chair near the flag staff. Wind blew through the shattered window overlooking the embassy grounds. When his hands came away from my body, they were wet and red. He forced my hands to cover the wound. Pain seared through me as I knotted fists to staunch the flow of blood.

Reto Poirier leaned low, his mouth close to my ear. "I thought these walls would provide refuge from evil men, but they are too strong. You will all die . . . because of me. This is something I cannot accept."

He turned away from me and vanished into the darkness of the corridor.

I looked down. The floor was a litter of ceiling debris and papers. The US flag had fallen from its position near the wall. Shards of broken glass littered its folds.

"My God. What do you want, Pope? Dental records?" Haas demanded. "We wait much longer, that's all we're gonna have left!"

The president blinked, then inclined a finger toward the door to the briefing room. "Thank you, Admiral."

"Sir?"

"You're done here," the president said. "Step outside."

Haas hesitated. Then he left.

The president leaned forward and unmuted the microphone. The light flicked from red to green. "Captain Ivers, this is the president."

Reto entered the Post Communications Center like a ghost. He knelt to lift Maya in his arms. Maya let go of Riley's hands and wrapped her arms around Reto's neck. He rose and carried her from the room and into the smoke-veiled corridor.

Riley struggled up into a sitting position and looked at the baton beside his boot. The emergency lighting flickered, and a rivulet of blood along the baton took on the same hue and thickness as oil.

Armando moved through the swirling tear gas on the main floor. Gaines and the Marines were being pushed back across the second-floor landing and up the stairs to the third floor. More Marines were positioned at the top of the third-floor stairs. Armando turned. At his gesture, the next three squads darted up the stairs.

High on the stairs above, Gaines tore the mask off a man and knocked him to the landing.

With a 9 mm in his right hand, Armando moved up the stairs behind the squads that would finally beat down the last resistance.

Daniel shifted the pack as he moved past a van maintenance bay and climbed stairs to a rooftop hatch. He released the latch and shoved the hatch upward until it locked open. Above him, the clouds had cleared, leaving only high thin cirrus clouds that moved quickly across the light of the moon.

That moonlight illuminated the gravel strewn on the rooftop. He took binoculars from the pack and knelt by the edge of the roofline. Even without the glasses, he had a clear view of the smoking embassy. His elevation allowed him to see the fires burning on the grounds, the naked flag mast, and the mob spilling inside.

Maya hugged her father tightly as he strode. The smoke was thicker in the corridor, and a nearby light flickered a last weak amber glow, then went out with a pop. The air was heavy, and it made Maya's chest ache. When she coughed, the sutures that knit together the ragged orbit of the exit wound in her side pulled and hurt.

As they walked down the corridor, Maya could see shapes ahead. Men locked in a surreal combat. Americans battled men with black masks over their faces.

The president rose from his seat, shouting at the bridge line device. He pounded the table with a fist as he made his point clear to Captain Ivers: "I have been personally assured that all American civilian and military personnel are safely out of the area! Recall your assets, Captain! Now!"

I moved from the chair to the floor. The glass in my window had not been safety glazed; it littered the ground in razors and shards. A piece the size of a dinner plate cracked under my foot and produced an edge as fine and as lethal as a surgeon's scalpel. Pieces of glass glittered as I picked up the staff that bore the American flag. There was a large razored cut across the red and white stripes.

With trembling hands, I slid the flag from the staff.

Rotor wash from the helicopters outside whipped through the sawtooth outline of the glass still in the window frame. Though no one could hear me, I spoke as I raised the butt of the flagstaff.

"It's not for me, Reto." I smashed the wood against the shards still in the window's lower sill. "And it's not for you."

The staff clattered to the ground. I took the top corners of the flag in my fists and staggered to the window, where broken pieces still glittered above and to the sides, like a macabre jagged overbite.

"We're doing this because it's right," I said.

The flag roiled out over the lip of the window, dangling outside the embassy from my third-floor window. It was illuminated by the golden light of bonfires and the burning Humvee. It was made luminescent by the soft glow of the moon overhead. And faster than thought, it was made brilliant by the swivel and glare of a searchlight from the Wasp's orbiting Seahawk.

"We're doing this," I said as the flag whipped in my hands, "because it's who we are."

The Seahawk pilot saw three things. The first was the expression on the Huey gunner's face as he jerked his head toward the embassy, responding to what must have been a frantic command from the Huey's pilot. The second was the spark and flicker of gunfire from multiple points on the embassy grounds as firearms unleashed a volley of hate toward the third-floor window.

The final thing he saw was the flag that leapt and curled from the lip of a third-floor embassy window. His copilot put the spotlight on the wall as the Huey spun for height and turned, bringing their gunner to bear on the face of the embassy.

"Wasp, this is Eagle," said the pilot. "We can confirm!"

Small arms fire shattered glass and exploded red puffs of brickwork around the man holding the flag.

Daniel watched the flag unfurl from the side of the building. He grinned and handed his binoculars to the man beside him.

Armando slammed the butt of his pistol hard against the head of a Marine trying to stagger up from the ground. Before him, Gaines fought a losing battle with three of his soldiers. They took turns hitting the tall American with batons and a two-by-four cut the length of a man's arm. Armando raised his 9 mm into aim on the back of Gaines' head.

But he lowered the weapon as two figures approached from among the melees in the third-floor corridor. He moved to the wall, to an area where light did not penetrate from the offices with open doors. Armando took off his gas mask to see them better in the darkness and waited patiently for Reto Poirier to come to him with his daughter in his arms.

A bullet tore across my arm. Blood sprayed the air and whipped across the flag and away. Wind tore one end of the flag from my hand. I nearly lost it entirely, the ends popping as the Huey completed a wide orbit that would bring the door gunner down level with me.

I raised from my crouch. I heard it over the dull thump of bullets impacting the bricks around me and over the crack of rounds as they narrowly missed. I heard it over the sound of the cloth twirling and popping in my good hand. It was my voice, crying out in anguish as I leaned over broken glass and gripped the cloth with my wounded arm again, taking hold at the far corner so that the flag was not just a torn and stained rag. It was something held aloft in a way even a child would recognize and understand.

Daniel watched the feed as Al Nivens gestured for his cameraman to get in tight on the flag. A tripod satellite feed antenna the size of a dinner plate sat on the roof behind them, beaming the image live.

"How's it feel?" Daniel asked.

"What?" Nivens replied.

"Having their lives in your hands."

"They were never in my hands." Nivens winced as gunfire struck Jackson Ford's shoulder and a crimson spray made the ambassador recoil. Ford clenched to the flag that much tighter as bullets shattered glass above him and the Malagayan Huey swung around.

"Get in close," Nivens said to the cameraman. "Direct to feed. Don't fuck this up."

Judge Sarah Everly followed the bailiff that had beckoned her from her office and stepped from her chambers into an outer office that should have been empty. Instead, she found a court reporter, two more bailiffs, and her secretary gathered around the small television perched on a filing cabinet. They parted when they saw her, the looks on their faces indicating they knew they were watching something unfold that would be of particular interest to the woman at the center of their working days.

"Your Honor," one of the bailiffs said, "it doesn't look good."

On the screen was Jackson Ford, his hair whipped by the approach of a Huey gunship.

The president fell silent as he followed the direction of Pope's gaze. He slowly sat as he turned, watching the images on the wall behind him flick, one after another, to live shots of the embassy in Malagar.

The Huey finished its airborne lunge. I stared at the door gunner as he brought his weapon to bear just fifty yards away. I did not release my grip on the flag. Some part of my memory recalls yelling a stream of profanity that was at once vile, defiant, and inaudible.

Sudden as the gray hand of God, the Seahawk plummeted between us.

Her rail-mounted machine guns pointed at the Huey. Downwash pummeled both craft. The orbit of their rotor blades seemed to be just inches apart. The Seahawk's descent startled the Huey gunner. He slipped from his rail and dangled from a safety line.

"YOU ARE IN THE AIRSPACE OF THE UNITED STATES EMBASSY!" The Seahawk pilot's voice boomed from an external series of speakers, surpassing even the rotor volume. "VEER OFF OR WE WILL OPEN FIRE! THIS IS YOUR ONLY WARNING!"

For a moment, the two helicopters danced back and forth, the orbits of their rotor blades close enough to promise entanglement and a fiery return to earth.

"Confirmed!" the communications officer said. "They've got a visual on the ambassador! There are Americans in the building!"

"Send them," Captain Ivers said.

Across the Wasp's flight deck, a trio of Seahawks leapt into the night sky.

The pilot and copilot of the Seahawk watched as the Huey's gunner pulled himself back into the cabin. The helicopter climbed and circled away over the outer embassy wall.

The voice of Captain Ivers came over their radio: "Eagle, disperse the crowd."

Lights flared from the Seahawk as pods shot canisters that burst midair, spewing a thousand pellets of combusting gas across the embassy grounds.

Reto walked with Maya cradled in his arms. There was little light in this part of the corridor.

Maya's hands tensed. He stopped. She stared at something that seemed to be only darkness, but then he saw the dark hollow of a gun muzzle emerge from shadows.

"Withdraw your men," Reto said in Spanish. "I surrender. I ask only that you provide medical care for my daughter."

Armando emerged behind the gun, smiling. "Shhh. The dead do not speak."

Something whipped through the air as Armando fired. The muzzle flash illuminated the corridor like a strobe. In the white-hot light, Reto saw Riley. The baton he held cracked across Armando's wrist. The boom of the pistol and the sound of the round tearing through drywall were immediately drowned out by Armando's scream, high-pitched and loud.

Armando cursed and kicked Riley. The Marine staggered backward without the strength to swing the baton again. Blood ran between Riley's fingers and slicked his side.

Reto gently lowered Maya to the ground.

Armando took the 9 mm with his left hand. He cried out again as he moved his arm. Bones in his shattered wrist were visible through the torn flesh. Armando struck Riley with the butt of his pistol. The Marine went to his knees. He looked up at the muzzle as Armando raised the weapon in his left hand.

Riley didn't blink.

Armando screamed at him as his finger found the trigger.

But Reto grabbed Armando's wrist, and his free arm slipped around the smaller man's neck. Reto forced Armando's hand to bring the 9 mm's barrel to a new aim.

"Some things must die to be reborn," Reto said as the barrel pressed hard against the hinge of Armando's jaw. "Are you among them?"

The muscles in Armando's jaw knotted. His teeth gritted in a sneer. Then the fingers of his left hand went slack, and the pistol fell from his grip.

Their camera recorded as US Seahawks touched down and Marines spilled out. The helicopters immediately dusted off and began a protective orbit while the Marines formed a line on the ground, advancing for the embassy as members of the mob fled through the main gate.

The cameraman turned to Nivens from his sat cell phone. "Every major network wants it! There's a bidding war! No one else is down here, man! Hang on . . . They wanna know if we can get interviews!"

Nivens looked at Daniel. Daniel nodded.

"Tell 'em hell yeah," Nivens said. Then he pulled a bottle of scotch from his pack while the cameraman turned away to continue the negotiations. "Not bad, Danny boy. I figure I owe you a case." Nivens cracked the bottle and took a deep pull, then extended it to Daniel. "How 'bout an installment?"

Daniel shook his head. "Al, I'm told that someday, that won't help."

"That'll be one sad day." Nivens took another swallow before spinning the cap and putting it back in his pack. He took the phone from the cameraman and moved into an animated discussion.

"It doesn't feel that way," Daniel said to no one in particular.

CHAPTER XXVIII

SECOND CHANCE

"Y'know, I think you're intentionally causing me more pain than I suffered when I got all these cuts and what, three . . ."

"Two," Doc Cassidy said.

"Two bullet wounds," I said.

"Marines have wounds. You have injuries," she said, carefully closing a suture. "And when I'm done, nobody's going to be able to tell you had these."

"Because you're a former Beverly Hills plastic surgeon."

"Right."

"Y'know, some scars might be nice," I suggested.

"How's that?"

"Be a nice memento."

BRIAN C. BAKER

"You mean from the time you put yourself on a bull-seye in front of what had to be *the* worst shots in the world?"

"They were gonna use a machine gun!" I protested. "Plus, are we not going to talk about the concussion-worthy impacts I endured when I used my head to smash through the roof?"

"That's your least vulnerable spot," she said.

"You're quoting something there."

"Paraphrasing, actually." She stepped back. "Done."

I pulled the bloody rags of my shirt back around me.

Outside the comm room, the sun was coming up. Light filtered into the building through office windows and the surprising number of holes in the ceiling and roof above. I limped past Marines from the Wasp, who had subdued, identified, and plasticuffed members of the mob that had been too slow or too recalcitrant to follow commands to depart the grounds. Armando was among them. Two Marines held him while a Navy corpsman from the Wasp tended to his broken wrist.

I knelt beside Riley. He'd been triaged and prepped for evac to the Wasp. "Richard," I said, "are you all right?"

"Never better, sir."

Gaines limped over with a Marine captain at his side. "Ambassador Ford," Gaines said.

I rose. The captain shook my hand.

"Captain Jose de la Hoya, Ambassador," he said. "Fourth Marine detachment from the USS Wasp. I've got helicopters inbound, sir."

"Captain, I'm not leaving," I said. "Reto Poirier is—"

"No, sir!" de la Hoya said. "My orders are to reinforce. Our ship's surgeons are ready to receive your wounded. With your permission, sir."

I nodded. Then de la Hoya turned and was gone, orchestrating the reinforcement.

I smiled at Riley as Marines and a corpsman lifted his backboard and carried him to a helicopter that waited outside.

"Mr. Ambassador," Gaines said. "If you'll accompany me, sir."

I followed Gaines down the stairs, across broken glass, and out where the embassy had once had front doors.

On the grass nearby the flagpole, there was a dark stain where the fallen American flag had been incinerated by the mob. I stopped for a moment, looking at the blackened and dead turf and the ashes that had once been cloth.

"Sir, we wanted you to see this." Gaines gestured to the flagpole.

In the distance, the sun rose. A wind moved across the grounds. It swayed the new lanyard someone had affixed to the pole.

From the front of the embassy, three Marines from our protection detail walked in step to the mast. White gauze wrapped one's forehead. Another had butterfly bandages over his cheek. They clipped the flag and hoisted it smartly toward the sky.

I recognized it. It was the flag that had been on a staff behind my desk. Holes were visible where it had been cut by glass or gunfire. At one corner, I could have sworn I saw a stain as red as wine.

Gaines turned to me as the flag topped the mast and the Marines moved back inside the embassy to continue their duties. "Mr. Ambassador," Gaines said.

I looked down. Gaines' hand was extended.

I shook it. Then Gaines walked down to the main gate to check on the Wasp Marines posted to sentry duty. I turned and found Reto waiting for me at the embassy entrance. We surveyed the wreckage together. There were places where fires still smoldered. The exterior of the building gaped where windows had been shattered. The barracks dribbled smoke into the sky. The radio mast was a set of skeletal remains that rose in dented and broken arcs from the ground and the broken back of the barracks.

"You asked me a question once," Reto said.

The sun was brass on the eastern horizon. I nodded, closing my eyes and feeling the promise of dawn on my face. It felt like the warmth of a sun I knew from a different, more private place.

"Do you believe"—my voice was a whisper—"in second chances?" I opened my eyes.

Reto was looking at me, smiling. "Yes. I do."

At the gate, Gaines waved a reporter and cameraman up the drive toward Reto and me. I recognized the reporter.

"Good," I said. "This is one for you."

I inclined my head to Nivens and his cameraman. Reto nodded and walked toward them.

They moved with Reto to a scenic part of the embassy, where smoke still billowed toward the sky. It made for a better visual spectacle. At the gate, Gaines and Daniel looked up to me. Daniel smiled, lifted a hand. I raised mine in return.

Daniel shouldered his pack and walked past the security fence and out of my field of view.

"Ambassador!" Harold called from inside the embassy. I heard him crunching and sliding across the broken glass. "Ambassador!"

He came through the doors with a large Marine ship-to-shore communications unit in his hand. Then he took a second and doubled over to breathe. He extended the receiver to me. "Took a while but . . ." He panted. "Wasp got through. She picked up . . . first ring . . ."

I held the receiver to my ear. I'd always imagined what this moment would be like. In my fantasies, it was a moment filled with loss. With the unraveling of important things. But that was in the past, from a life where I held tightly to the pretense that golden things could be panned from dark and septic water.

Now, all I felt was release.

"Hi, Sarah," I said. "There are some things I want to put on the record."